Too Soon A Man

By

Donovan Harrison

authorHOUSE™

1663 LIBERTY DRIVE, SUITE 200
BLOOMINGTON, INDIANA 47403
(800) 839-8640
WWW.AUTHORHOUSE.COM

First published by AuthorHouse 11/24/04

ISBN: 1-4184-8668-X (e)
ISBN: 1-4184-8667-1 (sc)

Library of Congress Control Number: 2004095502

Printed in the United States of America
Bloomington, Indiana

This book is printed on acid-free paper.

Dedication

    I dedicate this novel *Too Soon a Man* to my Mother who always read my work first, after my wife. During the time I was writing this novel, my Mother would read a chapter and say, "That is going to be a gooooood book." It was her favorite and after she could no longer read and correct my work, I would still read a chapter to her as she lay in a hospital bed dying of brain cancer. While I was reading the novel to her, I saw her laugh and I saw her cry. I hope *Too Soon a Man,* has the same effect on others. I regret that she did not live to see the final word written but if you are looking down one me, Mom, this one is for you.

    I would also like to thank Lillian Tubb who corrected the novel after my mother and to Carolyn Thomae who was the fourth in line to read and correct my work. I must thank my wife, Millie, who corrected my work first and was my harshest critic.

What is it like to grow up on a farm in Western Oklahoma shortly before during and after World War II? What's it like to be dirt poor and the youngest of five brothers? What's it like to chop cotton in the hot July sun and then pick cotton that fall when it is cold and windy and your back and legs hurt and your knees are raw from crawling on them? Ask Billy Harshburger, he can tell you.

Billy can tell you what it's like to fall in love with the neighbor girl whose father hates all Harshburgers and then face the father and tell him that you must get married.

Chapter One

Floyd don't see none too good, but he has the best pair of ears of any of us. Floyd's the oldest and I'm the youngest of five boys, and I ain't bragging none when I say I can count a bumble-bee's teeth at a hundred yards, but I sure can't hear nothing like Floyd can. That Floyd can hear a granddaddy-long-legs tip-toeing across a silk handkerchief.

Floyd's old enough to get himself a woman and go out on his own, but for some reason he hasn't. He's stayed on the farm, scratching these scrubby acres, knowing all the time it ain't no use. Ain't no way a man can get ahead. A man's mighty lucky just to stay even. What with Pa drinking corn whiskey all the time and never doing a lick of work, we have to work from sun up 'til we're plumb—-plumb tuckered out—-and then there ain't quite enough time to get everything done.

Me and Floyd had been choppin' cotton since sunrise on the river bottom forty. That's what we call it. But the Washita River ain't much of a river, a wide sand bed with a small trickle of water and a few muddy holes with catfish in them. But then we ain't much of a farm, either. This is the best piece of land we got and things grow tolerable well on it. Unless, of course, like often happens, it don't rain, then things just wilt and die. Or sometimes it rains and rains and rains. That's when that little old trickle of water grows until it overflows the banks and washes everything out. But sometimes when the weather is just right, we get a dang good crop on this chunk of land. But it don't happen very often.

I know one thing, when I get as old as Floyd, I'm going to leave here. Ain't no way I'm going to stick around, busting my back from daylight 'till dark. No sir. I'm going to a city up North someplace where it's cool and get myself a job.

It was halfway between morning and noon and the summer heat was already beating down on my bare back. Floyd's shirt was wet with sweat and our faded jeans had white half moons of salt on them. Our hoes worked up and down, breaking the thin, dry crust, cutting weeds, and bringing up the damp dirt. Gnats were swarming around our heads and I had three welts on my bare back

1

where sweat bees had stung me. I chopped and chopped and told Floyd all the things I was going to do when I growed up.

Floyd stopped choppin' and stood still. "Did you hear that, Billy?"

I told him I didn't hear nothing, and kept on talking and choppin'.

"Well, shut up and listen," he said.

I stopped choppin' and looked at Floyd. He was standing still, his wide shoulder back, his shaggy head turning from side to side, and I swear his ears were cocked like a big shaggy dog. His jaw bulged from a half plug of eatin' tobacco, and he spit once. We sometimes called Floyd the big Swede, but it ain't true. He's a full-blooded German like the rest of us Harshburgers.

"Hear that?" he asked again.

Then I heard it. A faint scream seemed to just hang there in the still air. It sounded like the time I was riding the blue filly after the cows, and she stepped into a prairie dog hole and broke her leg. She screamed and screamed until Floyd came out and shot her.

Pa was real mad at me for doing such a fool thing and he hung me up and whipped me until I passed out. I pissed blood for a long time afterwards and the thoughts of it still make me flinch.

"Don't you hear it, Billy?"

"Yeah," I answered. "What is it?"

But I was talking to empty air. Floyd had already started towards the house. He was running with that long loping stride of his that just eats up the ground, and I had to sprint to keep up. By the time we reached the locust grove just south of the house, I knew it weren't no use. I was falling farther and farther behind. I had outrun Floyd before in races, but today it weren't no use. Today I just couldn't keep up with that Floyd.

I wound my way through the grove and came out the other side. I thought Floyd had been running before, but now he was halfway to the barn and picking up speed all the way. His arms were moving like the pistons of a roaring freight train, and his heels were kicking up small puffs of red dust. That Floyd was really pounding his feet.

I had run too far and too fast in the heat and I just had to stop and catch my breath. As I looked out towards the barn, looked at the white leghorn chickens scratching in the dust, at old Molly standing with her ears forward, I saw where the screams were coming from.

Pa had tied Kevin's hands together around a corral post. Kevin was hanging there without any clothes on, his feet just off the ground, and the two twins were standing there watching him. Pa was behind Kevin, his shirt off, and he had a long wet knotted rope doubled in his fist. As I watched, he drew it back through the sand and stepped toward Kevin. He put all of his weight behind him as he brought the rope whipping forward to land on Kevin's bare back. Even in the distance I could hear the hollow, dull thud and Kevin's scream.

Kevin was sure tough, though. I don't think I could have lasted that long. I think I would have passed out by now. But he was still screaming when Floyd reached Pa.

Now, Pa's a big man and he's been knocked around a bit in one barroom or another. He can hold his own against any man or beast. And I remember the last fight between Pa and Floyd, a little over a year and a half ago. They fought half the morning. Floyd got the hell beat out of him. But Floyd did knock Pa down a few times, kicked him in the belly once so hard Pa had trouble getting his breath, bloodied Pa's nose, and blacked Pa's eye. Now, It's true Floyd had growed a bit, and pa's not been over eager to tangle with him since then, but in a regular knock-em-down and stomp-em fight, I'd still place my money on Pa. That is if I had any money to place.

But today, Floyd had up a full head of steam and was barreling in on Pa at top speed. As he reached Pa, Floyd's big fist went back to his shoulder and then forward. It catched Pa right in front of the ear and he floated in the air for a spell before he hit the ground in a cloud of dust.

When I got there, I saw Pa was snoring loudly through his open mouth and it was apparent he wouldn't be getting up for a while. I sure wish I could hit like that Floyd can. Wouldn't nobody pick on me or tell me what do.

Floyd and the twins cut Kevin down and stretched him out flat on his belly. He lay there moaning and whimpering with big red and blue lumps on his back. There was a lump in my throat and my eyes watered, from all the running I guess, as I saw Floyd's big, rough hands gently feeling along Kevin's back.

"He's got two busted ribs," Floyd said. He stood up, turned, and looked down at Pa.

Even with the hot sun beating on my back, I shivered. Man, I hoped to God Floyd never looks at me that way.

"Well, boys," he said turning his back on Pa. "We got to do it."

He turned and walked over to me. He reached out with his big hand and tosseled my head. I looked up at him and tried to smile, but he had a far-away, vacant look in his eyes.

"Better go to the house, Billy," he said, gently pushing me toward the old, weathered, rambling shack we call home.

I took a couple of steps towards the house, stopped and turned. "I don't reckon I will," I said, trying to keep my voice from rising. It ain't often I cross Floyd. "I don't know what you guys are up to," I continued, "but I'm a Harshburger, and I aim to be in on it."

Floyd looked me up and down as if trying to judge my size. "Okay, Billy. You will soon be a man grown and it's something we all gotta live with. Help tie Pa up."

Kevin was sitting up, slowly pulling on his pants, moaning and groaning, as I helped roll Pa over. Pa was still snoring and I could smell the familiar stench of corn on his breath.

A short piece from the barn grows a big cottonwood tree. It gives off a right nice shade and on one of its limbs we have tied a pulley. It's here each fall we hoist up a butchering beef on that pulley.

When Pa was tied up real good with his hands behind his back, I grabbed a leg and we carried him over to this tree. Then we tied his feet so he wouldn't kick none when he woke up.

"Go get a bucket of water and we'll see if we can wake him up," Floyd said to me.

I started to ask him if I was the only one what could carry a water bucket, but decided I had pushed as far as I safely could. I ran to the barn and got a milk pail, then to the stock tank, and dipped it full. When I lugged it back to the shade tree, I saw that Floyd had gone and gotten the rope, which Pa had used to whip Kevin.

"Throw it on him, Billy," Floyd said.

I drew back and heaved the whole bucketful right in Pa's face. Man, he came alive, thrashing and cussing. When he had calmed down, Floyd squatted beside him, the rope in his hand.

"You busted two of Kevin's ribs, Pa," Floyd said.

"Untie me, boy."

"Why wouldn't you leave like we asked you to, Pa? Me, Ma, and the boys would've left a long time ago, but we ain't got nowhere to go."

"Untie me, boy," Pa said, and I could tell he weren't talking no nonsense.

"We told you the last time," said Floyd, "when you beat Billy senseless, to never beat on one of us boys again."

"Untie me, or by God, I'm going to thrash every one of you to an inch of your life."

"No, Pa, if you keep whippin', you are going to kill one of us some day. No—Pa—you ain't ever whippin anybody again." Floyd began to fashion a noose in the end of the rope.

Pa looked at the noose and squinched his eyes. "You ain't got the guts."

"None of the other boys can remember how it used to be," Floyd said, his hands working on the noose. "But I can. Pa, you used to take me on your back when you went after the cows. I would hold you around the neck, and when you'd run I could feel the heavy pounding of your heart. I used to ride on your cotton sack while you pulled bolls. You'd throw me in the cotton wagon and then dump the sack on me, covering me with cotton, and laughing all the time. We chopped cotton together, just you and me. We talked about how we'd get a good crop some day and hit it big. You'd tell me about all the new clothes and things you'd buy me. And sometimes we'd race from the field to the house. See who could get to supper first, and you'd let me win.

"Yes, Pa, you were once a kind, gentle man. You were a big man, filled with big love. You worked hard, played hard, and laughed a lot. Those were the good times."

"Why, you goddamn gutless baby, you're crying," Pa said, and his booming laugh startled a blue jay, which was sitting in the cottonwood.

For a moment when Pa laughed I had some idea what Floyd was talking about.

"But none of the younger boys know you that way," Floyd said, taking a last turn on the noose. "All they know is you laying around while they work. Work all day as hard as we can and never get it all done. Never enough money to buy the things we need. And all the time you laying around, sleeping and drinking corn."

Floyd placed the noose around Pa's neck. "And when you do get up, it's only to knock hell out of Ma, or beat on one of us boys."

Floyd stood up and placed a wooden box under the pulley. "We warned you Pa, but you wouldn't listen," he said, as he threaded the end of the rope through the pulley.

"Help me stand him on the box, boys. Kevin, do you think you're able to cinch the rope to that snubbing stake?"

"You damn right," Kevin answered.

We stood Pa on the box He fought some and then slumped down, but Kevin pulled the rope tight and Pa stood tall.

"I don't know what happened to you, Pa," said Floyd, wiping his big arm across his eyes. "I've seen you change. Seen you become mean and vicious. Maybe the land was too much for you. Maybe the heat, the drought, the crop failures, used up all of the goodness that was in you. I don't know. I know you are no good to yourself or to anyone now."

"You're a passel of spineless bastards and you ain't got the guts to go through it," Pa shouted.

But Pa was wrong. Floyd stepped forward and kicked the box out from under him and quickly turned his back. Pa was wrong. Dead wrong. Floyd stood there like a big, shaggy faithful dog, looking out at the red hills with his bad eyes.

Chapter two

I waited a while and then I walked to Floyd. Floyd still stood there staring out at the red hills, a vacant look in his eyes. I reached over and took the sleeve of his shirt and tugged on it. "He's dead now, Floyd. He done stopped kicking."

"It's done then," Floyd said. "Now we have to finish it. Kevin, back in the corner of the barn there's a pile of old horse blankets. If you want to, you can go get a couple to wrap Pa in. Jim and Joe, you two can hook up Dolly and Molly to the wagon and Billy if you can rustle up some shovels and the pickax, we'll load Pa in the wagon and take him out to the pasture and bury him."

I took off then and ran to the tool shed. I stopped after I opened the door and just looked in. It was mighty dark in the shed after being out in the bright sunlight and it was kind of creepy after what we had done. I found the shovels and then I found the pickax and took them back to the tree where Pa was hanging except he weren't hanging no more. Floyd had taken him down.

Kevin showed up with the blankets and we wrapped Pa up good and about the time we were finished, the twins showed up with the wagon. We all grabbed a hold of Pa, all except Kevin, and we hoisted him up into the bed of the wagon. I put the shovels and pickax in the back with him.

Floyd helped Kevin get on the seat of the wagon and climbed up himself and took the reins. "You boys can ride in the back," Floyd said.

I looked in back of the wagon where Pa lay, all wrapped up in those old horse blankets and all dead and everything. I looked up at Floyd and said, "I don't think so. I think I'll just walk."

We picked a spot out in the pasture where it looked like we could dig and not hit any of that red sandstone that we have so much of. Floyd grabbed a shovel and started trying to dig but with the weather we had been having, the ground was dry and hard and he traded his shovel in for the pickax. Once Floyd got going good, the twins and I grabbed the shovels and started throwing dirt. It wasn't much dirt, just clods. Kevin tried to help, but with his busted ribs and everything he just couldn't do much. Finally

I said, "Kevin, just get out of our way. Go sit by the wagon or something."

"Why you little piss ant, it will be a cold day in hell when I can't do more work than you whether I'm busted up or not."

"The devil must be reaching for his fur parka now because this is one of those cold days in hell," I said, and I was trying to make up my mind whether to run or fight because it looked like he was fixing to come after me. I figured I could whip him today since he was hurtin', and I knew for durn sure I could outrun him with him having busted ribs like he did.

But as it turned out I didn't have to do either one because Floyd stepped in. "You ought not be doing too much, Kevin. Just take it easy for the next few days and give those busted ribs time to heal."

Kevin climbed out of the hole grumbling and walked to a wagon wheel and gingerly sat down. He sat there while we dug, and you could see from looking at him that he was mad at the whole wide world.

When we had the hole deep enough we all got a hold of Pa and dropped him in. He hadn't hardly hit bottom when Kevin grabbed a shovel and started scooting dirt in. "We can do that, Kevin," I said, "I know it hurts."

"He ain't ever going to do that to me again," Kevin said as he handed me his shovel.

We packed the dirt down tight and when we were through the top of the grave was level. That in itself was a surprising thing. Usually when you dig a hole and then fill it back up you won't have enough dirt or else have too much. But when we were through, the top of the grave was level with the ground.

"Kevin, do you think you're able to drive the team back?" Floyd asked.

"Hell yes. What are you going to do?"

"You boys go ahead to the barn, unhook the team and put the tools up. I'll be along in a minute."

"Load up boys. Let's go to the barn," Kevin said.

"I think I'll just stay with Floyd," I said.

"Get in the wagon, Billy," and I could tell that Kevin weren't about to take any nonsense so I jumped into the back of the wagon and sat with my feet dangling over the back. I looked over my shoulder and saw Jim help Kevin climb into the seat of the wagon and then Jim climbed onto the seat with him while Joe got in the back with me.

Kevin turned the wagon and we headed to the barn. I watched Floyd just standing there. Kevin drove the team slow so the bouncing wouldn't jar him too much but at last we rounded a red hill and the last I saw of Floyd he was just standing at the grave, his shaggy head bowed.

When we got to the barn, Kevin helped me put up the tools while Jim unharnessed the team. Since it was after lunch, Joe went to the house to see if he could find us something to eat. By the time the tools were put up and the team was taken care of, Joe returned with a basket that had left over breakfast biscuits and some fried chicken we had left over from the night before. We all dug in, and I think I could have eaten more but of course, we had to save some for Floyd.

We were all sitting on milk stools and not saying much when Floyd came walking in. He found a milk stool and sat down and began to eat.

"What are we going to do now?" I asked. "Are we going to make a cross or something to mark Pa's grave?"

"No!" Floyd said. "No, that's the last thing we're going to do, Billy."

"Well, just why in the hell not?"

"Don't cuss, Billy. You're too young. Twer'nt no other way, but what we did in the eyes of the law was murder. I know, if we hadn't hung Pa, it would just have been a matter of time until he would have kilt one of you boys. He was just like a dog that's gone rabid. But in the eyes of the law, it was murder." Floyd looked around at all of us and then continued. "If the law finds we kilt him and finds his body to prove it, then we're all in a heap of trouble. Kevin, you'll probably go to prison for the rest of your life. You're old enough. Joe, Jim, Billy, they'd probably send you boys to a reformatory. Me, they'd probably strap me into the electric chair."

"Floyd, what if someone asks about Pa? What do we tell them?" I asked.

"Just tell them that the last time you saw Pa, he was drunk and he had a fishing pole over his shoulder and was heading down the river." Again Floyd paused and looked around at all of us.

"I can't tell you how important it is that no one ever knows what happened to Pa. By this fall the grass will have grown back over his grave and no one will ever know where it is. It could be that none of us could even find it."

Kevin said, "I ain't telling nobody, that's for damn sure. The only thing I'm worried about is that little piss ant over there. He's got a mouth on him and that's for sure," and he pointed his finger at me.

Well, it riled me up a bit and without thinking, I reached out with my left foot and kicked the milk stool out from under Kevin and he hit the ground with a thump. The next thing I knowed Kevin was on me like a dirty shirt. He was astraddle of me and had already hit me in the eye before Floyd and the twins pulled him off.

"You oughten' have done that Billy," Floyd said. "Remember he's got busted ribs."

"I know," I said, standing up and dusting the dried cow shit off of me. "I just forgot. I'm sorry, Kevin."

Floyd and I went back to the river bottom forty and started back to choppen' cotton and the twins went back to fixing fence, and Kevin, Floyd insisted that Kevin take the rest of the day off but not go to the house where Ma could see him.

About six o'clock, Floyd and I went after the cows and as we brung em in, I saw thunderheads building in the southwest. We all had our cows to milk and I milked mine and one of Kevin's while Kevin sat in the corner of the barn and looked mad. Mad and miserable.

After we had milked the cows we carried the milk to the milk shed and separated the cream. We fed the separated milk to the calves and hogs and poured the cream into a cream can. Because of the clouds blocking the sun it was growing darker by the time we had finished so we went to the stock tank by the windmill, washed up and headed to the house for supper.

When I entered the house I smelled supper cooking and I knew we were going to have fried chicken again. Not that I minded fried chicken. In fact, I liked fried chicken. But we had had fried chicken every night for the past two weeks. The sad thing was we would probably have fried chicken for the next six weeks. That is until we had used all the fryers up. And when that happened I didn't know. I didn't know what we would have to eat.

Meanwhile we sat down to a supper of fried chicken, fried potatoes, lambs quarter greens and corn bread. Floyd asked the blessing, and we all dug in.

"Has anyone seen your Pa?" Ma asked.

Everybody shook their heads no with their heads lowered and I don't know about any one else, but when I shook my head no I kept my fingers crossed under the table.

Ma had finished eating but we were about halfway through when the rains came. I mean they came in torrents and the winds whipped the limbs of the elm trees frantically around the house. And then the rain changed to hail and it beat on the tin roof of the house with a roar.

"Billy, what happened to your eye?" Ma asked.

"Nothin'," I answered, and Ma looked at me and kind of smiled. Ma was one to let us boys solve our own problems.

"I hope your Pa isn't out in this," Ma said, leaving the table and going to the window and looking out. "I sure hope he's found cover somewhere."

"I'm sure he's not, Ma," Kevin said. "I'm sure he's found protection in the barn or granary."

"I sure wish your Pa wouldn't drink so much. Kevin, you don't look very happy," Ma said, and walked over to him and gave him a hug.

Of course Kevin with his busted ribs and everything, flinched and Ma felt it. She quickly backed away and said, "What's wrong, Kevin?"

Nobody said anything. We just kept on eating. "Somebody tell me what happened to Kevin?" Ma said, wringing her hands in the apron she always wore. "Tell me. What happened?" There was a long pause. "What happened, Floyd?"

"Pa gave Kevin a whippin'," Floyd answered.

"Why did he whip you, Kevin?"

"Durned if I know. I was nailing some boards up on the corral gate when he jumped me. Next thing I knowed was I was hanging on a corral post and Pa was whipping me."

"There had to be a reason, Kevin. There just had to be," Ma said.

"There was a reason, all right. The reason is Pa was a mean old son of a bitch," Kevin answered.

"Don't talk about your Pa that a way. Show him respect." Again there was a long silence. Finally Ma asked, "Where's your Pa, Boys?"

If the rest of the boys were depending on me saying anything they were barking up the wrong tree. I wasn't going to be no tattletale. Ma looked straight at me and asked, "Billy, where's your Pa?"

I looked at the floor and didn't say anything and further more I weren't going to say anything.

Floyd broke the silence saying, "Ma, when Pa whipped Kevin today he broke some of Kevin's ribs."

"I never ask what your Pa did, Floyd. I asked where he was."

Floyd continued, "Last month, Pa whipped Joe. Joe walked around addled head for over a week after that whippen'. Then two months ago, Pa whipped Billy. I don't know what he did to Billy but he peed blood for a week afterward. It was just a matter of time until he kilt one of the boys."

"I didn't need you to tell me any of that, Floyd. The question I asked was where is your Pa."

"Oh, for Christ sake, Ma," Kevin said, getting up from the supper table so fast his chair fell over. "We hung the mean old son of a bitch," and Kevin stomped out the door into the rain all hunkered over because of his busted ribs.

Ma stood there, her mouth open in shock. She turned abruptly and walked to the window and looked out. The hail had changed back to rain and it was still coming down hard and fast but the wind had died down. That's the way it is in Oklahoma. No rain or a bunch of rain.

With her back to us Ma said in a voice that was almost a whisper, "Tell me it isn't true, Floyd."

"I'm afraid it is, Ma. Twer'ent no other way."

"Oh Lord, what have I done? Where did I go wrong?"

Floyd stood up and walked to her. "It weren't your fault. You had nothing to do with Pa turning mean and vicious. There was nothing any of us could have done," and he started to put his arms around her. He started to give her a hug.

But Ma had other ideas. She whirled and pushed him in the chest and took a couple of steps backwards saying, "Don't touch me you, you monster! That's what you all are! Who else but monsters would hang their own Pa?"

"Ma," Floyd pleaded. "If I hadn't got back from the cotton patch in time, Pa would have kilt Kevin. You would have been burying a son for sure."

But Ma wasn't listening. "How could you boys do such a thing!"

Floyd pleaded, "Twer'ent no other way, Ma. Twer'ent no other way."

Ma looked out the window and watched the rain change quickly to a drizzle and then the drizzle stopped.

Floyd said, "Let's go check around and see what damage the hail has done while it's still light."

"Just a minute, Floyd," Ma said. "Get Kevin back in here."

Floyd did as he was told and Kevin came back in dripping wet.

Ma looked at all of us with her no-nonsense look. "Boys, I don't condone what you did but somehow I understand it. You may be right, Floyd, it might have been just a matter of time until your Pa hurt one of you boys mighty bad. But I still don't understand why you had to hang him. But you did and that's that." She sighed a deep sigh and her eyes turned steely gray. "Now you boys, don't you ever say a word about what you did to your Pa. Understand? Nary a word, ever."

"We weren't planning to, Ma," Floyd said.

"Well you'd better not. Now go on out and check the fields and see what the hail and rain did."

"Yes Ma'am," Floyd said, as he started out the door.

I got up from the table and started to follow the boys outside but Ma called, "Not you, Billy. You stay here with me."

The others left and Ma said, "You're so young, Billy. You're only twelve. You're too young to know what you done."

"I'm not too young either," I said. "I know exactly what we done. We hung Pa and he was asking for it. He was asking for it and we hung the son of a bitch."

"Don't cuss, Billy. Oh Billy!" she said and took me in her arms and about squeezed the breath out of me. "Let's go out on the porch and talk. I'll tell you of a side of your Pa you never knew."

Chapter three

As I followed her out onto the porch, Ma said, "Billy, your Pa used to be the kindest, gentlest man but of course you never knew him then. Your Father, Floyd Sr., and his two brothers, your Uncle Fredrick and your Uncle William, all worked for my dad. We had a large farm back in Pennsylvania and had a number of hired hands.

I took an interest in your Pa and he took an interest in me and one day he asked, "Rachel, would you like to go for a buggy ride with me after supper? Providing of course I can borrow your dad's horse and buggy."

"That would be nice, Floyd. Of course you must ask dad's permission."

My older sister, your Aunt Ruth, and I were very close and I told her about Floyd going to ask Dad for permission to court me.

"You're awful young to be courting, Rachel," she said.

"I don't care," I said. "I'm almost seventeen."

That night over supper after a lot of hem and hawing, Floyd asked, "Mr. Schmidt, I would like to borrow your horse and buggy and with your permission I would like to take your daughter for a buggy ride."

My dad liked Floyd and he thought he was asking to court Ruth so he didn't even hesitate before saying, "Of course you can borrow the horse and buggy but you will have to take Rachel along as a chaperone."

I glanced up quickly at Ruth and she shook her head no at me and motioned me to be quiet.

"I wouldn't have it any other way, sir," Floyd responded.

Floyd hooked up the horse to the buggy and pulled it up in front of the house. Floyd, being the gentlemen he was, helped Ruth into the buggy and then me. He then went to the other side and sat beside Ruth. As soon as we were out of sight of the house, Ruth and I traded places. It felt so good, sitting by Floyd and I wished I could feel that way the rest of my life. He made me feel so girlish and I felt so very safe with his big body beside me.

It was such a beautiful night, a new moon and the sky was filled with a million stars. Off in the distance we heard a hoot owl hoot and close by in the willows, we could hear the whippoorwills. When we crossed the bridge over the creek about a mile and a half from the house, Ruth asked Floyd to stop the team and he did.

Ruth said, "Now if you two will get out, I'll take the horses and buggy on down the road and turn them around. It will probably take me close to an hour to find a good spot to turn around in so you two behave yourselves."

Floyd jumped down and helped me down from the buggy. Ruth took the team on down the road and soon the clip clop of the horses hooves were lost to silence and Floyd and I stood on the bridge watching the stream go whispering by.

"The water is so clear and the creek is so pretty, isn't it, Floyd."

"It sure is, Ma'am."

"Floyd, you can call me Rachel if you'd like."

"Yes Ma'am, I mean yes, Rachel. Rachel, Rachel," he said, as if testing my name. "Rachel sure is a pretty name and it fits you. You're such a pretty thing."

"You sweet talker, you," I said, swatting him playfully on the arm. "Let's go wading in the creek."

"You think we should? Ruth will find a place to turn the buggy around and be back soon."

"Pshaw, when Ruth said it would take her an hour to find a place to turn around she meant she wouldn't be back for an hour. We have plenty of time."

So we climbed down the bank, sit down in the sand and took our shoes and socks off. We waded up the creek a ways and were wading back down when I stepped into some soft sand and would have fallen if Floyd hadn't grabbed me.

"You almost got all wet," Floyd said. "I don't know how you would have explained that to your dad."

"I don't know either, but I would have thought of something," I said.

"I'll make sure you don't fall in the water," Floyd said, taking my hand. Floyd was a shy one.

We waded on back to the bridge, picked up our shoes and socks and climbed back onto the road. We went to the bridge and sat down with our feet hanging over the edge. We brushed the sand off of our feet and put our shoes and socks on. Floyd reached over and took my hand.

"I don't think I'll fall now, Floyd."

"I know, Rachel. But I like holding your hand if you don't mind."

"I don't mind at all, Floyd. The truth is I kind of like it," and I smiled up at him. I think he would have kissed me then if he hadn't been so shy and if we hadn't heard Ruth singing 'The Old Rugged Cross' at the top of her lungs and the clippedy clop of the horses coming down the road.

"I'd like to do this again, Rachel."

"So would I, Floyd. Let's talk it over with Ruth."

"You two climb in and I'll drive until just before we get in sight of the house," Ruth said.

Floyd helped me into the buggy and then climbed in himself. I sat by Ruth with Floyd on the outside and Ruth started the team towards home.

"Ruth, would you mind if we did this again?" I asked.

"Mind?" Ruth said. "Mind? I love it. You know I'm the sneaky one in the family and I love putting something over on Dad."

"You're such a dear, Ruth," I said, and reached over and kissed her on the cheek.

When we got in sight of the house, Ruth stopped the buggy and Floyd took over the driving sitting beside Ruth.

The next time we went for a buggy ride Floyd and I didn't go wading but sat on the bridge held hands and talked.

Floyd said, "Fredrick, William and I are saving our wages. We don't use tobacco and we don't drink so we are able to save quite a bit."

"You mean I'm stepping out with a rich man?" I asked, teasingly.

"Oh, I wouldn't go that far," Floyd, answered. "But when we get enough saved, we're going out west to Oklahoma and get ourselves a farm of our own."

"Surely you don't have to go all the way to Oklahoma. Aren't there farms closer for sale?"

"But in Oklahoma they're giving land away for free," Floyd answered.

"I can't believe they're giving land away," I said.

"Well that is what they're saying but I expect that all the free land is gone by now," Floyd said. "But if they gave it away we ought to be able to buy it cheap, Fredrick, William and I. By the end of harvest this fall, we should have enough money to do it."

He had got up enough nerve to put his arm around me when we heard the clippedy clop of the horses and Ruth singing 'How Great Thou Art', at the top of her lungs.

The next time we went for a buggy ride and as we sat with our feet dangling off of the bridge, Floyd started off by putting his arm around me. We sat there in silence for a while watching the moon and stars reflect in the bubbling brook and listening to the stillness of the night with only an occasional call of the whippoorwill. I suddenly felt his breath on my face and felt his lips on my cheek as he kissed me.

"Floyd, that's not fair."

"What isn't fair, Rachel?"

"You kissed me and I didn't get to kiss you," I said.

Those few words were all the encouragement Floyd needed. Suddenly we were in each other's arms and all too soon we heard the clippedy clop of the horses and Ruth singing 'Rock of Ages'.

When harvest was done, my dad let Fredrick and William go, he didn't have enough work to keep them on through the winter. Soon, I got word that Fredrick and William had left. When I asked Floyd where they had gone he evaded the question. My dad still had enough work to keep Floyd busy, and so, he stayed on.

One Saturday Floyd went to town and when he came back we went for a buggy ride. Instead of trading places with Ruth when we got out of site of the house, Ruth climbed out of the buggy. "You two go ahead," she said, taking a quilt out of the buggy. "Just pick me up on your way back."

When we crossed the bridge, Floyd stopped the team and took me in his arms.

"Rachel," he said, "Now I'll tell you where William and Fredrick are. They are in Oklahoma. I got a telegram today. They have bought a section of land on the Washita River up river from Cheyenne about thirteen miles. They are in the process of building a half dugout. We all bought this land together with our savings and I'm now a landowner. I'm to meet them this spring with a wagon, a team of mules and a plow."

"Oh Floyd!" I said, "I'll miss you so much."

"The thing of it is, Rachel, I'll miss you also. Rachel, I'd like- - -, Rachel I think we ought to- - - Rachel, would you marry me?" he finally blurted out.

"Oh, Floyd!" I said, throwing myself in his arms. "Of course I will marry you. Just tell me when and where."

17

"How about next Thursday? I should have a team of mules and a wagon by then."

"You'll have to ask my father's permission," I said. "He's kind of old fashioned that way."

"I will. I'll have everything arranged and I'll ask him Thursday morning. Don't say anything until then."

"Dad is going to throw a fit," Ruth said when I told her. "He'll think you're much too young."

"I don't care," I said. "I love Floyd and he loves me and besides I'm seventeen."

"But you still need my help," Ruth said.

"It would make things a lot easier."

"Let's see. What can I get for helping you? Don't worry little sister, I'll think of something sometime when you least expect it. Just remember you owe me and don't you ever forget it."

Wednesday afternoon, Floyd went away and when he came back he had a team of mules and a wagon with a one-horse plow and a two-row planter in the back. My Dad should have expected something, but he didn't.

The next morning after breakfast, Floyd said, "Sir, I would like permission to marry your daughter."

"When?" was all dad asked.

"Today, Sir. I have the license and everything is arranged."

"Oh, no!" Mom said. "It doesn't give us time to plan for the church or anything."

"I know, Ma'am. But we don't want a big wedding or fuss. We've talked it over and we just want to get married by the justice of the peace."

I think my dad was thinking of all the money he had just saved and said, "Permission granted, Son. By all means, permission granted," and he shook Floyd's hand.

That after noon we stood before the justice of the peace and were married. Ruth, Floyd and I were the only ones there. Mom and Dad had it all arranged when we returned home but Floyd didn't even unhitch the mules.

"Ruth, you and Floyd can live in this room," Dad said, opening the door to an empty room. "It is much roomer than Ruth's room."

"But there is a problem with that, Father," I said.

"And what is that, Rachel?"

"I would like to live with my husband," I answered.

18

"What's that?"

"It is me, Rachel, Floyd married Father. Not Ruth."

He first turned gray and then his face turned red. "You sneaky little wench," he shouted. "You're no daughter of mine. Out of this house forever!" he continued to shout. "You too, Floyd! You double-crossing snake in the grass! Out! Out! Out, both of you!"

"I believe you owe me some wages, Sir," Floyd said in a mild manner. "I would like to think that my father-in-law is an honest man. I would like to think he would always pay his debts."

Dad stormed into the den and soon came out with a fist full of money. He thrust the money into Floyd's out stretched hand. "Here," he said. "Here's you damn wages."

"But sir," Floyd said, looking at the money. "This is much more than you owe me."

"I don't care. Out! Out! Out!" Dad shouted. "Be gone with you and good riddance."

We went outside and saw that Ruth was in my room. She opened the window and threw down my clothes. "Goodbye, little sister. Goodbye," Ruth called.

And that was the last time I saw her, Billy. I never saw her again.

Your Pa and I spent our wedding night in the back of a wagon with a planter and a one horse plow on our way to Oklahoma.

By the time Ma had finished telling her story it was dusk and she looked over at me and said, "Billy, that was such a long time ago. Here it is, 1941, but it seems like it all happened just yesterday."

The other boys returned and told us that the cotton crop had been hailed and flooded out, but the good news was that it was still early enough that we could plant again.

Chapter four

The ground was still too wet to work Saturday after the big rain so we worked on the fences until noon. We ate dinner and after dinner we carried buckets of water to the house from the windmill. We brought in the galvanized tub and Ma started water heating for a bath.

The tub bath was for Ma. Now don't get me wrong, all of us boys have bathed in that galvanized washtub from time to time, especially in the winter. But today the washtub was for Ma. It was Saturday and we were going to take the cream and eggs to town.

While Ma took her tub bath, us boys walked down the river carrying a set of clean clothes with us. Usually we had to walk down the river a ways where there was a deep hole of water but today there weren't no need to. With the recent rains, the river was flowing from bank to bank so as soon as we were out of sight of the house, we stripped down to the buff and dove in. The river water was well over my head, and there was a pretty swift current but it didn't worry me none because I'm a good swimmer. The other boys tell me I swim like a fish, and maybe it's true. I know I don't flounder along through the water like Floyd do.

When we were satisfied that we were clean, we got out of the river, shook ourselves dry, let the hot sunshine do its work and then we put on our clean clothes. By the time we got to the house with our dirty clothes Ma was clean and all spruced up so we hooked up the team, loaded the cream cans full of cream and egg cases full of eggs into the wagon and headed to town. Floyd drove the team and Ma sat up on the wagon seat with him but the rest of us boys climbed in the back with the cream and eggs and we headed to Cheyenne. Even though the fields were too wet to work, the road was dusty and red dirt fogged up from the wagon wheels. We met a pickup and then the dust really covered us up.

It took us a little over two hours to get there and when we pulled the team in front of the cream station—grocery store we were all about as dusty as we were before we took our baths, what with traveling over the dusty county roads and everything. But we pulled out our bandanas and began to wipe the dust from our faces and hands.

I thought I was as clean as the rest of the boys but I must not have been. Leastways not clean enough for Ma. She took my bandana from me just as I was about to put it into my back pocket and worked my face over some more. She must have found a dirty spot on my left jaw that wouldn't let go because she spit on my bandana and worked on the spot until my face burned.

Ma give me a dime and I headed off down the sidewalk of the main street of Cheyenne. I was heading to the drugstore where it was cool and I was going to buy myself a nickel coke chock full of cold ice. I rounded the corner to go into the drugstore and almost run head on into Betty Ann Payne.

Now Betty Ann lives across and up the river a ways. Her dad has close to a section of wheat ground plus a hundred acre hay meadow plus three sections of grassland back up in the red hills. He runs close to three hundred head of white-faced Herefords and has several hired hands who like to come to town dressed like cowboys but they ain't no more cowboys than I am. While they might work with the cattle a little more than we do they spend most of their days scratching in the dirt just like us. The only difference is they work the fields with tractors while we use horses.

"Watch where you're going, Billy," Betty Ann said. "You almost ran over me."

"Wouldn't been much of a loss if I had," I said.

"It might have been. I might have taken you down right here on the main street of Cheyenne and sit on you," Betty Ann said.

"That'll be the day when you can do that," I said.

"Or worse yet I might have grabbed you and kissed you in front of all these people," she said.

"And I might have blacked your eye like the last time you tried it," I answered.

"Well, I won't today but you can't ever tell. Someday I might. Bye bye, Billy Harshburger. I'll see you later if you're lucky," and she went walking away licking her ice cream cone and swishing her skirt in a saucy manner.

I don't like girls and of all the girls I don't like, Betty Ann Payne tops the list. But you can't let little things like that bother you so I went on into the drugstore, jumped up on a stool at the counter and when the waitress came to take my order I ordered a cherry coke. I could tell by looking at the waitress that she was more interested in the booth behind me than she was in fixing

21

my coke but she went ahead and fixed it anyway. As she made my coke I spun my stool around and looked at the booth behind me. There I saw three of Mr. Payne's hired hands sitting all dressed up in their cowboy outfits and I swear to God if one of them wasn't wearing chaps and spurs.

I took my time drinking my coke and eating all of the ice from the glass. I weren't in no hurry to leave the nice cool drugstore anyway. All too soon Joe stuck his head in the door and said, "Come on Billy, it's time to help load Ma's groceries.

"Can't we stay and go to the movie?" I asked as I helped carry sack after sack of groceries out and put them in the wagon bed.

"I'm sorry, Billy," Ma said. "We didn't get as much money for our cream and eggs and we can't afford a movie. I didn't even have enough money to buy all the groceries I wanted to."

Oh, well. Betty Ann Payne would probably have been at the movie and would ruined it for me anyway. I noticed one of the sacks of groceries I had carried out was chuck full of canning flats and I groaned because I knew what was in store.

We all loaded back up in the wagon and started the long dusty ride back home. We had gotten no more than a mile from town when Kevin said, "Say, Billy, didn't I see you talking to Betty Ann Payne?"

"You saw me talking to her, all right," I said. "And it was none too pleasant either." That's the problem with having so many brothers. You know that every time you do something one of them is watching you.

"I bet you were sweet talking her," Kevin said. "You little silver tongued devil, you."

"Tweren't neither," I answered. But I knowed I was in for a long ride home.

"Billy's got a girl friend. Billy's got a girl friend," Kevin started in and soon everyone except Ma joined in.

Like I said, I knew it was going to be a long ride home. But at last we got there and I carried the groceries in while Ma put them away. The other boys went after the cows. By the time I got the groceries carried in and the eggs gathered, they were in with the cows and I went down to milk.

It was dusk by the time we had finished milking, separating the cream, slopped the hogs and fed the calves. We washed up in the stock tank and went up for supper. I smelled it as soon as I went into the house. We were having fried chicken again.

The next morning was Sunday and we didn't work at all but by Monday morning it was dry enough to start plowing and planting but before I could slip out and help the other boys, Ma caught me.

"Billy, the green beans are ready to pick and can. I want you to stay and help me."

"Okay, Ma," I said. I knew there weren't no use arguing. It would be a losing battle because Ma usually got her own way. So I picked up a three-gallon milk pail and headed to the garden. When I had it full of green beans, I took it to the house and while Ma, snapped the beans and got them ready for the jars, I took another milk pail and went back to the garden. When I got it full I took it to the house but I had to snap this pail myself. Ma had already snapped the first pail and was putting the green beans into jars and getting them ready for the pressure cooker.

And that's how my day went, I'd pick the green beans and snap them while Ma put them in the jars and pressured them. When at last the day ended and I stopped picking and snapping so I could go and milk the cows, we had row after row of canned green beans setting on the table and ready to go to the cellar.

And so it went. Day after day I would pick green beans and snap them while Ma would can them. When the last green bean was picked and snapped, Ma sent me to the cornfield to gather corn. I picked the corn and shucked it and Ma cut it off of the cob and canned it. We now had corn on the cob along with our fried chicken for supper. Sometimes that's all us boys had for dinner. Ma would cook up a big old platter of corn on the cob.

By the time Ma had enough corn put away to last us a season, the green beans were ready to pick again. And guess who picked and snapped them.

By the time the green beans had shot their wad, the peaches in our orchard were ready to pick and can. While Floyd plowed up the old green bean vines and planted a fall crop, I picked and peeled peaches and cut them from the seed while Ma canned them.

The peach peelings didn't go to waste. No sir. Nothing went to waste on the Harshburger farm. Ma, with my help, cooked the peelings down and made jelly.

By the time the canning was done, the cotton was up and cultivated and was ready for choppen'. So it was back out into the cotton fields for Billy Harshburger.

We didn't work on Sunday and one Sunday afternoon I dug myself some worms, took my fishing pole down to a deep hole on the Washita River and started fishing for catfish. I caught several pan-sized catfish and as I fished, the water in the hole kept looking so cool and inviting. Pretty soon I couldn't help it. I set my pole in a forked willow stick, stuck the end firmly into the muddy bank, stripped off my clothes and dove in. I knew Ma and Floyd would skin me if they found out I was swimming by myself but I wasn't planning on saying anything and I doubted seriously that they would ever find out. When at last I came out and put on my clothes, I checked the bobber of my fishing pole. There weren't no bobber in sight, in fact there weren't no pole. I looked out in the middle of the water hole and there I saw my pole, zigzagging this way and that and moving this way and that. I got so excited that I jumped in after it, clothes and all. When I got to my pole, I grabbed a hold of it and started swimming back to shore. The way the pole tugged and pulled I knew I had a hundred pound catfish on the end of my line. When I got to the shore and pulled the fish up on the bank, I saw it wasn't no hundred pounds but it was a nice fish. I guessed that it weighed five or six pounds. We're going to have fish tonight I said to myself. I like chicken okay but catfish would be a welcome change of diet. But still yet there wasn't no way I was going to hide the fact that my clothes were wet.

When I brought the cleaned fish to the house, Ma already had the fryers kilt and dressed, but she set them in a cool place and cooked the fish instead.

This kind of started a routine. On Sunday I would dig worms and go fishing. Sometimes I would catch enough fish for supper, sometimes not. But one thing was always assured, before Sunday was through, I would go swimming in the deep hole on the Washita River without anybody knowing.

Chapter Five

The day before the Fourth of July, we loaded up the cream and the eggs in the wagon and Kevin took Ma to town. The rest of us went to the river bottom forty and chopped cotton.

"Sure looks like we're going to get a good cotton crop, Floyd," I said as our hoes went up and down, cutting the weeds and pulling damp soil around the tender young plants.

"It sure does, Billy. If nothing happens and we keep getting rains like we are we could get close to a bale an acre."

The twins had hooked onto a couple of exceptionally weedy rows and they were behind Floyd and me. "Floyd, if we do get a real bumper crop, do you suppose we could buy ourselves a pickup like the Paynes have?"

"I doubt that we get that good a crop, but if we do get a good crop you know how it goes, we won't get a very good price for it."

"Yeah, I know," I answered. "I remember year before last. We had a real good crop and it ended up we could hardly give it away. Then last year the price of cotton was high but we didn't hardly raise any. But if we do have a good crop and a decent price, do you think we could get a pickup? I'm getting awfully tired of riding the wagon to town. It takes so long to get there."

"I'd rather have a tractor, Billy. Our horses are getting old and sometimes I think they're not worth feeding all winter. I know one thing, we're going to have to get a younger team or a tractor."

By that time we had reached the end of the row. I picked up the file, which was sticking handle first in the ground, sat down on the ground, and began to sharpen my hoe. When I was finished I handed the file to Floyd and walked back into the scrub oak grove, picked up the gallon jug that had a wet sack sewed to it and had a big drink of cool water. It wasn't all that cool but it was a lot cooler than it would have been if it hadn't had the wet sack around it.

By that time the twins had come out the end of their rows and Floyd stood up and handed Joe the file. "Ready to make another round, Billy."

"Shouldn't we wait for Jim and Joe?" I asked.

"No. They just got here and we'll give them time to catch their breath. Let's skip two rows for them and we'll chop the next two rows."

"But they're the two weedy rows, Floyd."

"That's the point. The twins had the weedy rows last time and it's our turn this time."

"Now why in the hell should we favor the twins? We're ready to go and they're not. Let's take the next two rows."

"Don't cuss, Billy. You're too young. That's the way life is, you have to take the good with the bad. When you have the good be thankful, and when it's your turn to take the bad, well don't grumble. Just duck your head and get on with it. It's our turn to take the bad."

So we started chopping and when we were about half way through the field, the twins caught up with us and soon passed us. I didn't grumble when they went on down the field but it did burn me a little. But not as much as when the twins got to the other end and turned around and took the next two clean rows back.

"See that, Floyd. Jim and Joe took the clean rows back. We're going to be chopping the weedy rows all afternoon."

Floyd just laughed and said, "We're not getting paid by the row and it all has to be done."

It was about mid afternoon and I had just stopped for a moment to catch my breath and wipe the sweat off of my face when I heard the wagon come over the bridge and I knew that Ma and Kevin were home. It wasn't long until I looked up and saw Kevin coming to the field walking that long skinny stride of his and carrying a hoe over his shoulder.

We chopped until it was time to go get the cows and then Jim and Joe left to go get the cows and we chopped one more round before we went to the barn to milk.

The next day was the Fourth of July and Floyd and Ma both agreed that there wasn't anything so pressing that we couldn't take the day off. On a farm like ours, you never ever had all the work done. It was just that sometimes there weren't things just begging to get done. And this was one of those times. They sure didn't get any argument from me. I could take any day of the week off if they'd let me.

The day before when Ma and Kevin had gone to town, Ma had bought a big block of ice and two cases of soda pop. This was the one day of the year when we could have all the soda pop we wanted to drink. Again no argument from me as I guzzled an orange soda and turned the handle of the ice cream freezer. Jim came out to relieve me, and I let him take over. We were making the ice cream in the shade of a giant elm tree which grew just south of the house. I moved just far enough from the freezer that I could kick back against the trunk. I sat there and watched Jim crank the handle and drank my orange pop. This was the life. And of course for dinner, Ma cooked a big platter of fried chicken.

After we had all helped Ma clean up after dinner, we went out side and sat in the shade of the elm tree. Floyd took Ma a chair out to sit in but the rest of us sat on the ground and ate ice cream.

"This is liberty day," Ma said. "The birthday of freedom for Americans. But freedom hasn't been cheap. No sir, it hasn't been cheap at all. It has cost us a lot," and she kind of choked up and her eyes grew misty.

"No, freedom ain't cheap. It has cost not only American soldiers lives but other lives as well. During the World War, your Uncle Fredrick and your Uncle William went off to enlist. Floyd wanted to go with them but they talked him out of it since somebody was needed to run the farm and he had a wife and they both were single. They sent your Uncle William back because he had poor eyesight like you, Floyd, but they kept Fredrick.

"He wrote to us quite often and he would tell us where he was and what he was doing. Then pretty soon we got letters but the 'where he was and what he was doing' was blackened out so about all we knew was that he was okay.

"This went on for a year and a half and then we didn't hear from him. One day we got a telegram from the war department. When we opened it and read it we were informed that Fredrick had been killed in France.

"William saddled up and went to town that evening. Now none of the three brothers drank much but from what I heard, William got drunk. Mr. Payne and five of his hired hands were in town that night and they ran onto William in a bar. They started taunting him, calling him a dirty German.

"I'm an American," he said.

"One of them walked behind the bar and took down the American flag and held it out to William. 'If you're an American like you claim, then kiss this flag'.

"'Sure, I kiss it,' he said, taking the flag from them. And he did kiss it, not once but several times. Then he turned to Mr. Payne and handed the flag to him. 'Now you sons of a bitches kiss it,' he said, and the fight was on.

"They say the first lick William threw landed squarely on Mr. Payne's jaw and that he paralleled the floor and when he hit, he didn't move. They say that the next blow caught one of his hired hands in the breadbasket and he left the fight hunting for his breath. But the rest of the hired hands pulled their pistols and began to pistol whip William until he was unconscious. And even after he was unconscious, they kept beating him on the head.

"Then they put him on his horse, tied his hands to the saddle horn and sent him home. I never will forget hearing William's horse come plodding down the road. Floyd and I went to the door and looked out and saw William slumped in the saddle.

"We tried to doctor him. We tried everything we knew. But it weren't any use. He would just lay there and every once in a while he would snore. Finally Floyd hitched up the wagon and I put a stack of quilts in the bed. We loaded William in the wagon bed on the stack of quilts and took him to the doctor.

"He was in a coma for five days and was in the hospital for another two weeks before we brought him home. He was never the same again. If he were picking cotton he would pick and pick and pick until his sack was too full and he would still be trying to pick with the cotton spilling out of the sack. If he was plowing, your pa had to be there when he finished or he would keep plowing the same ground over and over again."

"What happened to him," I asked.

"I don't know, Billy. Nobody does. One day he wasn't here and we never saw him again. Your Pa went to look for him and he looked for him several days but he never did find him. He just wandered off somewhere."

"What about Mr. Payne and his hired hands. Did anything happen to them for treating Uncle William like that?" I asked.

"Why yes, Billy, they got theirs. The sheriff came out and asked your pa if he wanted to press charges and your pa said, no. You see, he didn't want any of them in jail. He wanted them where he could get to them.

"Your pa then waited for them. He waited along the side of the road. He was a very patient man. When he would catch one of them alone, then he would rope him and tie him to a tree. Then he would strip his clothes off and start to work on him with a buggy whip. It must have made a deep impression because when the hired hand was all healed up from the whipping, he left the county and was never seen again.

"He got them all but Mr. Payne and your Pa said that was okay, because Mr. Payne had nothing to do with it, him being unconscious on the floor and everything.

"So you see, the price of freedom is high and I hope we never have to pay it again. It cost the life of your Uncle Fredrick, it cost your Uncle William so much, and before that time, your Pa had been the kindest, gentlest man you ever saw."

"You mean Pa, changed after that?" I asked.

"Not so anyone could tell it. But I could. Something changed. He was still kind and considerate but it hardened him in ways that only I could see. He didn't start drinking until the thirties. That's when the depression hit. It was dry and dusty and it was seldom you could grow a crop and when you did, you couldn't sell it. I saw piles of cotton rot in the fields and the same thing with wheat. The government had a program where they would buy your cattle and then herd them up and shoot them. Your Pa refused to enroll in such a program. No, it was in the early thirties that I saw him start drinking corn and he changed from a kind, gentle man into the man you knew. I kept hoping someday he would quit drinking and change back into the man he used to be, to the man I loved. But it's too late now. Much too late."

After we finished our ice cream, all of us boys got our fishing poles, dug some worms and caught some grasshoppers and went fishing. It was hot. So very, very hot and the fish weren't biting. So it wasn't long until the cool water invited us in and we stripped off our clothes and went swimming.

The next morning it was back to the cotton field choppen' cotton for the rest of the boys but for me, the peaches were ripe again, and I picked and peeled peaches for Ma to can. I didn't mind too much though. It was much cooler under the elm tree peeling and slicing peaches than it was in the cotton patch.

Chapter six

It was the last week of July that we made our second cutting of hay. Floyd hooked up the team to the mowing machine and started cutting hay while Kevin, the twins, and I finished the last rows of cotton. Three days later we had the cotton chopped for the second time and I had a couple of days off while the hay dried, or would have had, if another bunch of peaches hadn't become ripe.

The twins and I picked, peeled and sliced peaches while Kevin and Floyd raked and piled the hay. By the time we got the peaches picked and canned, the hay was ready to haul.

Floyd harnessed up the team to the wagon and I drove. My job was to drive the wagon between two small stacks of hay and then stop the team. On one side of the wagon was Floyd and Jim and on the other side was Kevin and Joe, all with pitchforks in their hands. All I had to do was sit and watch as they loaded the small stacks of hay onto the wagon. Pretty easy job I had. It was about time I got an easy job around here.

When the wagon was full, I would drive the team up beside the haystack and then I had time off until the wagon was unloaded. While they unloaded the hay I found me a cottonwood tree with a nice shade and I sat and watched as the other boys pitched the hay onto the stack and tromped it down real good. I sat and watched and daydreamed of when I growed up. Maybe I would be a policeman or maybe I'd be a doctor. With the July heat settling in and smothering us, I knew one thing for darned sure. Whatever I was going to be, I was going to be up north where it was cool.

By the time the hay was all hauled in and stacked the apples were becoming ripe and Ma put me to helping pick, peel and can apples. You'd thought I was a darned girl, as much time as I spent in the kitchen.

It was the first day of August, and I was still peeling apples when I looked up at Ma and said, "You know school starts the sixth of August and I would sure like to go."

"Go you will, Billy. You might not be able to start when school starts but you'll be able to catch up if you're a little late."

"But, Ma, it's so much easier if I get to go to school when school starts."

This riled Ma somewhat and she said, "Billy Harshburger, you like apple pie in the winter time, don't you?"

"Yes, Ma'am."

"You don't think these apples are going to fall off of the tree and into the jar all by themselves, do you?"

"No, Ma'am."

"Well, I had better not hear any more grumbling about helping me can apples. You'll get to go to school when the apples are canned."

And I didn't say another word. I just kept on peeling apples. Pretty soon Ma asked? "Why do you want to go to school so powerful bad?"

"I want to get me an education, Ma."

"And what do you plan to do with your education, Billy?"

"I don't rightly know for sure but I do know one thing. I ain't going to be no farmer. I'm going up north where it's cool and get myself a job."

Ma looked at me and kind of smiled as she said, "You may be smarter than any of us."

School had just been going on for a week before the work was caught up and Jim, Joe and I got to go to school. We spruced ourselves up in our newest blue jeans, slicked our hair back real good and walked three quarters of a mile to catch the school bus.

We were close to the beginning of the bus route and we were some of the first ones on. I got a seat all to myself and had it to myself until the next stop when Betty Ann Payne got on. Even though there were plenty of empty seats, darned if she didn't plunk herself right down beside me in my seat.

"Well, well, Billy Harshburger, so you're finally coming to school."

I didn't feel that the conversation called for a response so I just sat there and stared out the window.

"Where you been, Billy? Why haven't you been coming to school?"

"They kept me home working," I answered.

"Working? Hah, I bet you've been spending your days down on the river fishing and skinny dipping."

"No I haven't. I've been working."

"I saw you down at that big hole in the river skinny dipping."

"You didn't either," but I felt my face turning red. Doggone that Betty Ann anyway.

"Yes, I did. What does your Mother and Father say about you swimming alone in that deep hole."

"Pa's not around anymore."

"Oh, where did he go?"

"I don't know. The last any of us saw him he was down on the river fishing," and I crossed my fingers and I thought I carried it off right well.

"Probably got drunk, fell in and drowned," Betty Ann said.

I didn't say anything and none too soon we were at the schoolhouse.

I had a new teacher for the sixth grade by the name of Mrs. Cole. She didn't take it kindly to me starting to school a week late and when I asked her what I had to do to catch up she really laid it out. Pages after pages of math, an unbelievable report in science and you wouldn't believe how much English she assigned.

After school I picked a bushel of tomatoes so Ma could can them tomorrow, went after the cows and when the milking, separating, and supper was over, I took a chair out on the porch, got a small table, opened my books and went to work. Ma brought me a lighted lamp when it started to get dark and I kept on working. By midnight my shoulders ached and my eyes burned but I was all caught up.

The next morning when I got on the bus, darned if Betty Ann didn't sit by me again.

Mrs. Cole didn't say anything when I turned in my catch up work the next morning, she just looked down her nose at me. But the next morning when she handed the papers back to me they were all marked with an A. "I'm real proud of you, Billy," she said. "You must have worked long and hard to get caught up like you did."

"Yes Ma'am, I did."

"Well keep it up and you'll do fine in the sixth grade."

It made me feel so good I was walking on cloud nine all morning. But at noon after lunch, things changed.

"Billy Harshburger," Bob Woods said, "I hear you're sitting by Betty Ann Payne on the school bus."

"It's more like she's sitting by me," I said mildly.

"I don't want you sitting by her. She's my girlfriend."

Normally I would have laughed it off and let it go but something about the tone of his voice irritated me considerably. Even though he was in the eighth grade and bigger than me I weren't going to take no lip off of him.

"You're talking to the wrong person," I said. "You ought to be talking to Betty Ann."

"I'm talking to you, Billy Harshburger, and if you don't listen I'm going to kick your butt," he said and he put his hand in my chest and shoved me backward.

That did it. I stepped forward and swung straight from the shoulder with my right hand and caught him in the left eye. While I was at it I followed through with a hard left hand and caught him in the right eye. I had learned a long time ago that if they can't see you they can't hit you. When I see I'm going to have to fight, the first thing I go for is their eyes. It has always worked for me and it worked this time too. Bobby Woods quickly brought his hands up to his face and that's when I put a left and then a right to the old breadbasket. He went down then and stayed on the ground crying and I simply walked away. I figured it was over with but I figured wrong.

When I went to the classroom after lunch break, Mrs. Cole met me at the door. "Mr. Davis wants to see you, Billy. You know where his office is don't you?"

"Yes, Ma'am." Mr. Davis was our principal and I knew the way to his office right well.

"You had better go to his office then."

"Billy, what's this I hear about you and Bob Woods getting into a fight during lunch hour?"

"Weren't much of a fight," I answered.

"That's what I hear. I heard you beat him up."

"Well, maybe," I said.

"What was the fight about, Billy?" Mr. Davis asked.

"He threatened to kick my butt so I saw no reason waiting, so I started kicking first.

"You've been in here for fighting before so you know what the punishment is, don't you."

"Yes, Sir. It's three swats."

"We might as well get it over with, Billy," Mr. Davis said reaching for his paddle.

"Wait a minute," I said. "Where's Bobby Woods. Don't he get three swats too?"

33

"Billy, he has two black eyes and you don't have a scratch on you."

"So I'm getting three swats because I'm a better fighter than he is?"

"You could say that," Mr. Davis said. "Bend over, Billy."

Weren't no use arguing, so I bent over and took my three swats. It didn't feel like he put too much into it though.

The worst punishment was on the school bus going home that evening after school. Betty Ann sit by me and said, "I hear you and Bobby Woods got in a fight over me, Billy."

"It weren't over you, Betty Ann."

"What was it over, then?"

"He threatened to kick my butt and I couldn't see no use waiting."

"But why did he threaten you, Billy?"

"Because you sit with me on the school bus."

"Then it was over me," she said excitedly. "Just think, two boys fighting over my affections. What a most wonderful thing to happen. How lucky I am to have two men love me."

"It weren't that way, Betty Ann." But she wouldn't listen to a word I said. Her mind was made up and there weren't no changing it. It was a very long ride home.

When I got home I picked Ma another bushel of tomatoes and by that time it was time to go after the cows.

When the milking, separating, hog sloping, and calf feeding was done it was time for supper. "Ma, Billy got a whippen' at school today," Joe said over supper.

That's the trouble with having brothers in school with you. Anything happens at school it comes straight home.

"Is that true, Billy?" Ma asked.

"Yes, Ma'am," I answered.

"What was it for," Ma asked.

"Fighting," I answered.

"Did you win?" Kevin asked.

"I'd say so. He has two black eyes and I don't have a scratch on me."

"Good job, Billy," Kevin said, slapping me on the back.

"Kevin, don't encourage him," Ma said. "Billy, you know what the rules are, don't you?"

"Yes, Ma'am," I answered.

"We'll take care of it after supper," Ma said.

I can't really say I enjoyed my supper much after that but when everyone was through eating we cleaned up the table. "Joe, Jim, I want you two to do the supper dishes. I have to take care of Billy."

"Yes, Ma'am," they said.

"Billy, go get you Pa's razor strap and let's go down by the barn."

I did as she told me and when I met her down by the barn she said, "Tell me about it, Billy."

"It's like this," I said, "Every morning on the school bus, Betty Ann gets on the bus and sits beside me. I don't invite her, she just plops herself down. I really wish she would sit somewhere else. I don't like girls and I don't like Betty Ann most of all.

"Anyway, Bobby Woods is stuck on Betty Ann and as far as I'm concerned he can have her. But today, right after lunch, he told me he was going to kick my butt if I sat by her on the school bus anymore. I would of agreed with him if I had any choice. But I don't. She sits by me, I don't sit by her. So anyway, when he threatened to kick my butt, I saw no reason to wait, so I hit him. Weren't much of a fight. He ended up on the ground crying and actually I felt a little sorry for him."

"You know what I have to do, don't you Billy?"

"Yes, Ma'am. I got three swats at school so I get six swats at home. It didn't seem fair at school and it don't seem fair now."

"Why?"

"There weren't no avoiding it. For some reason Betty Ann is going to sit by me on the school bus, and if I hadn't fought him today he would have fought me tomorrow."

"Never the less, you got a whippin' at school and a rule is a rule.

"Yes, Ma'am," and I bent over and she whopped me six times with the razor strap. It stung a bit, but I've had worse.

It was a far worse punishment the next morning, riding to school with Betty Ann sitting beside me and telling me what a hero I was for fighting for her.

35

Chapter seven

Things started going pretty good at school after the tussle with Bobby Woods that is except for Betty Ann. Every morning and every evening, no matter where I sat, Betty Ann plopped herself down beside me. But Bobby never said a word. Other than that, things went pretty good.

Every morning when I got off of the school bus, Larry would be waiting. We were the best of friends and had been since the first grade. We'd walk around the schoolyard and talk about the things we were going to do when we growed up and talk about what a pest girls were. Some times we would join the others in a game of 'tin can down' but mostly we stayed by ourselves and sat under a shade tree if the weather was hot, until the bell rang for us to go to class.

When we played 'tin can down', we played with not only the sixth grade but the seventh and eighth grade as well. To play 'tin can down,' there had to be someone who was it. We had an old tin can with rocks in it and the top smashed down flat so the rocks would stay. We drew a circle on the ground and then someone would throw the can. Whoever was it would run after the can and bring it back to the circle. Meanwhile the rest of us would go hide. When 'it' got the can back into the circle, they would start looking for us. When they found someone they would race back to the circle, put their foot solid on the can and say "tin can down," on whoever they had found. Then that person had to stay close by. When everyone was found, then the first person caught was the 'it'. However, if someone could sneak in to the can without being caught, then that person could pick up the can and throw it and everyone who had been found could run and hide again. Travis was the best at sneaking in and he could throw that can a country mile.

One recess we were playing and John, who had been the last one out of the schoolhouse, was 'it'. I hadn't hidden very well and was one of the first ones caught. Larry was the next one caught, he had hidden close to me, and then Betty Ann, Peggy Sue and Mary Beth. That's when Travis sneaked in and picked up the can. He reared back to sling that can to forever and away, but it slipped.

36

It flew right at me and before I could duck, it caught me right above the eyebrow. It knocked me down and I jumped right back up to run and hide but it wasn't any use. The can hadn't gone very far when it bounced off of my head and John grabbed the can, dropped in the circle, put his foot on it and started calling 'tin can down,' and he named everyone including Travis.

I didn't care much, blood was streaming down into my eye and I couldn't see. I pulled out my bandana and held it to the cut place and it stopped the flow of blood somewhat, but didn't do anything for the hurting. Betty Ann got me by one arm and Mary Beth got a hold of the other and they took me, over my protest, to Mrs. Cole.

"Billy Harshburger, have you been fighting again?" Mrs. Cole said when she first laid eyes on me.

"No, Ma'am," I answered.

Betty Ann and Mary Beth both explained to her what happened.

"Let me see," she said, pulling the bandana away, and of course the blood started flowing again. She turned kind of pale and had me put the bandana back to the cut. "You girls take him on down to Mr. Davis's office and I'll see if I can find some tape and bandages."

Mary Beth and Betty Ann did as she had told them.

"Don't tell me you've been fighting again, Billy," Mr. Davis said.

"No Sir," I said. "When I've come to your office for fighting, do I usually look like this?"

"No, Billy," he answered, kind of laughing. "Usually it's the other guy. You're pretty handy with your fists. I suppose you have to be when you have four older brothers. Tell me, what happened?"

Mary Beth and Betty Ann explained what happened.

"Let me see, Billy," Mr. Davis said.

I pulled the bandana away and let him have a good look.

"We really need to take you to a doctor and let him sew it up," Mr. Davis said.

"No, Sir," I said. "I ain't ever been to a doctor and I don't aim to start now."

"You 'haven't been to a doctor, Billy?" Mr. Davis said.

"No, Sir, I ain't," I answered.

Mr. Davis gave a deep sigh. "We'll patch you up the best we can, but you really need stitches."

Mrs. Cole came in about then with gauze and tape. They patched me up until it didn't bleed any more and then the bell rang and recess was over and it was time to go back to class.

"Billy, you been fighting again," Kevin asked. "What does the other guy look like?"

"No, Kevin. I ain't been fighting," I answered. "I got hit in the head with a tin can." And I went on ahead to explain what happened. It was the same after we had done the chores and went to the house for supper.

"You been in a fight again?" Ma said, when we sit down for supper and she saw the bandage on my forehead.

"No, Ma. I ain't been in a fight," I sighed. I went ahead and explained to her what happened and since the twins backed me up, she believed it.

A week later the bandage came off and we got our six-weeks report card. My report card looked much better than my forehead. My forehead had a long red scar across it but my report card had all A's except in English. In English I got a D.

"We're going to have to work on your English, Billy," Mrs. Cole said. "We're going to have to fix the way you talk and write. You're a smart young boy and there is no reason you shouldn't speak the King's language in a proper manner."

"I ain't got no King," I answered.

"You see, Billy. That's just it. Ain't isn't a proper word to use and you used a double negative also."

"I don't know what you're talking about," I said.

"What you should have said is 'I haven't a King'," Mrs. Cole responded.

I think every person has a teacher that influences him or her more than anyone else and I believe that was true for me also. That teacher for me was my sixth grade teacher, Mrs. Cole.

"Billy, Jim, Joe, you had better get your teachers to give you as many assignments ahead as they can. You're going to have to stay home next week. Kevin and I need you to help heading feed," Floyd said Thursday night at supper.

So Friday morning I went into Mrs. Cole's room before the bell rang and told her the situation.

"You mean they can't head feed without you, Billy?" Mrs. Cole asked.

"No, Ma'am," I answered. "On our farm we all have to do our share of work. That's how we make our living."

"So your Dad said you had to stay out of school next week? Is that right, Billy?"

"No, Ma'am. My oldest brother Floyd was the one. Pa disappeared last summer and we haven't seen him since."

"All right, Billy. I hate for you have to miss school. But if you must, you must. Come to me after school and I'll have next week's assignments outlined for you."

I did, and she did.

We started heading feed the next day, Saturday. Again I drove the wagon with Floyd and one of the twins on one side and Kevin and the other twin on the other. While I drove the wagon down the rows, the other boys would cut off the heads and toss them into the wagon. When the wagon was full, I drove the team up to barn and they forked the heads into the granary.

One hot afternoon the boys had just started cutting the heads off and throwing them in the wagon when Dolly stepped close to a rattlesnake and it buzzed. The horses had been more restless and harder than usual to handle all day and when the rattler buzzed, that's all it took, and they were off.

"Whoa! Whoa!" I shouted, standing up and sawing on the reins. But I might as well have been talking to the wind for all the good it did. "Whoa! Whoa!"

When we got to the end of the field, I tried to turn them down a little road we had there but I couldn't do that either. When I saw we were going through the fence, I grabbed hold of the wagon seat real good with both hands and hunkered down. All three strands of the barbwire snapped when the horses hit the fence and I heard the broken wire zinging around my head. The horses reared and I grabbed the reins and hauled back on them hollering, "Whoa! Whoa!" For a moment I thought I had them under control but Molly and Dolly were of a different mind and they took off again.

The pasture was real bumpy the other side of the fence and all I could do was hang on and ride. The front wheel of the wagon dropped off into a small ditch but that ditch was large enough to rock the wagon up on two wheels. For a long moment it looked like the wagon was going to turn over and I was trying to decide whether to try to ride it out or jump. I looked at the pasture and looked at the prickly pear cactus bed we were going through and I tightened my grip and decided that in the wagon was the place to stay. At last the wagon dropped onto all four wheels with a bone-jarring thud, and I was glad I had made the decision I had.

It might have been fun if I hadn't been so scared. As it was, my heart was pounding a million times a minute, and every time we hit a big bump and the wagon went airborne, and I had to grab another hand hold on the wagon seat, my heart went to beating a little bit faster.

At last, we were out of the rough pasture and racing over fairly smooth grassland and I could turn loose of the wagon seat and take the reins again.

I knew what was ahead, and I didn't like it. Over the next rise and at the bottom of the hill was a deep canyon. I didn't know if the horses would stop at the canyon or not. The mood they were in, I wondered if they wouldn't just keep on going and pile up in the bottom of the canyon. I knew one thing for sure, I wasn't going over. If I couldn't stop them by then, I was jumping. That was for sure. That was for darned sure.

Again I stood up and leaned back putting all my weight on the reins and hollering, "Whoa! Whoa, damn you! Whoa!"

We were going uphill, the horses were old and I think they had about run all they wanted to anyway. Whatever the reason, they began to slow down and I kept working the reins. Soon they were at a trot and then they stopped and stood there, their heads down and their sides heaving.

I got down from the wagon and walked up to their heads, stroking their heaving sides all the way and talking to them nice and gentle. At last I got them calmed down and checked them over. The barbed wire had cut them on the chest and the front leg but the cuts were shallow and they were bleeding only a little.

I climbed back on the wagon seat and turned the team around. I met Joe, Kevin, Jim and Floyd about half way back to the field and they were all running in the direction I had gone.

"We were coming to gather up the remains," Kevin said, breathing hard. "But I see you rode it out okay.

"There wasn't anything to it," I said. "I just hung on tight until I could get them back under control."

"Is the team okay?" Floyd asked, walking up to the horses and looking them over.

"I could find only a few scratches from the barbwire," I answered. "I think the horses are all right."

"I wonder what made them run away?" Jim asked.

"Didn't you see or hear that rattler that Dolly almost stepped on?" I asked.

Jim's face went a little pale and he said, "No. No I didn't. I guess we'd all better watch where we're stepping."

We went back to the field and again began to head feed, cut the grain from the top of the maze stalks, as if nothing happened. The work went slower with everyone walking more careful and watching where they stepped. I leaned back in the wagon seat nonchalantly and hoped against hope that no one noticed my shaking hands holding the reins.

After the feed was headed, Floyd hooked the team to the binder and started bundling the stalks. Us other four boys followed behind putting the bundles in shocks. And then we hauled the bundles in and stacked them.

I was working with Kevin shocking feed when I asked him, "What are we going to do with the feed we headed and stored in the granary?"

"You know as well as I do, Billy. We're going to feed it to the horses and cows this winter."

"Kevin, what are we going to do with these bundles we're shocking?"

"We're going to feed it to the horses and cows."

"Wouldn't it have been a lot easer and faster to have bundled the feed with the heads on it? After all we're going to feed it all to the horses and cows."

Kevin stopped and looked at me with a quizzical expression on his face. "That's a good question, Billy. I don't have a good answer. Floyd's kind of the boss around here since Pa's gone and he decided to head the feed and then bundle it because that's the way Pa did it. I suppose Pa did it that way because he was taught to do it that way by his pa."

"It doesn't make any difference with me," I said. "I was just curious."

We got to go back to school at the beginning of the next week. I pretty well had all of my work caught up and it wasn't near the struggle it had been when I first started to school that year.

When I got on the bus that first morning, sure enough Betty Ann plopped herself right down in the bus seat with me. "Well, look whose back. Billy boy is going back to school. Where you been, Billy? Isn't the water a little chilly to be swimming?"

"I've not been swimming, I've been helping get in the feed."

"Yeah, yeah, I bet. You probably been down at the hole fishing. Are the fish biting real good, Billy?"

41

"I ain't been fishing, Betty Ann. I mean I haven't been fishing. I've been working." Doggone that Betty Ann anyway.

A few nights after we had started back to school, we got a real heavy frost and I knew the cotton would open, the leaves would fall off so we could reach the bolls real good and school would turn out for cotton picking.

Chapter eight

The Saturday before we started picking cotton, Ma used her cream and egg money to buy canvas. Even though the next day was Sunday Ma finished making cotton sacks which she had started the night before.

"Here's yours, Billy," she said, handing me a cotton sack. Before I had always picked cotton using a six foot sack but when I looked at the sack she had made me, I saw it was a good ten foot long.

"Isn't it somewhat longer than I usually use?" I asked.

"You're a bigger young man than you were last year. We expect more out of you, Billy."

I didn't like the sound of that but I didn't say anything.

That night after supper, Floyd said, "Since Pa isn't around anymore, I think we should have a family discussion on cotton picking."

"What are you suggesting, Floyd?" Ma asked.

"Before, we all picked to support the family and that was okay then. But now we're all older and we need money for our very own. What I'm suggesting is this. When we weighd our cotton, we keep track of how much we each pick. When we sell the cotton then we each get paid by the pound for picking and only the profits go to the family and the farm."

"That sounds like a damn good idea to me," I said, without thinking.

"Billy Harshburger, don't you dare cuss in this house! Especially in my kitchen," Ma said.

"Yes, Ma'am. I'm sorry," I said.

"How much would we pay ourselves for picking," Kevin asked.

"In town Saturday, I heard the going price was a dollar seventy five a hundred," Floyd said.

"Sounds fair to me," Kevin said and all the rest of us agreed except Ma.

"I never heard of such a fool notion," Ma said. "Your Pa would never have agreed to such a thing. Your Pa felt that a roof over you heads, plenty to eat and clothes to wear was pay enough."

"But Ma, Pa is gone," Floyd said. "The cream and egg money feeds us with the help of butchered beeves, butchered hogs, and frying chickens. Would you agree to it if we agreed to buy our own clothes?"

"Well, that might be okay. If you bought your own clothes." She was silent for a while and then she said, "You know I always pick some. Does that mean I'd get paid?"

"Of course, Ma," Floyd said.

"What if I didn't want to. What if I felt my share should go into the family fund?"

"You'd get paid anyway," Floyd said. "You could use the money to buy yourself new dresses and ribbons or whatever you wanted."

She sat there again in silence thinking things over. "Okay. I guess since I'm outnumbered I might as well agree."

The next morning we each got a pair of cotton gloves, picked up our cotton sacks and walked to the river bottom forty. Ma was with us. She had put on a pair of Pa's overalls and had her gloves in one of the big pockets and her cotton sack over her shoulder.

The cotton looked as good as we thought it would be. It stood waist high to the other boys and shoulder high to me and Ma. The stalks were full of cotton boles and boles went from the ground clear to the top and over half of them were open. We strung out across the field, each of us picked a row and started down it snapping the boles off and putting them in our sacks, boles and all.

The first two hours went pretty good and I picked a hundred pounds of cotton and according to my calculations, I made a dollar seventy-five. But it was then I began to hurt. First is was my back and then the back of my legs. Then my shoulder began to chaff where the cotton sack strap went around my shoulder. I dropped to my knees and crawled along my row. Then my knees got raw and began to hurt. I thought seriously about sitting on my sack and taking a rest. As tall as the cotton was no one could see me if I did. Then I thought of the dollar seventy-five a hundred and of all the things I was going to buy with my money and I kept on picking. When my knees hurt too bad I stood up. When my back began to kill me, I dropped back to my knees and so the morning went.

At lunch time we stopped and sat on our full cotton sacks at the scales where we weighed the cotton and ate the lunch we had brought to the field. Ma had cooked an extra large batch of biscuits for breakfast and then she had scrambled a big skillet of eggs. She had covered the biscuits on top and bottom with a liberal portion of sandwich spread and then placed scrambled eggs between the top and bottom.

I knew this would be our fare for lunch throughout cotton picking but I didn't care. I was so hungry after a morning of picking cotton that the biscuit and scrambled egg sandwiches were right tasty.

After lunch I didn't want to go back picking cotton, I was hurting so much, but everyone else got up, weighed the cotton and dumped their sack in the wagon and I knew that they were hurting as much as I was, so I weighed my sack, dumped it into the wagon and started down another row. After all I was making a dollar seventy-five a hundred of my very own.

Ma stopped picking in the middle of the afternoon and went to the house to fix supper, but us boys kept on picking until it was time to bring in the cows and do the chores.

When we got to the house after doing the chores, Ma was back in her dress and had supper on. I would have enjoyed supper a lot more if I hadn't been so tired. After we had eaten and helped Ma clean up, I slipped into the big room where all us boys had our beds and lay down for a spell. I thought I'd just lay there a while and rest up but the next thing I knew, it was morning and Floyd was shaking my shoulder to wake me up and I knew that today would be the same as yesterday. Darned if I was going to be a farmer when I grew up! One day was just about the same as the next.

We had turned our old wagon into a cotton wagon by putting two by fours up right on the side, braced them up real good with more two by fours and lined the sides with chicken wire. I guessed it was close to two o'clock when we filled the wagon with cotton. Floyd hitched up Molly and Dolly and took the cotton to the gin at Cheyenne. The rest of us kept on picking and piling our cotton on the ground. Again Ma quit in time to go to the house and cook supper, and the rest of us boys kept on picking until it was time to go and do the chores.

With four of us doing the chores rather than five it took a little longer, and we were later than usual getting to the supper table. Floyd hadn't got back from town yet so we ate without him, however Ma did put the food back on the stove to keep it warm for him.

Even though I was tired and sleepy I was determined to stay up and wait for him. I sat out on the front porch, swatted mosquitoes and watched down the road. Listened for the sound of Molly and Dolly's hooves on the hard packed road and watched for Floyd to come home.

It was well after dark when I heard the hoof beats and I got up and went to the corral to help Floyd unhook the team. When we had the horses rubbed down and grained, Floyd and I went to the house.

"How did it go?" I asked, as Floyd sat down to supper.

"Pretty good," he answered. "The price of cotton was fair so I sold this bale. I may not sell anymore for a while. People were talking that with the war in Europe, cotton prices are going to go up."

When I first started cotton snapping I thought that in a few days I would get used to it and it wouldn't hurt so bad. I was wrong. I never did get used to it and it always hurt. The first two hours of a morning in the cotton field and I hurt from the stiffness and soreness from the day before. After I had that worked out, I hurt from what I was doing today. I never complained or said a word about it though. I knew if I did, they would call me a 'sissy' or a 'wimp', and I figured that everyone else was hurting the same as I was.

But sometimes when I was struggling to get out of bed of a morning I thought about playing sick. Playing sick and staying home for the day. Nobody would ever know. I had done that last year several times and nobody ever found out. However, I think Pa suspected it, but even if he did, a whippin' wouldn't hurt no more than bole pulling did. And besides that, he was often sick himself. Drunk more than likely. But then I would remember that I was getting paid this year. Remembering that I was making money of my very own and with the thought of it, I would fight my way up until I was standing on my hind legs. I had never, ever, in my whole life had any money of my very own, only a nickel or a dime that Ma gave me. The way I had it figured, I had made close to a hundred dollars and today I was going to make more.

I'm not bragging none when I say that I'm fast with my hands. That's the reason that I've never been hurt much in a fight. I can hit them several times before they can swing one blow and usually by then they are extremely discouraged.

46

Besides having fast hands being handy in a fight, fast hands are right handy snapping cotton. Especially when you're getting paid by how much cotton you snap. I could pick more cotton in a day than Ma or the twins and I think I could have picked more cotton than Floyd except the cotton sack would get heavy and slow me down. I know I could never have matched Kevin. He has fast hands like me and besides he is bigger and can zip that heavy cotton sack right on down the row.

We picked cotton every day except Sunday. Sunday, 'the Lords Day,' as Ma called it, we took off and rested. We even picked cotton on Thanksgiving.

At noon on Thanksgiving Day, that 1941, we were sitting by the wagon on our cotton sacks eating our biscuit and scrambled egg sandwiches when Ma looked around at us boys and said, "We have so much to the thankful for. Nineteen forty-one has been good to us. We had a good feed crop and we have a good corn crop in the fields waiting to be harvested. We're gathering a good cotton crop and we're getting a good price for it." Again she looked around at us boys, her eyes resting on each one of us for a long moment before she said, "The thing I'm most thankful for though, is my boys. I'm thankful that all of you are here and not across the seas fighting in the war that's going on."

"About the fair price for cotton," Floyd said, "The price of cotton is going up every day and I haven't sold any except that first load. Do you think I ought to sell?"

"Whatever you think, Floyd," Ma answered.

"I'm getting kind of nervous," Floyd answered. "We have twenty-nine bales we haven't sold and I'm afraid the price will go down. I think I'll sell when I take this load to town."

But he didn't. When he took the next bale to town, the price of cotton had gone up even more and so he hung onto them.

We were about through with the first picking and it was Saturday December the sixth. School would be starting back up in another week but I could see that we would have it all snapped by then for the first time, but we would be starting over again, picking the boles that hadn't been open when we went through it the first time. Of course the second picking wouldn't be near as good as the first. And of course there was still corn in the field to be harvested.

The wagon wasn't quite full when we stopped picking that Saturday but we took Sunday off anyway. Monday morning we finished filling the wagon and Floyd hitched up the team and took the cotton to town. We kept on picking and piling the cotton on the ground.

It was middle of the afternoon when I looked up and saw Floyd coming to the field driving the team much faster than he should have, them being old and everything. Even at that distance I could see that they were all lathered up and were about done in.

"We're at war!" he shouted as he came on into the field. "We're at war with Japan and Germany. Cotton prices are sky high and I sold every bale we had."

It was then that Ma sat down on her cotton sack and started crying. "Don't cry, Ma," I said, walking to her and putting my arm around her. But it didn't help. She just kept on crying.

"I'm going to Oklahoma City tomorrow and join the army, Floyd said. "Those Germans and Japs will be sorry they started this war when they have to face Floyd Harshburger."

"Especially when they have to face two Harshburgers," Kevin said. "I'm going with you."

"How about me?" I asked. "I'm a real good fighter."

"Yes, you are," Kevin said, "But you're too young. You're only twelve years old and Floyd and I will have this war over by the time you're old enough. Shoot, I suspect we'll have it finished by the time you're thirteen."

Ma didn't beg or plead with Floyd and Kevin not to go. She had too much dignity and was smarter than that. Ma just sat on her cotton sack and cried and cried and cried.

Chapter Nine

Kevin and Floyd packed what little clothes they had, Ma made them plenty of biscuit and scrambled egg sandwiches, and they started hiking down the road to catch the train at Red Moon. It wasn't much of a hike, only about six miles.

The railroad track went from Pampa, Texas, to Clinton, Oklahoma. We had two trains a day go through. One going west and one going east. One of them was a coal burning freight train that pulled a passenger car behind its freight cars. The other was a small, diesel switch engine, labeled the Doodlebug, which pulled only a passenger car and sometimes a freight car. On one day, the steam train went from Clinton to Pampa while the Doodlebug went from Pampa to Clinton and the next day they would do the reverse. On any given day a person could go east or west if they chose, but they either road the Doodlebug or the freight train.

The day before I had seen the smoke from the freight train heading east, so today I knew Kevin and Floyd would catch the Doodlebug. They planned to ride it to Clinton where they then planned to catch a bus.

It was in the evening of the fourth day after they had left that I looked up from separating the cream and saw Floyd walking down the road, suitcase in his hand.

I saw him go into the house and a short time later he came down to help us finish the chores. "What happened, Floyd? How come you're home? Why aren't you getting ready to go out and fight the Japs?"

"My eyesight, Billy. They wouldn't take me because of my eyesight. I told them I could still fight, even with my bad eyes, I even offered to step outside and show them I could fight. But because of my bad eyes, they wouldn't take me."

"But they kept Kevin?" I asked.

"Yeah, they kept Kevin. Doggone I wish I could have stayed with him."

When I started to school again after cotton picking, the other boys just kind of shunned me. In fact, everyone shunned me except Larry. And of course, Betty Ann. I would just as soon that Betty Ann had of shunned me.

Larry was good to have around. It felt good to have one true loyal friend.

One day during lunch hour shortly after we were back in school, Larry and I wandered out to the drinking fountain that was outside by the windmill and storage tank. The drinking fountain was only a pipe sticking out of the ground with a spout on top of it. To get a drink, one just turned a valve wheel and water came spurting out the spout. When you were through getting a drink, you were supposed to turn the valve off. A lot of times the kids would forget and let the water keep spurting out onto the ground and the ground around the fountain was always wet and muddy. I let Larry get a drink first and as he did I saw Bobby Woods, Travis, John, Ralph, and Troy coming our way. They are just thirsty, I thought as I bent over to get myself a drink.

"Stop that!" Bobby said.

"Stop what?" I asked.

"Stop drinking out of that water fountain," Bobby said. "My friends and I have to get a drink too and we don't want to drink after no dirty German.

I sighed. I thought Bobby Woods knew better. I really did, but I guess some people never learn. He walked right up to me his fist clenched at his side.

My right fist shot out and caught him in the left eye. Like I say, I have fast hands and before he could do anything, my left fist hit him in the right eye. I put a left and a right into his breadbasket and just for good measure, I followed through with an uppercut to the chin. Then I stepped back and let him fall. I wasn't mad, I really wasn't. Excited, maybe, but I wasn't mad. It was just that I wasn't going to take nothing from anyone.

It was then that Travis said, "My Daddy's out whippin' Germans and now I'm going to whip me one," and he started towards me.

I didn't back up. Not on your life. I never back up from a fight. Travis and I had never fought. We each, at one time or another, had fought everyone else in school, but we had never fought each other. I didn't like the idea of squaring off against him. He was big, he was fast and he was tough. I had seen him fight several times and I saw that he was utterly ruthless. I would have given anything to be anywhere else but where I was. But Travis left me no choice. The only choice I had was either fight or run and I wasn't about to run.

Might as well get it over with, I thought. I felt in all likelihood I was fixing to take a beating. That Travis was tough. I knew he had seen me fight before and he knew I went for the eyes first, so this time I did something different. I faked a left towards his eye and it worked. He was ready for it and he quickly raised his hands and when he did, I quickly came in with a right to his stomach with all the power I could muster. Then I followed with a hard left and then a right to the same place. Hitting his stomach was like hitting a board but I heard him gasp and it did slow him down some. He swung a left hook, which I partly blocked with my right hand, and I put a hard left jab right on his nose. His nose started bleeding and I liked the results so much that I put a right in the same place and I felt the bone of his nose break and I knew the fight was about over. I started a left for his eye but before it landed, the others piled into me and I went to the ground. And that made me real mad. It just wasn't fair.

Larry jumped in to help me but it was no use. I had seen Larry in fights before but I had never seen him win one. Larry helping me was worse than no help at all. He just kept getting in the way.

They had us down in the mud and were pounding on us something fierce and I was beginning to hurt real bad. I tried to cover my head and face with my fists and arms and someone reached down to pull my hands away. When he did, his finger got too close to my mouth. I opened my mouth, reached my head up and latched onto it and hung on biting as hard as I could. The howl of pain was music to my ears and made the beating I was taking almost worthwhile.

Above the howl of pain I heard Betty Ann screaming, "It's not fair, all you boys picking on Billy and Larry. I'm going to go get Mrs. Cole."

"No need to come and get me," I heard Mrs. Cole say. "Go get Mr. Davis. Boys! Boys! Stop that fighting right now."

I felt their grip on me let up as they turned me loose. I saw John's face swim into view and I couldn't help it, I uncorked a good one. John went up in the air and over backwards.

"Billy, you too," Mrs. Cole said. "Stop that fighting."

We all stood up then but I noticed they all stood well out of my reach.

"Just look at you boys," Mrs. Cole said. "What a bloody, muddy mess. What was the fight about anyway?"

"Nothing," I answered.

"It must have been about something," Mrs. Cole said. "Oh, well," she said with a sigh. "We'll let Mr. Davis sort it out. Come on boys, let's go to Mr. Davis's office."

I led off. I figured I knew where Mr. Davis's office was better than anybody. I hurt all over but I stood up real straight and refused to let them see me limp even though my leg was killing me.

We met Mr. Davis hurrying towards us before we got halfway there. "Do you know what the fight was about, Mrs. Cole?" Mr. Davis asked.

"No," she answered. "I asked Billy and he said 'nothing'. All I saw by the time I got there were Bobby and Travis laying on the ground. Troy, John and Ralph had Billy and Larry down on the ground beating on them."

"Thank you, Mrs. Cole. I'll take it from here. Come on boys, let's go to my office."

Once in his office, Mr. Davis asked, "Now what was the fight about?"

"Nothing," I answered.

He asked each one in turn and they gave the same answer I did.

"You boys all know the punishment for fighting, don't you?" Mr. Davis asked.

"Yes Sir," I answered. "Three swats."

"Okay," Mr. Davis said, picking up his paddle. "Who's going to be first?"

"I'll go first," I said. "But you might as well give me twelve swats and we'll get it over with."

"Twelve, Billy? Why Twelve?"

"Well, three for this fight. Bobby and Travis I've pretty much settled with but for those other three sons of bitches I haven't settled the score. But one by one I will. I'll catch them by themselves and then I'll have three swats coming. Count them up. That's twelve swats. Let's go ahead and get them out of the way."

"I see your point, Billy," Mr. Davis said, laying the paddle down. "Perhaps I'll make an exception this time. Perhaps I won't give anybody swats."

You could see everyone's face light up when he said that, but mine didn't. I knew there was a catch there somewhere.

"You boys are going to have to settle this among yourselves some how," Mr. Davis said. "We can't have you fighting every time you get together. So what we'll do is this. When recess comes, rather than going out, you'll stay in Mrs. Cole's room. At lunchtime you will take your lunches to Mrs. Cole's room and eat your lunch there and then you will stay in. I'm sure that given enough time, you boys can settle your differences peaceably. Do you understand me, Boys?"

"Yes, Sir," we all mumbled.

"We'll do this until you work out your differences. When you do, you come to me and say so. After you've apologized to each other before me and have shaken hands and have promised no more fighting, then you can go out at recesses and lunch hours. Until then all of you will be staying in. If it isn't settled by spring when school is out, then we'll start again next fall when school starts up again. Now I'm going with you to clean up and then I'm taking each of you to class."

We stayed in during the afternoon recess but I didn't say anything to any of them and they didn't say anything to me.

"You been fighting again, haven't you, Billy?" Ma asked when I got home from school.

"Yes, Ma'am," I answered.

"And you got three swats, so go get the razor strap."

"No, Ma'am. I didn't get three swats."

"Oh? How did that happen? Tell me about it, Billy."

So I told her about it. I told her from the start when they demanded that I not drink out of the fountain until Mr. Davis told us we would be missing lunch hour and recesses until we had it settled.

Ma sighed. "I'm afraid that you, Jim and Joe are in for a rough time. I'm afraid that we all are until the terrible war is over and maybe not even then. Well, you go on out to the cotton field and help Floyd, Jim and Joe with the second picking of cotton."

That night after supper I was out in the yard when I saw car lights coming down our driveway. That itself was puzzling. When the car pulled up into our yard and stopped, I saw Mr. Woods get out, followed by Bobby, Travis, Troy, Ralph and John.

I shouted, "Floyd, Jim, Joe, get out here. I might need some help." It was mighty gratifying to see all three of them come bailing out the front door of the house, followed by Ma.

Mr. Woods chuckled, "I don't think you'll need any help, Billy. But it's nice to meet the rest of your family. I understand that my boy and these other four boys got in a fight with you today."

"Yes, sir," I answered.

"Mind telling me what it was about?" Mr. Woods asked.

"No Sir, I don't. They told me not to drink out of the water fountain because they didn't want to drink after a dirty German," I answered.

"That's pretty close to what they told me. They told me they ganged up on you. Is that true?"

"Yes, Sir, they did, and I didn't think it was fair."

"I agree with you, Billy," Mr. Woods said. "They told me also that you were going to catch them by themselves and beat up on them. Is that true, Billy."

"Yes, Sir. I did make such a promise," I answered. "And I aim to keep it."

"I don't blame you, Billy. Now is your chance. Your brothers and I will see that no one interferes and you can take them on one at a time. Is that agreeable to you Mrs. Harshburger?"

"I don't condone fighting," Ma said. "But if that's the only way to settle it, it sounds fair to me."

"It's settled then," Mr. Woods said. He turned to Bobby and said, "Bobby, you want to be first?"

"No, Sir," Bobby said. "He done whipped me twice and I'm not hankering for a third whipping."

"Then apologize," Mr. Woods said.

"I'm sorry, Billy," Bobby said. But I could tell it wasn't coming from the heart.

"Travis?" Mr. Woods asked.

"He hurt me powerful bad today, Mr. Woods. I think I can whip him this time, but not without getting hurt. I'll pass," Travis said with a wry grin. "I'm sorry, Billy." Again I couldn't tell, but I don't think that his apology was sincere.

"Troy, do you want to fight him?" Mr. Woods asked.

"Heck no. I would have a hard time whipping him with two hands but now I'd have to fight him with one. He done almost bit my finger off. I'm sorry, Billy."

So that's whose finger I had between my teeth, I thought with great satisfaction.

"John?" Mr. Woods asked.

"No," John answered. "He just got a little bit of me when he poked me in the face, but that little bit let me know that I don't want no more. I'm sorry, Billy."

"Ralph?" Mr. Woods asked.

"I can't whip him. If I were to step up to fight him, the only thing I'd get would be a beating. I'm sorry, Billy."

"Mrs. Harshburger, I thought you had five sons, yet I only see four here," Mr. Woods said. "Don't you have another son?"

"Yes, I do," Ma, said. "He's off to basic training for the army. He's getting ready to go across the sea and fight the Germans."

I looked at the five boys who had fought me and I saw their mouth drop open. They looked sheepishly at the ground and then Travis stepped forward.

"I am truly and deeply sorry for what we did today, Billy," Travis said, shaking my hand, and I could tell it was from the heart. The others rushed forward, shook my hand and apologized all over again.

"What can we do to make it up to you, Billy?" Travis asked.

"Just be my friend," I answered.

"That won't be hard to do," Travis said. "In fact I think I might enjoy it." Then he said with a grin, "I still think I can whip you though."

"Anytime you want to try it, come ahead," I answered.

"No. No. I don't think I'll even try. Even though I whipped you, I'd get hurt doing it. No, let's just let it lie. Let's not find out whose the toughest," Travis said, slapping me on the back.

The first thing the next morning we all met in Mr. Davis's office and told him we had settled it, that there wouldn't be anymore fighting between us.

"I'm glad," he said. "Fighting is a poor way to settle anything. Actually it doesn't settle anything at all. It just decides who's the biggest, toughest, and fastest. All other things should be settled other ways. More peaceful ways."

When I left Mr. Davis's office, I left with Larry and five new friends.

Chapter ten

It was Saturday when we got the first letter from Kevin. It was just afternoon and we were all ready gathering up our clothes and getting ready to take a bath in the galvanized tub. It was a little over a week before Christmas and much too cold to take a dip in the hole at the river.

From the house I saw the mail carrier driving his car down the road and I saw him stop at our box and then take off again in a cloud of dust. I went running to the mailbox to see what he had left. Besides the Sears and Roebuck catalog, I saw we had a letter. The letter was from Kevin. I knew better than to open it and start reading. I knew that only Ma could open the letter, that was the rule, and I also knew Ma would read it to us, so I hustled back to the house as fast as I could run.

When I reached the house, baths were postponed while Ma opened the letter and read it to us.

Dear Ma, and Brothers,

I hope this finds you well. For me I have good days and bad days. You know how I am when it comes to taking orders. I never took orders at all until I joined the army. Now I take orders most of the time. It is hard for me to do, but when I'm ordered to do something, I swallow once and maybe twice and do it.

Like the other day, I was ordered to pick up a cigarette butt and put it in the butt bucket. Now I haven't learned to smoke yet and I knew it wasn't mine. I thought seriously about refusing, but I swallowed twice, picked it up and did as I was told.

All this marching and saluting, I don't see how its going to teach me anything about how to fight the Germans, and I know I'm going to be fighting the Germans. When they found out I could speak German real well, they decided then where I was going to go. Not only that, but they gave me the rank of PFC. That's private first class, one step above private.

I'm going to close now, I have to pull KP tomorrow and I know they will have me up by three thirty.

Love to all,

Kevin

After we all had time to discuss Kevin's letter, we took our baths, harnessed up Molly and Dolly, loaded the cream and eggs into the wagon and headed to Cheyenne.

On our way back home, Jim hollered, "Stop, Floyd. Look at that," and he pointed to an old John Deere tractor setting under a tree with weeds growed up around it.

"I don't see anything," Floyd said.

"See that tractor setting there with the weeds around it?" Jim said. "I bet we could buy it real cheap."

Floyd spotted it and said, "I bet we could. It don't look like it will run."

"But Joe and I have been studying things like that at school. I bet we could get it running. There's a house up there and I bet the guy who lives in the house owns the tractor. Let's go see if he'll sell it."

Floyd turned the team up the driveway and when we got to the house, the guy came out into the yard to meet us.

"Do you own that old John Deer tractor?" Floyd asked.

"I sure do," he answered.

"Would you sell it?" Floyd asked.

"Sure I'd sell it. I can't get the dad burned thing to run."

Floyd and he started dickering and the guy who owned the tractor had met his match. That Floyd could dicker a person out of his shirt and then get him to throw in a dime to get it washed. In the end, we wound up owning a tractor that wouldn't run and the guy had ten dollars in his pocket.

Even though the next day was Sunday, Floyd and the twins talked Ma into letting them take the team and drag the tractor home. It looked funny when they returned home to see one of the twins driving the tractor while the other one walked with Floyd driving the team.

"Don't reckon you'll plow very fast like that with the tractor," I couldn't help saying.

"You just wait, Billy," and I could see it was Jim driving the tractor. "You just wait and you'll see how much we can plow with this tractor."

I helped them get the tractor into a shed out of the weather and the twins immediately went to work on it.

Ma came down to the shed and saw what the twins were doing. "Boys, this is the Lord's day. It is a day of rest."

"But we're not working, Ma. We're playing."

"It looks like you are enjoying it. I suppose it will be okay. Go ahead, play with the tractor. It's not going to hurt anything."

There wasn't much farming to be done in the winter other than shelling corn and the chores. The twins spent every spare minute after school working on the tractor.

Then Christmas vacation came and the twins worked on the tractor all day long. They had that tractor tore into a million parts and if that wasn't enough, they went to town and bought some more parts. Then they cleaned all the parts and started putting it back together.

It was New Year's Day and Ma had just sent me out to get some more wood when I heard a loud explosion from the shed. My first thoughts were that the twins had blown the shed to smithereens. A quick glance showed me the shed was still standing but a powerful lot of gray smoke was coming from it. I started running to the shed to help them put the fire out. Floyd passed me before I was halfway there but neither one of us had made it to the shed before we heard another loud bang and then the steady pop, pop, pop of the John Deere tractor.

Floyd stopped and I caught up with him. "They got it running, Billy," he said. "I can't believe it. They got it running."

"It sure sounds like we got ourselves a tractor," I said, grinning at him. About that time, I heard kind of a grinding sound and looked back at the shed to see the tractor lurch backwards out of the shed with Jim at the wheel and Joe riding the tow bar. They backed out a good ways and then the tractor came to a stop. I saw Jim messing with the gearshift and then the tractor inched forward very slow. Jim stopped the tractor and found another gear and the tractor went faster. By that time they had the tractor headed in the general direction of Floyd and me. They stopped the tractor again and when it started forward again it almost died, but Joe reached up and pushed forward on the throttle and that old John Deere started coming towards us powerful fast. I didn't know whether they could drive well enough to miss us, this being the first time either one of them had ever had hold of the wheel of a motorized vehicle, but I didn't hang around to find out. I run and Floyd run with me. I got behind a tree and Floyd stopped, turned around and came back to the tree with me. The twins went by, laughing and waving but they were having trouble making the tractor go in a straight line.

Ma came out of the house and we went to her and watched as the twins went down our road to the mailbox.

"I see they got it running," Ma said. "I guess we have just sprung forward into the modern age of farming."

"That is if someone will learn how to drive the fool thing," Floyd said.

"I think Joe is about to master the art of tractor driving," I said, as I saw them coming back up the road towards the house and the tractor was going in a much straighter line than when it had left.

They turned the tractor around and brought it to a stop. "Want a ride, Floyd?" Joe shouted above the steady pop, pop, pop of the engine.

"Not me," Floyd said. "You ain't ever going to catch me on that durned thing.

"What about you, Ma? Want a ride?"

"Riding on a tractor is just so much foolishness," Ma said. "But if you're old like I am then you might as well be an old fool. I don't mind if I do."

Jim got off of the tow bar and Ma got on. I was kind of amused to see Ma hanging onto the tractor seat for dear life as Joe took her to the mailbox and back. When they got back, I saw Ma was grinning from ear to ear.

"Want a ride, Billy?" Joe asked after Ma had stepped down.

"No, I don't want a ride," I said. "I want to drive it."

"I don't know, Billy," Joe said.

"Come on," I said. "If you can drive it then I can drive it. You just have to show me how."

"Well, okay," Joe said, climbing down from the tractor while I climbed upon the tractor and Joe got on the tow bar.

"Billy, that pedal by your left foot is the clutch. Put your foot on it and push it down."

I did as he told me.

"Now push the gear shift to the left and bring it back."

Again I did as he told me.

"That lever up there is the throttle," he said, pointing. "Let out on the clutch gently and push forward on the throttle."

Again I did as he told me and the tractor lurched forward and then settled to a snails pace. "Joe, I want to go faster than this. I want to go real fast like you did." I said over the pop, pop of the motor.

"I think we'd better work up to that, Billy," he said. "But we will put it into a little faster gear. Push in on the clutch, let the tractor come to a complete stop and then move the gear shift forward and to the right."

I did as I was told and the tractor started going backwards. "You have it in reverse, Billy. You pushed the gearshift straight forward. Push in on the clutch again. There that's right. Now pull it back until you can move it to the right just a little bit and push it forward."

I did as he told me and when I let out on the clutch that tractor reared up in front and when it came down it took off like a scalded skunk. "Whoa!" I shouted. "Whoa! Joe, I don't want to go this fast." About that time, the front wheels hit in the sandy road and the tractor made a hard right turn, the right rear wheel came a frightful distance off of the ground and I started out across the rough field.

"Joe!" I shouted, "I don't want to go this fast. What do I do?" But Joe didn't answer. I took a quick look over my shoulder and saw that the reason Joe didn't answer was because Joe wasn't there any more. I had to look quickly forward to see where I was going and I saw the bank of the Washita River was coming up mighty fast. I thought about jumping but then I thought again. If the jump from the tractor didn't kill me, Jim and Joe would if the tractor wound up in the river.

But if I didn't do something and do it real soon, the river was where I was going to wind up. The riverbank was coming at me powerful fast. I have to confess, I panicked.

I turned the steering wheel hard to the right and again the tractor made a sharp turn with the wheel coming up off of the ground. I was racing down the field and I took a quick glance to the place where I had left Joe and saw Joe sitting in the middle of the road rubbing the side of his head.

I wanted out of the field and it was apparent to me that I was going to have to turn the steering again to the right to get there. It was also apparent to me that the last time I had turned the steering wheel too much and too fast. This time I turned the steering wheel gently to the right and the tractor came around just as pretty as you please. I was getting the hang of steering the tractor right well. Now if I could just learn how to stop it.

I saw that I would soon be out of the field and onto the road so I started turning the steering wheel gently to the left and the tractor came up out of the field and started down the road just as pretty as you please. I looked up and saw Jim running towards me.

He stepped out of the road into the field as I drew closer to him and when I went by, he jumped on the tow bar, grabbed a hold of the seat and hung on. When we were about to the yard where Ma and Floyd were watching us, he reached over my shoulder, got hold of the throttle and pulled it all the way back. The tractor popped a couple more times, sputtered and died.

"So that's how you stop the darned thing," I said.

"That's one way," Jim said. "It's not the best way. The best way is to push in on the clutch and take it out of gear."

"How did you like your first tractor driving lesson, Billy?" Floyd asked.

"I don't think Joe cared for it much but I was about to get the hang of it," I answered.

About that time Joe walked into the yard, the side of his face and head all skinned up. "Did he break anything?" he asked Jim.

"No," Jim answered. "The only thing I can find wrong with it is the tank is about dry." He turned to Ma and asked, "Can we have some kerosene?"

"Some what?" Ma asked.

"Some coal oil. This tractor runs on coal oil."

"Sure, boys. Go ahead. Just make sure you leave me enough to cook supper and breakfast."

"We'll only take a little, Ma," Jim said. "But next Saturday we'll use the tractor to pull the wagon to town and we had better bring back a couple of barrels of kerosene."

I watched as Jim and Joe took turns practicing driving the tractor all evening but I didn't even ask them to let me take my turn.

Chapter eleven

When school started back up again after Christmas vacation I knew I was in for the long haul. With the exception of getting Good Friday off before Easter, I knew I was in for a steady grind. No more time off until summer.

Kevin got a furlough at the end of basic training and he was able to come home for a short while. I was really surprised when I saw him come walking up the driveway in his soldier suit. Ma had sent me out to bring in an armload of wood for the night and I was the only one outside when he came walking into the yard.

"Hey, Kevin," I said, shaking his hand. It looked to me like Kevin had put on weight and it looked like most of it was muscle. I looked at him and said, "What are you doing home? How come you're not out there fighting the Germans? You've not whipped them yet, have you?"

"No, Billy, they ain't whipped yet. I've just finished basic training and I have a few days off."

I looked at his arm and said, "What does the two stripes on your sleeve mean?"

"They really don't mean a lot. They simply mean that I'm a corporal for right now."

"What do you mean for right now? Aren't they on there to stay?" I asked.

"Billy, those stripes have been sewed on and ripped off so many times they're about worn out."

"How come they keep taking them off?"

"The first time I made corporal, a private in my squad objected to me giving him an order. He tried to hit me but I ducked real fast and the next thing he knew, he was on the ground. I didn't put him on the ground hard enough because he came right back up and when he came up he had a switchblade knife in his hand. I got a little over excited and when I took it away from him, I broke his arm. Then of course I broke the knife and threw it away.

"Two sergeants came up and grabbed a hold of me and I was still a little excited and I didn't notice the stripes on their sleeve. All I knew was two guys grabbed me and I didn't appreciate it one little bit so I started swinging. I won the fight but lost my stripes and was a private again. Every time I build up a little rank, something would happen and I'd lose it again. Is everybody else inside?"

"Yeah," I answered. "Come on inside where it's warm."

We went inside and everyone else was as surprised and happy as I was to see Kevin home.

"You're not home to stay, are you?" Ma asked hopefully.

"Nah, Ma. I've just finished basic and I have a short furlough. I have to be in Texas a week from Monday.

"What in the world are you going way down in Texas for?" Ma asked.

"I'm going to learn how to be a waist gunner in a bomber, Ma. I'm going to fight this war up in the air. That way I won't have to walk. Down in Texas is where I'll be trained."

We sat up and talked late into the night with Kevin telling us one soldier story after another. It sure was exciting, the stories he told, and he hadn't even left to fight the Germans. I sure wish I were old enough to fight the Germans.

Kevin took off his soldier suit that night before he went to bed and next morning he tried to put on some of the work clothes he had left behind when he went off to basic. Neither the pants nor the shirt fit. They were all much too snug.

"Looks like you might of growed a little, Kevin," I said.

"Either that or my clothes have shrunk since I've been away. Floyd, you got some extra clothes I could wear?"

Floyd give him his extra set of work clothes and Kevin put them on. They were too big but at least Kevin could wear them.

Kevin had gotten home Friday evening and the next day being Saturday, Jim, Joe and I didn't have to go to school.

After we ate breakfast and did the chores, nothing would do but that Jim and Joe had to show Kevin our tractor.

"Will it run?" Kevin asked when we were in the tractor shed.

"You bet it will," Jim said. "Joe and I had to work on it from the bottom to the top. But we got it running. Here, I'll show you." He closed the petcocks at the side of the engine, grabbed hold of the cast iron flywheel, and with effort, spun it. The John Deere fired right up and I listened to the pop, pop, pop of the engine.

"I'm impressed," Kevin said. "Looks like we have a couple of mechanics in the family. That tractor will be real handy when it comes plowing time this spring."

"Do you want to go for a ride?" Jim asked.

63

"Sure," Kevin answered. "But I don't see no saddle and there's only one seat. I don't see how it's going to happen. I'm sure not going to sit in that seat and try to drive the durned thing myself."

"I'll drive, and you stand on the tow bar and hang onto the seat," Jim said.

"Or, better yet," Joe said with a grin, "if you really want a ride, let Billy drive."

"Don't listen to them, Kevin," I said. "They're going to tell you a bunch of exaggerations and a pack of lies. There isn't a word of truth in it," and I ducked my head as Joe told Kevin of my first, last and only tractor driving lesson.

"And you haven't tried to drive the tractor since, Billy?" Kevin asked.

"No I haven't. They won't let me and I don't want to," I answered.

"Better give it a few more shots, Billy," Kevin said. "I'll bet that if you would give it a few more tries, you'd become a first class tractor driver."

That was just like Kevin. When he and I fought, he was always pounding me into the dirt and then helped me up and encouraged me to fight better.

Kevin got onto the tow bar while Jim crawled upon the tractor. Jim carefully backed the tractor out of the shed and started down the driveway. When he got to the mail box instead of turning around and coming back, he turned west and soon the pop, pop, pop of the tractor died in the distance.

"We might as well cut wood, boys," Floyd said. "There ain't any other work that's pressing to do."

We went down to the river and Joe pulled up dead limbs for Floyd to chop or break into firewood. As soon as there was an armload, I gathered it up and carried it to the house. I put the first armload in the wood box by the stove in the house. When I got back they had already cut much more than I could carry. I took the next armload up onto the porch and started a stack there. When I went back for the third armload, there was chopped wood all over the place and I took as much as I could up to the house and stacked it with the other wood on the porch. As I stepped off of the porch, I heard the tractor and looked down the driveway and saw it coming to the house with Kevin driving.

"How do you like driving the tractor, Kevin?" I asked when they got to the yard and Kevin pulled the throttle back to idle.

"It's all right, Billy. It's all right."

"Joe, why don't we hook the wagon to the tractor and pull it down by that woodpile Floyd and Joe are making?" I asked. "We could load up the wagon and bring all the wood to the house at once."

"I don't know what Floyd would think of it," Joe said. "We've never done it that way before."

"That's because we've never had a tractor before," I answered. "Besides we're having to move on down the river farther and farther and it's getting a greater distance from the house."

"It sounds like a good idea," Kevin said. "Billy, let's you and me gather up the bucksaw and the other two axes and put them in the wagon. With all of us working I bet we can cut enough wood to last all the rest of the winter."

While Jim drove the tractor to the wagon and hooked it up, Kevin and I gathered up the wood cutting tools and carried them to the wagon. When everything was loaded up, Jim started to get on the tractor but Kevin stopped him.

"Jim let's let Billy drive the tractor."

"I don't know about that. I remember the last time he was a hold of the steering wheel."

"That's okay, Kevin. Jim doesn't want me to drive and I really don't want to."

"Billy, get your butt up in that tractor seat," Kevin said. As I climbed onto the tractor, I wondered how anyone could even think about disobeying Corporal Kevin Harshburger when he spoke in that tone of voice.

Jim got on the tow bar, had me push in on the clutch and put the tractor in second gear himself, this time.

"Now gently let out on the clutch," Jim said and I did as he said and the tractor started forward. "Now push forward on the throttle, that's right, that's just right," and he left me and walked the wagon tongue back to the wagon and climbed on the seat beside Kevin.

The tractor was moving just about the same speed a person could walk and that was fast enough for me. It was a lot easier to steer in second gear than it was in road gear and I handled it right well even if I say so myself and soon we were at the wood pile that Floyd and Joe had cut.

With Floyd chopping, Joe cutting the limbs off of the dead trees, Jim and Kevin cutting the bigger logs and me loading the wood on the wagon we had a wagon full of wood shortly before noon. Nothing would do but Kevin had me drive the tractor back to the house and I found second gear myself.

We stacked some of the wood on the porch but the rest, we piled on the ground behind the house. After the wagon was unloaded and Joe had pulled the wagon down close to the milk house, I just stood and looked at all the wood we had cut and hauled that morning. It was apparent to me that we wouldn't be cutting wood any more this winter.

I knew that Kevin had to leave in the latter part of next week, but I sure wish he could stay around. Everyone else wanted to do things as they had always done them and Kevin was the only one who would listen to me when I had an idea.

After lunch, everyone took baths and put on their going to town clothes. Kevin put on his uniform and we loaded the cream and eggs and headed to Cheyenne, the tractor pulling the wagon, Ma and Floyd on the wagon seat, Joe driving and Jim, Kevin and I sitting in the back. The trip to town went a lot faster with the tractor pulling the wagon, rather than Molly and Dolly.

When we reached Cheyenne, I went to the drugstore to buy me a cherry coke with my own money I had made picking cotton. When I got back to the cream station—grocery store, Ma had bought all her groceries and the boys were all there and had most of them loaded up. I carried a couple of bags out and when I put them in the wagon I noticed two brown boxes in the wagon and I could tell at a glance, it wasn't Ma's.

I didn't say anything even though my curiosity was killing me. I didn't say a word or ask a question, which was quite a feat for me.

When we got home I carried in the groceries with only Floyd helping me. Jim, Joe and Kevin took in the boxes and again I didn't ask any questions.

When the groceries were carried in I went into the living room and there was Kevin and Jim tinkering with a brown wooden box with a dial and knobs while Joe strung wire out the window and up on the roof. I couldn't take it any longer so I asked, "What is going on here?"

"I bought you guys a radio," Kevin said. "I used my savings from my army pay. Now you can keep track of what's going on in Europe and the Pacific. Joe's stringing out the aerial now."

I stepped outside and looked and sure enough, there was Joe up on the roof stringing wire. When I went back inside, Kevin was just finishing fastening the aerial to the back of the radio. We all gathered in the room and watched Kevin plug it into the dry cell battery. Then Kevin turned it on and I kind of jumped as voices of people I didn't know blasted into the room. It was a miracle sure enough. People a thousand miles away talking to us in our house. We stayed up late that night listening to the radio.

We listened to the radio all day Sunday and Monday I didn't want to go to school. "Billy," Kevin said. "Do you want to be a farmer all your life?"

"No, sir. I want to go get me a job as soon as I'm old enough."

"Then you had better get all the education you can get. The better education you have the better job you'll get. Take me for instance. If I had more education than I've got I'd be leaving to go and learn how to fly a bomber. I'd dearly love to do that. But I don't, so all they'll let me do is fire a gun out the doorway while some other guy has control of the airplane. I know I could learn to fly just as well as the next person, but they won't even start to teach me.

So I went to school. Flying an airplane sounded to me like a pretty neat job to have. But I swear that day was the longest day of my life as I waited for the last bell to ring, so I could catch the school bus home.

And sure enough, Betty Ann plopped right down beside me and chattered all the way. Right irritable.

Chapter twelve

At last school was out for the summer and was I ever ready for it. For a month almost everyday had been a beautiful spring day with the sun shining and the birds singing in the elm trees outside our classroom window. I was ready for school to be over with for that year. I was tired of sitting at my desk all day and I was ready to be outside again.

It's funny how that works. I was so anxious to get out of school that spring and yet by the first of July walking down the cotton row with the hot sun beating down on my bare back, I was counting the days until school started again, and I could be inside out of the sun and sitting down.

That spring the tractor made the plowing and planting go a lot faster and even though Floyd still used Molly and Dolly to cultivate, the tractor didn't help at all with the cotton choppin'. It was still hot, sweaty, tedious work.

It was the middle of July when we bought the Burns farm. Mr. Burns was close to ninety years old. I never knew his wife, she was dead before I was born and his children and grandchildren were all in California.

It was evening and we were all sitting out on the front porch when we saw him coming down our driveway in his old green pickup. He parked his pickup in our yard, got out and came gimping up on the porch. We welcomed him, offered him a seat and he sat down.

"My tractor's busted," he said. "I was plowing up the wheat stubble and she just stopped running." He sat there in silence before going on, "That's going to happen to me one day. I'm just going to stop like my tractor did."

"Pshaw, Mr. Burns," Ma said. "You're a healthy man. You'll keep running for years."

Mr. Burns just looked at her for a while and then said, "I'm afraid that's just wishful thinking, Mrs. Harshburger. We all think we're going to live forever, but we don't."

"Let Jim and I look at your tractor, Mr. Burns," Joe said. "I bet we could get it running again."

"The thing of it is, I don't care if the tractor ever runs again." Mr. Burns sat there in silence for a good moment and then said, "I don't have all that many years left and I'm tired of farming. I had a bumper wheat crop and I got a top price for it. I want to go to California where my kids are. I was wondering if you would want to buy me out, since my land joins yours?"

"I don't know," Floyd, said uncertainty. "You grow wheat and we're row croppers. We don't have the equipment for wheat farming."

"You didn't understand me, boy," Mr. Burns said to Floyd. "I want to sell you everything. I want to sell my wheat drill, combine, even the old tractor that don't run. You'd be buying thirty head of whiteface cows with calves on them, a saddle horse and saddle, a team of four draft horses, all under twelve years old, my house, barns, everything."

Floyd's eyes lit up when he mentioned his team of young draft horses and then his eyes fell as he said, "We couldn't afford it. Besides you'd probably want too much for it anyway."

"Now don't you start dickering with me boy. Leastwise not until I name a price."

"How much would you be asking?" Floyd asked. Mr. Burns named a price.

"But Mr. Burns," Ma said, "You can't sell your whole farm, machinery, livestock and buildings that cheap."

"Yes I can. It's my farm and I can sell it for whatever I want to. I've probably got enough money saved up to last me the rest of my life. I want to go to California, and I want to go now. You don't have to give me all the money now, just what you can afford and each summer after wheat harvest, send me what you can."

"You'd trust us to do that?" Ma asked.

"Of course I would," Mr. Burns said. "Don't forget, I was living here when you, Floyd Sr. and his brothers moved out here. I know there isn't a more honest family around. I really liked Floyd Sr. until he started drinking and got mean. Where is Floyd Sr. anyway? I haven't seen him around for a long, long time."

"We haven't either," Floyd said. "Of course you know he was drinking that corn that the Biggs Brothers made. One day he hiked down the road to get some more corn to drink and we haven't seen him since."

I had held my breath when Mr. Burns had first asked about Pa, but I thought Floyd carried it off right well. Then Floyd and Mr.

69

Burns got down to working out the details of selling the farm, Mr. Burns selling and us buying.

All this money talk and details got boring so I walked down by the river and watched fireflies blinking in the willows. I knew one thing for sure. I knew that our farm had just gotten bigger which meant there would be more work for Billy Harshburger to do. Oh, well. The farming ground was in wheat and at least you didn't have to chop wheat like you did cotton.

Two days later we hooked the tractor to the wagon and we all loaded in and went down the river to the Burns' place. We went to see what we had bought. Us boys were interested in the machinery and livestock, but Ma wanted to look the house over and I'll have to say, it was a pretty house. It was clapboard the same as all other houses around, but Mr. Burns had put a storage tank so the windmill would pump water into it and he had run a pipe under ground to the house so that the house had water right in the kitchen and Mrs. Burns, when she was alive, didn't have to carry water.

"It's a right pretty house," Ma said. "It's not as big as ours but we could live in it."

Floyd had just come in the door and he had heard what Ma had said. "Do you want us to move down here?" Floyd asked.

Ma thought for a while and then said, "No. No I reckon not. Your Pa built our house for me and I reckon that's where I'll spend the rest of my life." She was silent for a while, moving around the house and looking at it. "This would be a good house for you, Floyd, should you ever take a wife."

"I guess it will set empty for a while," Floyd said. "Leastwise on my part. I haven't found a woman yet who I'd even think of marrying."

"And you won't, Floyd," Ma said. "Not until you start looking. Not until you start courting."

"I don't have time for that, Ma. I've always had too much work to do."

Ma sighed and stood in the middle of the room looking around. "Maybe Kevin would want to live here. Maybe when the war's over and he comes back from England, maybe he'll take a wife and want to live here." Again she was silent for a while. "Maybe Jim and Joe will get married and want to live here though it don't hardly seem big enough for them."

"It looks plenty big enough to me," I said.

70

"You don't understand, Billy," Ma said. "Jim and Joe haven't ever been separated in their whole life. I suspect when they get married, they'll still live together. This house isn't big enough for two families." Then Ma looked at me with a funny look and I didn't like it.

"What is it, Ma," I asked. "Why are you looking at me that a way?"

"Maybe it will be you, Billy. Maybe you will get married and live here. Don't you think that little Betty Ann Payne would like living here?"

I could tell she was teasing me but it kind of rankled me anyway. "Ma," I said. "I don't even like girls and of all the girls I don't like, I don't like Betty Ann most of all."

"That will change, Billy. That'll change."

"Even if I do someday like girls, and I'm not saying I will, but even if I do and I do get married, I'll not be living here."

"And why not, Billy? Isn't the house good enough for you?"

"Oh, the house is plenty good enough. I would like to live in this house if it weren't where it is."

"Billy, don't you want to live next to your family?" Ma asked with a hurt tone in her voice.

"It's not that, Ma. It's just that I don't plan on being a farmer. I plan on getting myself an education and going up north and getting myself a job."

I left the house then and walked out through the trees. I saw the twins over by some machinery looking it over and I wasn't nearly as interested in machinery as they were so I walked on down to the corral. In the middle of the corral stood a kind of bluish roan looking young filly and as I looked at her, she looked at me. She looked kind of lonesome so I stuck my hand through the corral and started talking to her. Sure enough, she came right to me. I petted her nose and blew in her nostrils so she would know me next time and she nickered.

"Why don't I take you out for a run," I said and she nodded her head up and down just as if she understood me. I went into the tack shed to find the bridle and I not only found the bridle but a saddle and blanket as well.

I had ridden Molly and I had ridden Dolly from time to time but I didn't much like to. They were too wide and it stretched me in the crouch to sit astraddle of them. I had never in my whole life sat in a saddle.

I took the bridle down from the nail on the wall and walked up to the saddle horse just as pretty as you please. She took the bit as if she were anxious and when I had her bridled, I led her up to the tack room door. It was a struggle to carry the saddle and blanket out. Again she stood there and let me put the blanket on her but I had to try three times before I was able to get the saddle on her back. I figured out how to cinch the saddle and I soon had the filly saddled and started leading her to the gate, right proud of myself. We had taken only a few steps when the saddle became loose and started to roll. I stopped her right quick. I didn't want that saddle to fall off and have to heave it on her back again.

I looked at the cinch and I couldn't see anything wrong except it was loose. I reached to tighten it and I saw her puff her sides out and I knew what had happened. I unbuckled the cinch and tried to tighten it but I couldn't. Not with her sides all puffed out like that. "That's okay old girl," I said. "I have plenty of time and you have to relax sometime," and I waited her out and soon her sides went in and then I pulled on the cinch as hard and as fast as I could. I saw then that I had the cinch pulled down to where it had been before and I buckled it up. I led her on out the gate and climbed aboard. The stirrups were let out much too far for me to get my feet in them and it made it right unhandy when she started crow hopping. But I found out how handy it was to have a saddle horn and I rode it out just fine. When she had settled down, I rode her up to the house.

Floyd and Ma were just coming out and Floyd looked at me and said, "Billy, how did you manage to do that?"

"It weren't nothing," I said. "She likes me."

"Do you like her?" Ma asked.

"I sure do, Ma. Isn't she just about the prettiest thing you ever saw?"

"Then you can have her," Ma said.

I started to thank her but before I could say anything, Floyd interrupted, "Providing you do certain things."

"What's that, Floyd?"

"You use her to help the family, and you feed and take care of her."

"I will, Floyd. I will."

"You can start out by checking on the cows. We bought thirty head of whiteface cows with this farm and a bull. Ten of the cows have calves and the other twenty are due sometime during the two months. You can go check on them now and then ride the filly home. Is that okay with you, Billy?"

"That's just fine with me, Floyd. She needs to be rode," and I started to rein her away towards the pasture, but Ma stopped me.

"Billy?" Ma said.

"Yes, Ma?"

"What's her name?"

"Oh, I don't know. Blue, I guess. Yes, Blue fits her just fine. She's the Blue Filly.

Chapter thirteen

The spring of that year a late frost had killed most of the fruit blossoms and since we didn't have to help Ma can fruit, I started to school when school started. I didn't have to scramble to catch up in school work as had so often happened, but simply started to school with the other kids of my seventh grade class. Not only was this a change, which I was happy to see, but there were other changes as well.

I didn't notice it at first but Larry did, he had two older sisters. It was the first recess of the first day back in school when Larry nudged me in the ribs with his elbow and said, "Look at Betty Ann."

I looked at her and said, "Yeah, I'm looking at her. So what?"

"I mean really look at her. Look at her chest. Betty Ann's growing titties."

I really looked then and sure enough, when she turned just right you could see them poking out against her loose summer blouse. I was astonished. I couldn't help it. I stared. The magnets of Betty Ann's chest drew my eyes. Betty Ann was talking to the two Marys, Mary Lou and Mary Beth at the time. Betty Ann glanced my way and I knew it was going to be powerful embarrassing if I kept on looking at her, but I couldn't pull my eyes away. Betty Ann turned back to the other girls and continued to talk and then she suddenly turned and looked me straight in the eyes with a puzzled expression on her face. I quickly looked elsewhere.

I was so very confused. All my life I had disliked girls, didn't want to have anything to do with them, didn't want to be around them and I paid them very little attention, Betty Ann most of all. But now I felt my heart thumping in my chest and this funny feeling all throughout my body. We had just gotten out for recess but it was a hot August day and maybe I'd been standing in the sun too long. Something sure was wrong. It was like a meteor had fallen from the sky and hit me on the head because suddenly I didn't hate girls anymore.

I was in a daze all the rest of the day. I had disliked girls all my life, and suddenly it wasn't true anymore, and I didn't know what to think of it. Throughout the day I had trouble keeping my mind on my lessons and my eyes off of Betty Ann. She got up to turn in an assignment and when she sat back down, her skirt rode half way up her tanned brown thigh. I was sure it wasn't the first time such a thing ever happened but it was sure the first time I had noticed. It went against my grain but I had to admit that Betty Ann was a pretty thing, what with her bobbed brown hair, bangs on her forehead and underneath the bangs her flashing black eyes.

It was all so confusing. Just this morning I had disliked girls and now all of a sudden I thought Betty Ann was the most beautiful thing around. She was even prettier than my blue filly.

When school was out for the day and I got on the school bus, Betty Ann, as usual, sat down beside me. But it didn't seem like she plopped down in the bus seat as she usually did, but flowed into the seat gracefully. That really set my head swirling. I didn't know what to say, I didn't know what to do with my hands so I wouldn't touch her, and I didn't know where to look so I wouldn't look at her. I wanted to look at Betty Ann, wanted to look at her terribly bad, but instead I scrunched against the side of the bus and looked out the window and watched the cotton fields and the maize fields go drifting by. It was okay that I didn't know what to say because Betty Ann talked enough for both of us. At least some things were still the same.

"Are you mad at me or something, Billy?" Betty Ann asked. "You're awful quiet."

"No, I'm not mad at you," I said, still staring out the window.

"I'll bet you're sick. Here, let me see," and she slid over against me. She turned and put her hand on my forehead. Her body was against mine and I felt her soft, young breasts against my shoulder. I felt her breath on the side of my face and I felt her hand on my forehead.

"Nah, you're not sick," she said. "You don't have a fever."

And that shows you what she knew. She didn't know anything because I felt the trickles of sweat tickling down my sides, chest and stomach.

In one sense, the bus ride home took forever and a day and in another sense it was over all too soon. My feelings were bouncing like a rubber ball dropped on the sidewalk of Cheyenne. For the first time ever, I enjoyed sitting on the bus with Betty Ann and listening to her musical chatter. But also, for the first time ever, I didn't know what to say. I especially didn't know what to say to a beautiful wonderful girl like Betty Ann. I wouldn't dare let her

75

know that my feelings for her had changed. If she even guessed that my feelings for her had changed she would laugh at me and make fun of me. Or worse yet, pity me. I was afraid if I said anything, anything at all, she would know. I wondered if girls had some sixth sense and could read boys minds. I sure hoped not. I wondered if Betty Ann could tell by looking at me that I had changed. Maybe I had changed on the outside as much as I had on the inside.

We reach the intersection in the road where Jim, Joe and I got off of the bus. I tried not to touch Betty Ann when I stood up to get off. She turned sideways in the seat to let me by but it was still too crowded and I brushed against her as I stepped into the aisle.

"Bye, Bye, Billy Harshburger," she called as I started down the aisle. "See you in the morning."

I just grunted and went on down the aisle. The feeling of her body was still with me as I stepped down the school bus steps onto the hard packed road and watched the bus disappear into the dusty distance. I stood there with a lonesome heart. Jim and Joe had already started home, and I had to run to catch up.

I thought of Betty Ann as I saddled up Blue and went to check on the whiteface cattle at the Burns' place. I found all thirty of them and I saw all their calves. I thought of Betty Ann as I dismounted to open the barbed wire gate into our pasture and led Blue through. I mounted up again and herded up the milk cows and took them to the barn to milk. I did my share of the chores and I ate supper in a daze. After supper, we helped Ma clean up the kitchen and then we all went into the living room to listen to the news on the radio.

Usually this was the best time of the day for me. I would sit on the floor by the radio and as the news reporter would give a detailed description of our troops fighting the Japs or Germans and it was like I was there fighting with them. Sometimes there would be a report from the front lines and I could actually hear the rifle fire and the artillery rounds going off. It made me wish I would hurry up and grow up so I could join the army and go fight.

When they told about an air raid over Germany, I just knew that Kevin was in it and I envied him. I wished I were old enough to be with him. With him and helping man the machine gun. I bet if I were with him pointing out the German fighters and making sure that he had plenty of bullets for his machine gun, why I bet we would shoot down hundreds if not thousands of German fighters.

In my minds eye I could see them bursting into flames and going down in smoke.

But not tonight. Tonight was different. When the reporter told of the action in the skies over Germany, instead of seeing myself beside Kevin helping him fight off the German fighters, I saw myself holding the hand of Betty Ann as we walked the red hills together.

I gave up and went out side. The night sky was filled with a million stars and the sliver of a new moon floated above the western horizon. The wind, which always blows in Oklahoma, had died to a gentle breeze. In the far distance I heard the lonesome hoot of a hoot owl and the yap, yap, yap of the coyotes. I looked up at the bright band of the Milky Way and in the stars I saw the smiling face of Betty Ann Payne.

I had to admit it then. No way around it. I had to admit that I was in love with Betty Ann. Helplessly and hopelessly in love. Hopeless because Betty Ann's father owned a lot of land and was a very rich man. He owned horses, cattle, wheat fields and alfalfa meadows. He didn't have any cotton fields, which, in my opinion, showed that he was a very smart man. He had influence in the local government and at the state level as well. A very prominent citizen. There was no way he was going to let his only child have anything to do with a poor boy like Billy Harshburger. I bet he didn't even know that Betty Ann sits beside me on the bus. I bet Betty Ann didn't tell him.

But dreams are your own and are free. They don't even require a payment in courage. You can just dream them. Dreams brought pleasure and in them anything can happen. Your dreams are truly the only thing you really own.

At last I went inside, climbed the stairs and went to bed. I went to sleep thinking of Betty Ann. In the first half of the night Betty Ann and I lived in the house on the Burns place. We were so very happy and our days were filled with love and our nights were filled with passion. It was a wonderful life we lived.

The second half of the night Betty Ann and I lived up north and I had myself a job. We lived in a small cottage with a picket fence and a yard filled with flowers. I liked the second dream much better. All too early, the rooster crowed and woke me up. My brothers had just begun to stir when I dressed and went outside to do my chores. I thought of Betty Ann as I milked and separated

77

the cream. I thought of her as I ate breakfast, packed my lunch and started the walk to the school bus stop.

When the bus stopped to pick up Betty Ann I scooted over in the seat and let her sit down. I truly enjoyed her animated chatter all the way to school. Occasionally I would glance at her out of the corner of my eye and my heart would swell and a lump would come in my throat.

Yes, I was secretly in love with Betty Ann and because it had to be kept a secret, I ignored her when I could and when I couldn't, I teased her and was especially mean to her.

Chapter fourteen

The last day of school, before school turned out for cotton picking was a bitter sweet-day for me. I was tired of sitting in the classroom and was ready to be outside, even if it was in a cotton field, except school was out for five weeks and that would be five weeks that I wouldn't be seeing Betty Ann. The ride home with Betty Ann chattering beside me on the bus was over all too soon. It was with a lonesome heart that I stepped into the aisle and off of the bus.

The cotton was even better this year than it had been last year and just before noon of the second day we had the wagon full. Joe hooked the tractor to the wagon and headed for the gin in Cheyenne. He got back before supper but after the chores were done, which burned me some since I had milked some of his cows. I just know I could have driven the tractor to town just as well as Joe. Maybe not as fast, but just as well.

"I sold the cotton, Floyd," Joe said over supper. "I was afraid with this year's cotton crop coming in, the prices would drop and I sold it for the same price as we got last year."

"Good, Joe," Floyd said. "You probably did the right thing."

"There's something else, Floyd. The price of cotton picking is up. It's now two dollars a hundred. Don't you think we should pay ourselves the same thing?"

"Definitely," Floyd answered.

My ears perked up to that. I had already picked well over a thousand pounds and at two cents a pound meant I had over twenty dollars coming and I hadn't even spent all of last year's money. I had it tucked away between my mattress and springs in an old Prince Albert tobacco can.

"There's one more thing we need to discuss, Floyd," Joe said.

"What's that?"

"Since we bought the Burn's place we've got more work than we can handle. We've got the wheat up real nice, like we need to put a fence around the field and see if we can buy some steers to graze the wheat. Someone needs to start looking around at the cattle sales. We need to do all this besides getting the cotton crop out while the price is still up."

"I know," Floyd said. "Doesn't seem like there's enough hours in the day to get everything done that needs to be done."

"That's what I'm talking about, Floyd. We've more work to do than we can get done. That's why I hired the King family to help us snap cotton today while I was in town."

"You did what?" Floyd asked, startled.

"The Kings had only ten acres of cotton and they already have it snapped. They were at the gin looking for a boll pulling job and I hired them."

"I don't know about that," Floyd said. "We've never done that before. We've always picked our own cotton."

"Floyd, we're farming twice as much ground as we did before we bought the Burns' place. We're doing all we can do and if we don't hire out some of the work then there is much of that work that won't get done."

"I suppose you're right. When are they going to show up?" Floyd asked.

"In the morning."

Floyd sighed, "Well, its too late now, what's done is done. I would have liked to think about it, though."

Me, I didn't see anything to think about. It sounded like a damn good idea to me. I know I was getting paid two cents a pound to snap cotton but the sooner the cotton was picked the better I liked it. I knew I might not make as much picking cotton as I did last year but there had to be an easier way to make money. Besides Mary Lou King was in my class in school and she was kind of cute. If it hadn't been for Betty Ann, I think I would have fallen in love with Mary Lou.

The Kings showed up the next morning at daylight, just as we were finishing the chores. We had eaten breakfast long before daylight and as soon as the chores were done we headed to the cotton patch.

There were four of the Kings. There was Mr. and Mrs. King, Mary Lou and her older brother, Ted. Mary Lou had her long blond hair tied into a ponytail, which hung down below her straw hat. I had never seen her in anything but a dress at school but today she must have had on one of Ted's outgrown shirt and a pair of his outgrown blue jeans. She sure looks cute, I thought, as I walked to the field beside her. But I bet she can't pull bolls worth a durn.

80

I was soon to find out how wrong I was. Everyone took a row of cotton and Mary Lou took one beside me. I couldn't believe how fast her gloved hands flew up one cotton stalk and down the other as she picked the bowls. I worked as hard and as fast as I could trying to stay up with her but she steadily pulled farther and farther ahead. We were about a third of the way down our rows when I started to gain on her. I caught up to her at the halfway mark and slowed down some so I could pull bolls beside her.

She stood up, stretched her back, shook the cotton down in her sack, bent back over and lunged against her cotton sack to move it forward.

"Sack getting pretty heavy?" I asked.

"Yes," Mary Lou answered. "I can stay up with everyone until my sack gets too heavy to pull."

"I know what you're talking about, Mary Lou. I was that way last year but this year I'm so much bigger and stronger that it don't hardly slow me down none."

"It sure looks like you've gotten bigger and stronger, Billy."

My head swelled with pride to hear Mary Lou talking like that. "I tell you what, I'll pull my row on out and then come back to meet you on yours."

"Would you, Billy?"

"Sure," I said and then I really dug in. I snapped cotton as hard and as fast as I could and tried not to show any strain as I pulled my heavy sack on down the row. When I got to the end I turned around and started down Mary Lou's row, again I snapped cotton as fast and as hard as I could. I stood up and stretched my back just before I met Mary Lou. I looked at her, all bent over snapping cotton. The top button of her shirt had come undone and I could look down it and what I saw made me swallow hard. Mary Lou didn't have a bra on and it was evident that she was quickly becoming a young woman. Her breasts were bigger than Betty Ann's, and I was in love all over again.

When we got to the cotton scales everyone else was there too. Ma and Mrs. King weighed their sacks first and Floyd emptied them in the wagon while Mary Lou and I weighed ours. Floyd wouldn't empty our sack though. "If you're old enough to pick it, you're old enough to dump it," he said. He did, however, throw our sacks into the wagon and Mary Lou and I climbed up and shook our own sacks out. When our sacks were empty we got down, draped our sacks over our shoulder and started following Ma and Mrs. King to the other end of the field.

Floyd, Joe, Jim, Ted and Mr. King dumped their sacks, turned around and started picking down the row away from the scales. When they got to the end they would simply turn around and pick back to the scales. But Ma, Mrs. King, Mary Lou and I walked to the other end and picked back towards the scales. There was no way we could drag two rows of cotton in our sacks.

We all sat on our sacks and had lunch together but by the middle of the afternoon we were pretty scattered out. Mary Lou and I were faster at cotton picking than Ma or Mrs. King and, of course, the men picked two rows before they weighed in. Mary Lou and I met Ma and Mrs. King walking to the end of the field about half way up our rows. We met the men picking down their rows about two thirds of the way to the scales. When I got to the end of my row I did as I had been doing all day and turned and helped Mary Lou finish her row.

We weighed our sacks and wrote the weights down in the tally book. We helped each other load our cotton sacks in the wagon and then jumped in to shake them out. The cotton was packed pretty well in my sack and Mary Lou had hers emptied before I had mine. I had just shook the last bowl of cotton out of my sack when I suddenly felt a hard shove in the middle of my back and I went sprawling in the cotton pile. I rolled over and saw that Mary Lou was laughing at me. "What's wrong, Billy? Did you trip over your own feet?"

"You know what happened," I said. "Here, help me up," and I put out my hand to her. Darned if she didn't fall for it and reached out and took my hand. A hard pull and she was in the cotton pile with me. We wrestled around a bit and I ended up slightly on top of her holding her down. I looked at her face, her smiling lips. I looked into her blue eyes and as I watched, I saw her eyes turn even a darker blue.

"Are you going to kiss me or what, Billy?" Mary Lou breathed.

Now I had never in my whole life kissed a girl not counting Ma. And then I had only kissed Ma on the cheek. But I had never kissed a girl on the lips and I wasn't rightly sure that I knew how. I had seen it in the movies, though, and I figured I'd do as they did. I took a deep breath, closed my eyes bent down and put my lips against hers.

When I raised back up Mary Lou said, "Come on, Billy. You can do better than that. You're not going to your own hanging. You're just kissing a girl. Relax and let's try it again."

I did and this time the kiss went on for a long while. "That's much better, Billy. Did you like it?"

"I liked it very much, Mary Lou. Let's do it again."

"No, Billy. We'd better get out of here and get our butts to the end of the field and start picking cotton. People will wonder if we stay here too long."

That night when we sat down to listen to the news I couldn't concentrate again, so I went outside and wandered around. For a while I listened to a pack of coyotes howl back in the red hills. The night was clear and there were a million stars and I jut stayed outside and watched them for a while. At last I went upstairs to go to bed with the taste of Mary Lou's lips still on mine. That night it was Mary Lou and I who lived in the Burns' house, and it was Mary Lou who lived up north with me.

The next day was the same as the day before, except Mary Lou and I would sneak a kiss every chance we got. When others weren't scattered out or if they were too close to the scales, we would just walk behind the wagon and hold each other and kiss before we walked to the other end of the field. I worked harder than ever just so I could have time alone with Mary Lou. When the day was over and Floyd tallied the days picking, I was pleasantly surprised at how much cotton I had picked. It made cotton picking a lot more fun to know at the end of each row, there waited for me, a kiss from Mary Lou.

One afternoon a short time later, Mary Lou and I weighed our cotton and dumped it in the wagon. As I shook the cotton from my sack I looked at the field and saw that everyone was picking cotton side by side at the far end of the field. When my sack was empty I threw it to the ground and grabbed Mary Lou. We fell laughing into the cotton in each other's arms. As I began the kiss I suddenly felt Mary Lou's tongue dart into my mouth. It sent shivers clear to my toes and I drew back quickly.

"How'd you like that?" Mary Lou asked with a mischievous grin.

"I liked it," I answered.

"That's called a French kiss," she stated.

"Why haven't we done it sooner?"

"I wanted to wait until I knew you better," she said.

"Let's do it again," and we did. As our tongues entwined my hand reflexively went to her right breast and I squeezed it.

She tore her mouth away and said, "No, Billy. No."

I quickly jerked my hand away.

Mary Lou looked at me with her dark blue eyes and said, "I didn't mean that, Billy. I meant don't squeeze so hard. Be gentle, they're kind of tender right now."

We kissed again with me gently squeezing her breast. We were both breathing heavily when we broke the kiss and I looked out and saw the cotton pickers were a lot closer. How time flew when I was with Mary Lou.

"We'd better go, Mary Lou."

She rose up on one elbow and looked out over the cotton patch. "Oh, my," she said.

I crawled out of the wagon on shaky legs, threw my cotton sack over my shoulder and nonchalantly walked to the other end of the field with Mary Lou and started picking cotton towards the scales.

It was in the middle of the fourth week of cotton picking when it became apparent that we were going to finish the first picking of cotton. Most likely that day. We would go over the field one more time picking the few newly opened cotton bolls, but the Kings would leave us and go somewhere else to pick. There was a festive mood in the air for everyone but me. Me, I had mixed emotions. On one hand I was happy that the biggest part of cotton snapping would be over for another year but on the other hand, I wouldn't be seeing Mary Lou until school started in a week and a half.

"What will you do when this cotton is picked, Mary Lou?" I asked.

Mary Lou sighed, "Go to another field and pick cotton until school starts."

I looked at her with pity. I didn't have it so rough after all. "Do you know where you'll go next?" I asked.

"I heard Mom and Dad talking about checking with Mr. Woods. Last we heard, he had fifty acres left to pick. What will you do, Billy?"

"Floyd was talking about fixing the fence around the wheat field so we can put cattle on the wheat. Building fence is a lot easer than picking cotton except I don't get paid for it."

"You get paid for picking cotton?" Mary Lou asked.

"Sure. Don't you?"

"My Dad does but Ted and I don't. He says that a roof over our heads, clothes on our back and good food is pay enough."

We were at the scales by then. Mary Lou and I weighed our cotton, wrestled our sacks into the wagon and emptied them. I looked down the field and saw there were only two rows of cotton left and the pickers were much too close so we threw our sacks to the ground, jumped down and met behind the wagon for a tender goodbye.

She and I walked to the far end of the field and started picking towards the scales. With everyone picking the last two rows were picked, weighed and dumped in the wagon. Joe hooked up the tractor and we all rode to the house on the cotton. When we got out of the wagon at the house, Joe left with the cotton heading for Cheyenne. It was late in the afternoon and I knew I was going to have to help milk Joe's cows again. I wondered why everyone thought that Joe was the only one who could drive a tractor.

While Mr. King and Floyd went into the house to settle up, Mary Lou and I sat close in the shade of a large cottonwood holding hands leaning back against the trunk.

All too soon Mr. King and Floyd came out. "Well, I guess it's time for me to go, Billy," Mary Lou said, releasing my hand and standing up. "I'll see you when school starts."

"I'm looking forward to it, Mary Lou," I said as I watched her climb in the back of their homemade model A pickup with her cotton sack and soon she was lost in the dusty distance.

Chapter Fifteen

When at last school started again, I was the first one out of our house to go and wait for the school bus. Today I was going to get to see Mary Lou. I licked my lips remembering the kisses we had shared while picking cotton and I hoped for one or two more kisses before the day was over. Some of the eighth grade boys had girl friends and they walked around the school grounds with their arm around them during recess and lunch hour. I looked forward to doing the same with Mary Lou. Darned that bus, would it ever come?

Jim and Joe were at the stop when I at last heard it climbing the last hill before it came to our bus stop. When at last it stopped and opened its doors for us, I climbed aboard and sat down where I always sat.

The next time the bus stopped, Betty Ann Payne got on and sat in the seat with me. I was comfortable with it. I didn't have to worry about how I looked at her nor about accidentally touching her because I had a girlfriend who I was madly in love with.

"Did you pick a bunch of cotton, Billy, or did you spend all your time swimming and fishing in that deep hole on the river."

"You know darned well it's too cold to swim, and no I didn't fish at all. I spent four weeks picking cotton and the rest of the time fixing fence."

"How could you get the cotton picked in just four weeks? Wasn't the crop any good?"

"It was the best crop ever," I said. "But this year for the first time ever, we hired some pickers."

"Who did you hire? Some Mexicans. I bet that's it. You hired some Mexicans and I bet Billy Harshburger has a little Mexican girlfriend."

"No. We didn't hire Mexicans. We hired the Kings."

Betty Ann stopped laughing and smiling then and asked, "How did you and Mary Lou get along in the cotton patch?"

"We got along fine," I said and I could feel my face turning red.

"I see," Betty Ann said. She then turned and faced the front of the bus and for the first time ever, she didn't say a word all the way to school.

When the bus stopped at the schoolhouse, I would have been the first one off if it hadn't been for Betty Ann. I stood up to get off and she stood up in front of me. She gripped the back of the seat in front of us with one hand and the back of the seat behind us with the other and just stood there letting everyone on the bus file past. When Jim and Joe came up, they stopped to let us out.

"Go ahead, boys," Betty Ann said. "We're in no hurry."

When the last one had filed past, Betty Ann stepped into the aisle and strolled to the front of the bus as slow as could be. I didn't know Betty Ann could walk so slowly. But at last I made it off of the bus and as soon as my feet touched the ground, I took off looking for Mary Lou. I looked back once and saw Betty Ann just standing there watching me with her hands on her hips. Well, who was she anyway. She didn't own me. Nobody did. With those thoughts in mind I hurried to the side of the schoolhouse looking for Mary Lou.

And I found her. She was strolling across the lawn with Bobby Woods. Bobby had his arm around her shoulder and Mary Lou had her arm around his waist.

I stood there in astonishment. I didn't know what to think. I felt like I was going to cry, but I knew I wouldn't. I wouldn't let myself. Then I got mad. For a moment rage and hurt fought a battle royal in my soul. Finally I walked up to them, ready to either forgive them or beat Bobby Woods to a pulp. They were so occupied with each other that I was right close before they saw me.

"Hi, Billy," Mary Lou said.

"What is this, Mary Lou? I thought you were my girl."

"I was, Billy. I was. But now I'm Bobby's girlfriend."

"But Mary Lou?" I said, struggling to keep the hurt from my voice."

Mary Lou took her arm from around Bobby's waist and turned to face him placing her hand on his chest. "Be a dear, Bobby, and walk over there by that tree and let Billy and I talk for just a moment."

"But Mary Lou," Bobby protested.

"Run along, Bobby. I'll be along in a moment."

"How could you forget me so fast, Mary Lou?" I said. "After all we did in the cotton wagon."

"We didn't do nothing, Billy. We just kissed and petted a little. It didn't mean anything. Remember, we went from your cotton field to the Woods. Bobby and I picked cotton together."

"But you and Bobby didn't do what we did, did you?"

"Yes, Billy we did and we still do. We do everything you and I did and more. Bobby has a car. Course he's not old enough to get a driver's license, but it's okay as long as he stays on the country roads. He comes to see me in it, and he takes me for a ride."

"I can't help it if I don't have a car, Mary Lou."

"But Bobby does. We go for long rides and sometimes we park on a hill and sit for hours. We don't have to worry about where other people being around us or anything. We're all alone by ourselves."

"But Mary Lou, I'm in love with you. I dreamed about you and us being together every night."

"You'll get over it, Billy," she said, patting me on the cheek.

"No I won't Mary Lou. I never will. I can't stand the thought of you in Bobby's arms. I can't live with the thoughts of you kissing him like you kissed me. I just can't stand it. I just can't live with it. I'm going to go home after school today and take the shotgun and blow my brains out."

"Really, Billy?" Mary Lou asked.

"Yes, Really," I answered.

"Would you do me a favor?"

"Sure, Mary Lou," I said hopefully.

"Could you not do it right after school? Could you wait until Bobby and I get there?"

"No need, Mary Lou. You and Bobby aren't going to talk me out of it."

"Oh, we're not going to try to talk you out of it, Billy. I just want to watch."

It was then that rage took over. I'd never hit a girl and I promised myself that I never would but right then I came real close to breaking that promise. I sure wanted to hit Mary Lou. I just stood there looking at her and it was kind of funny. As I looked at her I wondered why I had never noticed. I wondered why I had never noticed that she had buckteeth.

I turned and walked away then. Walked away with my heart pounding rage. My arms were shaking and my knees felt weak with rage. Blinding rage. I almost ran over Betty Ann when I rounded the corner of the schoolhouse.

"Did you find Mary Lou?" Betty Ann asked sweetly.

"Oh, shut up," I answered.

"My, we are testy this morning aren't we?"

The bell rang just then and I hurried to class.

When school was out, I got on the bus and as usual, Betty Ann sit beside me. This surprised me somewhat because I didn't figure she would want to have anything to do with me.

She didn't say anything for a long while, which was another surprise. The bus driver started the engine and we started down the road with me glumly looking out the window.

"Poor Billy Harshburger," Betty Ann said.

I turned to her quickly thinking she was making fun of me again and I wasn't in the mood, but then I saw the look of concern on her face.

"Mary Lou got into you bad, didn't she?"

"I've had better days," I answered. "I don't know, Betty Ann, things were a lot simpler last year when I hated girls. Maybe that's what I ought to do. Learn to hate girls all over again."

"Now Billy, don't go judging all girls by what Mary Lou did. I would have warned you if I'd only known. Mary Lou is a heartbreaker. She delights in getting a boy head over heels for her and then dumping him. She'll do the same thing to Bobby as soon as she gets tired of riding around in his automobile."

I looked at her and said, "I thought you and Mary Lou were friends."

"We are, but I know her. I don't have to approve of everything my friends do."

"You wouldn't do that, Betty Ann? You mean you wouldn't love a boy just because he had a car?"

"No, Billy, I wouldn't. If I loved a boy, I'd love him whether he had a car or not."

"Sounds like you're the girl for me, Betty Ann," I said, teasingly. "I sure don't have a car and I don't see one in my near future."

Betty Ann laughed. "I could never be your girlfriend. My dad would skin me alive. But I'll tell you what, Billy, if I can never be your girlfriend, I'll always be your friend. Okay?"

"It's a deal, Betty Ann," and we spit in our palms and shook hands on it. "I'm kind of tired of girlfriends right now anyway."

I got off of the bus and walked home. I went into the house hoping I could find myself a snack before I saddled up Blue and went to check on the cattle and bring the milk cows in. I looked for Ma and found her sitting in a chair crying. It was evident to me that my bad day wasn't over yet.

"What's wrong Ma? Why are you crying?"

"We got a letter from Kevin, Billy," Ma said, handing me the letter. "We got this too," and she handed me a newspaper.

"What happened to Kevin, Ma? Did he get hurt?"

"It's all in there, Billy. Read it."

I opened the letter and begin to read:

Dear Ma and Brothers,

I came through the operation just fine although I have to tell you I'm half a foot less than I was when I left home. No, I didn't shrink, I'm just as tall as I ever was, I was just joking and a poor joke at best. Today the doctors took off half of my right foot. Now I'm not handicapped or anything, when the foot heals I'll be able to walk just as well as I ever could, just not as fast. I'll never be able to play third base for the Brooklyn Dodgers.

How it happened is told very well in this newspaper I'm sending you but I would like to give you my thoughts and comments.

Two German fighters just showed up out of nowhere and began to shoot up our plane. One of the bullets hit me in the foot. I was the least hurt of anyone and they called me a hero for saving the other crewmen's lives, but I ain't no hero. When I landed that bomber on the emergency airstrip in England, I was thinking more or less of Kevin Harshburger's hide.

How could I fly that bomber without any training? I'll tell you right off, it weren't easy. But I have always been around the cockpit when the plane took off and landed and I watched the pilots and seen what they did. Both the pilot and copilot protested at first but I never paid them any mind. They even ordered me back once, but it is just another one of those orders I disobeyed.

I explained to them that since I was riding in this thing, I wanted to learn as much as I could about what made it go and how they kept it up in the air. I just knew I could fly a plane as good as anybody if I just got the chance and as it turned out, I could. Well, maybe not quite as good as the pilots, but then you have to take into consideration that the plane was all shot up and everything.

After the fighters hit us and I got to the cockpit I found both pilots slumped over and unconscious. The plane was in a shallow turning dive so I quickly unbuckled the pilots, got them out of the seats and took over. I just did what I had watched the pilots do and I got the plane under control. When I found the emergency landing strip in England, I just lined the plane up and set her down. I didn't try to anything fancy like put the wheels down or anything, I just tried to put her down in as few pieces as I could and I did. I wasn't able to walk away but I was able to hobble away so I guess it was a good landing.

Ma, I know you would have liked for me to take the medical discharge they offered me but I just couldn't. The Germans ain't whipped yet and I plan to stay in this war until they are. You know me. I'm like all the other Harshburgers and we never leave a fight until it's over. Sorry, Ma.

Ma, this next paragraph is to my brothers and you don't need to read it unless you want to. Brothers let me tell you this; I personally saw those two sons of bitches who shot up my plane go down in flame even if our airplane was bobbing all over the air like a fishing cork when a fish is biting.

Love,
Kevin

I folded the letter and put it back in the envelope. I then opened the newspaper until I saw the picture of Kevin and began to read.

Sergeant Kevin Harshburger
America's Newest Hero

When Sergeant Harshburger's bomber was attacked by two German fighters, Sergeant Harshburger not only sent the two fighters to a blazing death, but he also flew the bomber back and landed it when he saw that all the other members of his crew, including the pilots, were severely wounded. It might be added that Sergeant Harshburger was seriously wounded also. Even though Sergeant Harshburger had never had formal training as a pilot, he brought the plane back and landed it thus saving the lives of his comrades in arms.

When the Sergeant was told that he would be up for a medical discharge and would be going home as soon as he got out of the hospital, he said, "No, I ain't. The only way you'll get me home before this war is over is in chains. The only place I'll be going when I get out of the hospital is back into a bomber and behind a machinegun. I ain't going home until the Germans are whipped."

Hats off to Sergeant Harshburger. If we had an army of Sergeant Harshburgers, Hitler would be taken care of fast.

"Ma," I said, "Kevin is a real live hero. Just think my brother is a hero. I bet he'll be getting all kinds of medals and everything. Why are you crying? Aren't you proud of him?

"I don't want my son to be a hero," Ma said. "I don't want him hurt. All I want is for him to be back home. All I want is for Kevin to be out of danger." And she started crying all the harder.

Chapter sixteen

It was a week before school was out for Christmas and Jim and Joe were all excited. They were usually pretty cool characters and nothing much excites them. But they had found an old model A coupe that wouldn't run and they thought they could fix it.

"I don't know if we can afford it," Floyd said over the supper table. "We are kind of short on money right now. You know we put about all our money into those steers we bought and put on the wheat ground."

"I know," Joe said. "But we got the guy down to fifteen dollars."

"Are you absolutely sure you can make it run?" Floyd asked.

"We're not absolutely sure, but we're pretty sure," Jim said.

"Of course you'll have to spend money on parts," Floyd said. "How much do you figure the parts will cost?"

"I think twenty dollars. We can't rightly say for sure, but twenty dollars should cover it."

"I'm sorry, boys," Floyd said. "I wish we had an extra thirty-five dollars, but we don't."

"Well, it was just a thought," Joe said. "A car sure would be nice to take the cream and eggs to town in. It would be a lot faster than the tractor."

That's the trouble with farming. You're always broke. If a farmer has a good crop and sells it for a good price, then he will turn right around and plow it right back into the farm like we did by buying the steers.

After supper we all cleaned up the kitchen for Ma and then we went into the living room to listen to the radio. Again it was one of those nights when I couldn't concentrate. I was thinking of Mary Beth. I'd been watching her at school and I thought she was mighty cute, what with her freckled face and red hair. Now if I had a car and knew how to drive it, I'd just bet I could walk up to her and say, "Mary Beth, if you're not busy, how would you like to go to the movies with me this Saturday night." Then she would say, "Yes." Then if I had a car, I could pick her up and we would go to the movies and then on the way home, we'd park on the top of some hill where we could watch the road in both directions and who knows what would happen. If I just had a car.

Finally I gave up trying to listen and went upstairs where we boys had our room. I knelt down beside my bed and reached in between the mattress and springs and pulled out the tobacco can. I dumped the money out on the bed and counted out the money I had left from cotton snapping. I saw I had a hundred and twenty dollars left. I counted out thirty dollars and put the rest back into the tobacco can and slipped it again between the mattress and springs.

It wasn't that I didn't trust my brothers because I did. I really did. But if they didn't know where my money was and if they didn't know how much I had, well, I figured it was the best way to keep honest people honest.

I went back downstairs and saw that Jim and Joe were still in the living room listening to the radio so I called them into the kitchen. "Here," I said, handing Jim fifteen dollars. "Buy the car." I handed Joe another fifteen dollars and said, "Buy the parts."

"Billy," Joe said, "where did you get all that money?"

"It's what I had left over from cotton snapping," and I crossed my fingers in case I had implied that was all the money I had left over.

"Well, thanks, Billy," Jim and Joe said together.

"But there's a catch to it. As soon as you get the car running, you guys have to show me how to drive."

"No problem, Billy. We'll teach you to drive just as soon as we learn ourselves," Joe said.

"And," I said. "When I learn to drive, I get to use the car some."

"But, Billy, you're not old enough to get a driver's license," Jim said.

"You two are old enough, but I bet you don't have a license either."

They just kind of looked at each other then Joe said, "You're right, Billy. But when we get the car running we'll work something out."

The next day after school while I saddled Blue and went to check on the cows and steers, Jim and Joe started the John Deere and went after the car.

All the whitefaces, their calves, and the steers we had bought were grazing contentedly on the wheat pasture and they weren't

94

hard to find. I counted them as I rode through them on Blue and saw that they were all there. It was a little early to bring in the milk cows so I rode the fence line. I found a wire loose from the post and sagging, so I took my wire pliers, which doubled as a hammer, and a staple and fixed the fence. By the time I had ridden the fence and fixed the places that need to be worked on, it was time to herd up the milk cows and take them home.

I brought the cows in and shut them in the milking lot. I had just unsaddled the blue filly and turned her loose when I head the pop, pop, pop of the John Deer. I looked down the driveway and saw the tractor pulling the Model A coupe, one twin driving the tractor and the other twin driving the car. I watched as they pulled the car to its new home.

By the time school was out for Christmas, the twins had that car broken down into a million pieces. I was with Ma down at the shed where the twins were working on the car when she looked around in amazement and asked, "Do you boys think you'll ever get it back together again?"

"Yes, Ma," Joe answered. "We'll put it together just like we took it apart."

"Do you think it'll ever run?" Ma asked.

"Yes, it'll run," Jim, answered. "We've already found out what was wrong with it to start with but since we had it apart we thought we'd go ahead and give it a complete overhaul. We're going to pour new bearings, grind the valves, — —"

"Stop, boys. I don't know what you're talking about and you're making my head hurt. I just ask if you're sure you're going to be able to make it run and it sounds like you are. I'll have Floyd hook up the team and take me to Cheyenne this morning so I can try to get gasoline ration stamps."

"I sure wish Floyd would learn to drive the tractor," Jim said. "Then he could take you to town and back a lot faster."

"Well, he's not going to," I answered. "That Floyd isn't going anywhere he can't walk or ride behind a team of horses. But I'll hook up the tractor and take you to town, Ma."

"I know you would, Billy. But you're the only one who can ride Blue so we need for you to check the cattle."

Jim said, "Ma, you might should also get ration stamps for the Burns place. That H Farmall runs on gas and not kerosene like our John Deere."

"I thought the tractor on the Burns' place was broke and wouldn't run."

"Jim and I have been looking at it and we don't see much wrong with it," Joe said. "I think the truth of the matter is that Mr. Burns was just tired of farming and wanted to go to California."

Jim said, "If we can afford it, order gas for the Burns gasoline storage tank."

"How much would it cost, Boys?"

"I figure about fifty dollars," Joe said. "Of course if that is more than we can afford we could just half fill it."

"I'll talk it over with Floyd," Ma said, and we started to the barn where Floyd was working, Ma to get Floyd to hook up the team and take her to Cheyenne and me to saddle Blue.

Surprisingly enough, Floyd didn't give any argument when Ma broached the subject of filling the gasoline storage tank at the Burns place.

"If it's machinery, those twins can make it work," Floyd said. "It would help out a lot on the plowing if we had two tractors."

While Floyd hitched up the team to take Ma to town, I packed myself a lunch and saddled up Blue. We left at the same time, Ma and Floyd going to Cheyenne and me to the Burns place. Before Floyd and Ma had gotten gone, Joe came running out to the wagon with a five-gallon can.

"Bring us back some gasoline," he said. "We'll need it to start the car.

It didn't take me long to find the cattle and I rode through them counting. It was while I was riding through the white-faced cows that I noticed one of the calves was still a bull. I don't know how that little sucker had escaped me. I uncoiled my rope and caught him on the second try. Blue was becoming a pretty good roping horse and she kept the tension tight on the rope when I jumped off, ran up the rope and threw the little bull down. I pulled out my pocketknife and went to work with his mama bellowing, kicking dirt and threatening me with all kind of dreadful consequences. When I was through, I took the rope off of his neck and got up off of him. He jumped up and ran to his mama. He'd gone down a bull but came up as a steer.

I rode on down to the Burns' house and ate lunch and then I started some badly needed repairs on the corrals. It was late afternoon and I had just saddled Blue to take the milk cows in, when I first heard, and then saw, the gasoline delivery truck coming down the Burns' driveway and I knew Ma had been successful in getting the gasoline rationing stamps. I watched as the truck pulled up to the storage tank and filled it with gas.

True to their word, the twins had the car running three days later, the day before Christmas. It was in the afternoon and I had just ridden down to check on the house, barns and corrals after checking the cattle when I heard a car coming down the driveway. I wondered who was coming to the Burns house and then it came in sight and I saw it was our model A coupe and that the twins had it running.

It was going slower than I thought it should even though the motor was wound up pretty good and there was smoke coming out of the exhaust pipe. Jim, who was driving at that time, waved at me as he went past and he drove the car up to the gasoline storage tank.

"I thought the car would go faster than that," I said when both twins got out.

"Oh, it will go a lot faster," Jim, said. "I haven't really caught on to this driving and I only had it in second gear. And that's where I'll keep it until I get to be a better driver."

"I noticed it was smoking a lot more than I expected it to," I said.

"It'll do that until the rings seat," Joe said, as he took the hose down from the gasoline storage tank and started fill the gas tank of the car. "Rest assured, Billy, we have a good car. As soon as it gets broke in and we learn to drive it better, why we'll think we're driving a new car."

"That's tractor gas," I said. "Are we supposed to be putting tractor gas in the car?"

"No, we're not," Joe, answered. "But we're not going to tell anyone are we, Billy?"

"I'm sure not going to tell anyone," I answered. Of course they knew I wouldn't. All of us Harshburgers have a streak of outlaw in us and my streak is wider than anyone's. Anyone except Kevin. Kevin, he's all outlaw.

"Especially don't tell Floyd," Jim said. "Floyd would skin us alive if he knew we were using good plowing gas to run around in the car. But how else are we going to learn how to drive except by practice?"

And practice we did. Several tank fulls of tractor gas later, the car stopped smoking and all three of us could drive pretty good.

The day before school took back up after Christmas break, Jim, Joe, and I took turns driving to Cheyenne. When we took turns driving home, Jim and Joe had shiny new driver's licenses. I didn't have one of course, I was too young, but I could drive better than either one of the twins.

Chapter Seventeen

I was just a little smaller than the twins and quite a bit smaller than Floyd, course a lot of people are smaller than Floyd, but when it came time to drive the tractor, I was big enough. I guess that is why I sat on the tractor day after day after day. First I listed the cornfield, then the maize field and then the cotton field. When that was done, it was time to start planting and I started all over again. I'd fall to sleep at night with the pop, pop, pop of the John Deere still echoing in my head.

True to their word, the twins had the Farmall running just after school was out that spring. We used it on the Burns place. We used it to pull the combine when we harvested the wheat. Mr. Burns also had a wheat truck, which he had left when he went to California and with a little tinkering, the twins soon had it running. I think those twins could make a willow log run if they could just find the parts.

When it came time to harvest the wheat, it was the twins and I who did it. Floyd said he didn't know nothing about wheat so while we were harvesting, Floyd hooked up a team and cultivated on the home place.

I didn't have a driver's license so I worked in the wheat field while Jim or Joe hauled the wheat to town. I mostly drove the Farmall and pulled the combine while one or the other of the twins rode the combine. It was sure different to hear the hum of the engine of the Farmall rather than the pop, pop, pop of the John Deere.

With the war on, wheat brought a good price and Floyd had them sell it. And we had a good crop too. Floyd figured we were getting somewhere between fourteen and seventeen bushels an acre. The way I figured it, we were soon going to be rich. But, of course, we never were.

From time to time that spring when we took the cattle off of the wheat and put them on grass, Floyd had me saddle up Blue and cut out anywhere from five to fifteen steers and drive them to Red Moon where we put them in cattle cars to haul to the sale in Oklahoma City. With meat being rationed, the steers brought a good price. But did Floyd keep any of that money? Oh, no. He either bought seed or more white-faced heifers with it.

As soon as wheat harvest was over, the twins and I found ourselves in the cotton patch choppin' cotton. And then we had a good rain. As soon as the wheat field was dry enough, Jim and Joe helped me hook up the oneway plow to the Farmall and I started plowing the wheat field. I started around the wheat field with the oneway plow throwing the dirt to the right and cutting a furrow on the left and when it took me what I judged to be two and a half hours to make the first round, I knew I would be plowing the wheat field for several days. But that was okay with me, because when I got to the north end of the field I could see Floyd and the twins choppen' cotton on the river bottom forty.

I had to admit that for once I had the better job. There was a draw back though. I was all alone. There wasn't anybody to talk to but myself or the tractor. Oh, well, one has to do the best with what one has and the tractor and I had many conversations. It also gave me a chance to dream. What, with things going the way they were, and with Floyd plowing all our profits back into the farm, we just might get as big as the Payne's. It didn't make any difference though because as soon as I was out of school I was heading up north. With the hot sun beating down on my bare back, going north where it was cool was my favorite day dream.

The second day of plowing, the sun was straight overhead, so I stopped by a shade tree where I had my lunch stashed and ate. After eating I was a little sleepy and was tempted to take a short nap. But I didn't. Billy boy, I said to myself, this field isn't going to get plowed with you sleeping, so I cranked up the Farmall and crawled back aboard. I thought in a little while I would wake back up, but I didn't. My eyelids grew heavier and heavier. I started singing and it helped some. I sung up every song I knew and even made up a couple and then I started singing the songs over again but my eyelids started growing heavy again. I stood up and drove and that too helped but before long my eyelids grew so heavy they slammed shut.

I suddenly woke up with the sensation of falling, and when I became aware of where I was, I found myself wedged between the steering wheel and the iron seat of the tractor with my feet hanging off. I quickly scrambled back on the tractor and looked to see where the tractor was going and I was a little surprised to find the tractor was heading down the field like it was supposed to. I looked back to see what kind of a mess I had made plowing. The field behind me looked just as it should and I knew I hadn't been asleep for long. But I had dozed off long enough for me to almost fall off of the tractor.

I wasn't sleepy anymore. I tell you, not one bit. My heart was pounding a million times a minute. The thoughts of me falling off of the tractor and the plow running over me and cutting me into a million pieces was enough to keep me wide awake all afternoon.

I mentioned the incident to my brothers while we were milking and while Jim and Joe made some wiseass comment or other, Floyd was quiet for a long while.

"Billy," he finally said. "We're powerful short handed around here as it is. We need all the help we can get to get all of the work done, and we need you. If you fall off of the tractor and the plow runs over you, it will cripple you or worst yet, kill you and you won't be any good to anybody. Next time you get sleepy, stop the tractor and get off. Walk around a bit. If that don't wake you up, then take a nap. Don't run the tractor when you're so sleepy you might fall off. We can't afford to lose a tractor driver. I'd rather lose a hour or two of plowing while you take a nap than to lose a tractor driver altogether."

"I won't do it again, Floyd. That I can promise you. It scared me too bad."

"And for God's sake, Billy, don't tell Ma. She thinks we expect too much out of you already. She thinks you're just a boy."

"Well, I'm not a boy. I'm a man and I plan to keep on doing a man's work around here."

It was in the afternoon two days later that the sleepies got me again. I had stayed up later than usual the night before and I was paying for it now. I tried singing and I tried standing up and I tried standing up and singing, but it wasn't any use. The hot sun on my bare back, the steady drone of the engine lulled me towards sleep and I felt my eyelids getting heavier and heavier. When I got to the north end of the field, the end that was close to our land, I stopped the tractor, killed the engine and got off. I walked around a bit but it didn't help. I was still drowsy. I know what will wake me up, I said to my self and started hiking up the river to the deep hole.

Actually the walk up to the hole woke me up but since I was already there I stripped off my britches, the only clothes I wore, and dove in. I swam across and back again and then stood on a sandbar to catch my breath with the cool water up to my chin. I thought I heard a horse neigh and I wondered if Blue had gotten out and followed me. I didn't hear it again and decided it was just my imagination. I really ought to get back to the plowing, I thought, but one more trip across the hole and back wouldn't hurt anything. I swam across, kicked off of the far bank to come back and went under water for a spell. I came up in the middle of the deep hole, blew the air out hard, shook the water out of my eyes and saw Betty Ann bending over to pick up my britches.

"What the hell do you think you're doing!" I shouted. My yelling at her made her jump and she turned to face me.

"You shouldn't be cussing in front of a woman, Billy," she scolded.

"Okay. I'll ask it nice, what do you think you're doing?" I had worked my way to the sandbar and was standing on it but I continued to move my arms as if I were treading water.

"I told you I knew you were skinny dipping when you were supposed to be working, but you wouldn't believe that I knew. Do you believe me now?"

"But you're not going to tell anybody are you, Betty Ann? If you do I'll just deny it." All the time we had been talking I had been working my way to more shallow water but hunkering down until only my head was above water and working my hands as if I were treading water.

"I bet no one knows that you go swimming in the deep hole all by yourself, do they?"

"No, and I don't care for them to find out." Even under the circumstances I was in, I couldn't help but notice that Betty Ann was a lovely thing. Her red halter top with her breasts straining it to the limit, her short, short red shorts which she filled out so well, her lovely legs, narrow waist and all tanned a golden brown.

"But they're going to find out. They're going to find out that you go skinny dipping in the deep hole all by yourself."

"You wouldn't tell them, Betty Ann, would you? If you do I'll just say it's something you made up." All the while I was scrunching down farther as I worked my way to shallower and shallower water.

"No, I'm not going to tell them but you are."

"Now why would I do such a fool thing as that?"

"How else are you going to explain it when you have to go home bare naked when I ride off with your pants?"

102

"Ride off? Do you have a horse here?"

"Yes. I have old Stocking tied in that thicket up there," she said pointing.

I looked where she was pointing and sure enough I saw a horses tail flicker as it swatted flies. I knew if I could get just a little closer and with Betty Ann still thinking I was in deep water, I knew I could be out and on her before she could get to her horse. What I need was just a little more time and I knew the only way I could get time was to keep her talking. I also knew that wouldn't be hard to do because that Betty Ann sure liked to talk.

"Betty Ann, why do you want to do such a mean thing to me?" I asked, making my voice whine.

"Oh, I don't know. Maybe I want to get back at you for all the mean things you did to me at school."

"But Betty Ann, I didn't ever do anything as mean to you as you're threatening to do to me." All the while working my way closer and closer.

"Maybe I just want a souvenir. That's it. I've got myself a souvenir. Maybe I'll tack these britches to the wall of my room and the next time you deny skinny-dipping to someone I'll just invite them to my room."

I didn't know whether Betty Ann was teasing me or not. To be truthful I don't think she had made up her mind either. I think on one hand she was seriously considering riding off with my pants and throwing them in a canyon somewhere. I doubted seriously that she even considered taking a pair of old wore out dirty britches home with her and tacking them on the wall of her room. But on the other hand she was thinking of just dropping my pants and running to her horse and riding away when she got tired of the game.

Betty Ann may not have been sure what she was going to do but I was darned sure what I was going to do as soon as I got the chance. I was now squatted down in very shallow water and I was afraid that if I went any closer to shore, my knees would break the surface. So when she said, "Bye-bye Billy Harshburger," I put both hands on the sandy bottom, pushed with my arms and legs and came exploding out of the water and two lunging steps forwards and I was on shore.

Betty Ann squealed took a step backwards, stumbled and fell. Three long strides and I were on top of her before she got a chance to move. I got astraddle of her thighs, put my hands on her shoulders and pinned her flat in the sand. She lay there laughing.

"You sure put one over on me, Billy. I thought you were still in deep water and would have to swim ashore." She was looking me in the face and then her eyes wandered down my body. "Oh, my, Billy. I've seen you swimming nude before and you never looked like that." Her eyes came back to my face and the laughter died and was replaced by a smile. "Are you what they call aroused?"

Of course I had another name for what had happened to my body but I felt myself blush as I nodded my head, yes.

"Do I do that to you? I do, don't I. I make you aroused."

I didn't answer her but bent over and kissed her on the lips. It wasn't much of a kiss as she was still smiling.

"Just think, I can do that to you."

I bent over and kissed her again. This time she kissed me back and the kiss went on for a while.

"I liked that," she said, when at last the kiss ended. "I have never been kissed by a boy before."

"And you're not kissing a boy now," I said. "You're kissing a man. Here, let me show you what a real kiss is like."

Her eyes watched me in anticipation as I stretched my self the full length of her body, my legs on top of her thighs and my body against hers. I lowered my mouth to her lips and a short time after the kiss started, I probed her lips with my tongue. Her mouth reflexively opened and I plundered her with my tongue. I wasn't quite expecting the reaction I got from Betty Ann. She threw her arms around my neck and clutched me around the waist with her legs and her body arched up to mine and she was all movement beneath me. I felt rather than heard a guttural groan come from deep within her throat. She tore her mouth away saying, "No, Billy, no. We can't."

"Why, Betty Ann."

"We just can't." And her body was still moving beneath me, betraying the message her lips were delivering. "Stop, Billy. Stop now. Please."

"But I don't want to stop, Betty Ann."

"I don't want to either. But we must, Billy. We must. We have to be strong. Get up and put your clothes on."

Reluctantly I stood up on shaky legs. I reached for my britches, turned my back to her and put them on. When I turned back around, she was gone. A few moments later I heard a horse splash across the river, and then I heard the thundering hoof beats as she raced out towards the red hills as if the demons were after her. Demons she could not outrun.

All the while as I was plowing down on the Burns' place, when it got to about what I guessed was two o'clock in the afternoon, I would stop the tractor and hike down to the deep hole and go swimming. I never again that summer saw Betty Ann on shore but I could still see her in my minds eye and I could feel her warm, vibrant body against mine.

Chapter Eighteen

I was at the road intersection plenty early when school first started my sophomore year of high school. Jim and Joe were with me and they were as anxious as I was. They would be seniors and this was the first day of their last year of school.

I got on the bus and saw that the seat where Betty Ann and I sat was empty so I sat down and scooted over to the side of the bus so Betty Ann would have room to sit when she got on. Was I surprised when Betty Ann got on, walked down the isle, said, "Hi, Billy," and went on by to sit with Kathryn, who got on the bus before I did. I sat there on the bus all the way to school completely bewildered. I kept glancing back at her and saw she was talking to Kathryn and never once did she glance my way.

When we got to school, Betty Ann rushed off of the bus and took off across the school yard, her loose skirt swishing around her legs and her white sandals kicking up small puffs of red dust which were blown away by the wind. I walked up the cement steps into the school house, walked down the cool, dimly lit hallway to the sophomore lockers, picked one and opened the door so that the other sophomores would know it was taken and then went outside through the back door.

There I saw Betty Ann. She had her arm around the waist of Bobby Woods and he had his arm around her shoulders. They were strolling across the scrubby lawn, talking. At least Betty Ann was talking and Bobby Woods was listening.

I just stood there and watched and I was surprised by how I felt. It wasn't rage I felt, I wasn't mad or anything. I was just terribly, terribly hurt. Hurt and confused. It was true that Betty Ann and I had agreed long ago that it would be best if she and I were only friends and Betty Ann had even gone so far as to say, because of her father, we could never be anything more. I could live with that, or so I thought. But the feelings I had from watching Betty Ann and Bobby, I suddenly wondered.

I couldn't understand it. I could whip Bobby Woods every day of the week and twice on Sunday. I could run faster than he could and I could beat him arm wrestling. I made straight A's in my classes where Bobby was happy with a C. It seemed that we always like the same girls but the difference was, he got them. What did he have that I didn't?

Of course Bobby had a better car than I did and he never seemed to worry about rationing stamps. His father farmed ten times the amount of cotton we did and he was also a prominent member of the community. But Betty Ann had claimed those things didn't matter to her. But I wondered now if what she said was true. I wondered if down deep they really did. Of course I had to also admit that one thing Bobby had going for him was that Mr. Woods and Mr. Payne were the best of friends.

I stepped back into the hallway of the schoolhouse before they saw me. I knew I couldn't face them right now.

When I had seen Bobby with Mary Lou years back I had felt different. It had been a little bit of hurt and a whole bunch of rage. But today it was different. Today there was no rage. There was just hurt. Deep down, dull aching hurt. I felt betrayed and I knew there was no reason for it. Because of her father, Betty Ann and I could never be more than friends.

Somehow I made it through the day without anyone noticing or if they did, they didn't say anything. The morning was spent enrolling in our classes and buying our books. I couldn't afford the new books but had to buy the old many times used books and just hoped that all the pages were still in it.

That afternoon we went to our afternoon classes and as luck would have it, Betty Ann was in every one of them with me. I knew what that meant; it meant that she would be in my morning classes also.

When I got on the bus to go home, Betty Ann again walked passed the seat I had saved for her and sat by Kathryn, but I had expected it. I even welcomed it. It was a lot easier to ride home alone than to sit by Betty Ann knowing she was going with Bobby Woods. Jim, Joe and I got off the bus and started the walk home. I had nothing to say but they talked all the way home, telling each other how great their last year of school was going to be.

When I walked into the house through the kitchen door intending to see if I could find me a cold biscuit and butter, the kitchen was quiet and where Ma was usually bustling around, it was empty. I looked into the living room and found it empty. Puzzled, I stepped out on the porch and there I found Floyd and Ma. I felt, rather than saw, the twins step out on the porch behind me.

Floyd and Ma were just sitting there, Floyd holding Ma's hand. She wasn't crying or anything, just sitting there her dry eyes focused on the red hills far beyond the river.

"What's happened?" I asked.

"Kevin's been kilt," Floyd answered.

"What!" and I couldn't help but shout. "I don't believe it. Kevin's too tough to get killed."

Ma handed me a telegram and I read it to myself:

> To the Harshburger Family:
> Subject: Sergeant Kevin Harshburger
> We regret to inform you that Sergeant Harshburger is reported missing in action in the skies over Germany and is presumed dead. His plane was shot down and observers saw no parachutes before it was lost from sight heading towards the ground.

I handed the telegram to Joe and as he started reading it to Jim I could not stand to hear those words again. I took off running. I ran down to the corral, saddled Blue, led her out of the corral and climbed into the saddle. We went thundering out into the pasture.

After about a half a mile, I slowed her down to a walk. Soon we were in the red hills and I rode a little farther before I pulled Blue to a stop and sat there in the saddle looking around at a strangely empty world. I thought of Kevin and I remembered how he always loved the red hills.

When he and I were young and didn't have work to do, we would come wandering out into the red hills together. Floyd was more like a father to me than a brother and the twins always stuck by each other, so that left Kevin and me. I remembered one time when we were exploring a canyon right after a rain. We had come upon a bank of the canyon that was covered with gypsum crystals sparkling in the sunlight. We had gathered them and put them in our pockets until our pockets were full and we had claimed that they were diamonds. When we got them home and took them out of our pockets, but try as we might, we could never get them to sparkle again as they had in the bank of the canyon.

And that was Kevin. Kevin so full of life, so full of fun and he had such a complete disregard of rules of any kind. Like the gypsum crystals, Kevin would never sparkle again. He was gone. Gone forever.

And I wished a man could cry. I wished I could break down and cry like a woman. But a man couldn't. For a man to cry showed weakness. Men had to be strong and manly. But as I remembered Kevin I felt a lump forming in my throat and I couldn't help it, the lump came out a sob. I felt the tears streaming down my face and I was ashamed. Ashamed that I wasn't strong enough to keep from crying and I was glad I was out here deep in the red hills and alone so no one could see me.

The edge of the sun was almost touching the western horizon when at last I kicked Blue lightly in the ribs and we moved on. I gathered up the milk cows and herded them home. By the time I got the cows to the milking pen I had scrubbed away the tears and all other evidence of crying with my bandana.

There was nobody at the corrals when I got there so I unsaddled Blue and turned her loose. I went up to the house to get my brothers.

As I stepped in the door, I heard Joe say, "Ma, you know what the bible says. It says 'an eye for an eye and a tooth for a tooth'. Those German bastards killed Kevin and Jim and I are going to make them pay."

"Please don't go," Ma pleaded. "I don't want to lose anymore sons."

"You ain't, Ma," Jim said. "But when Joe and I get over there you can damn well bet there are some German mothers whose going to lose their sons."

"We really need you on the farm, boys," Floyd said. "I don't know if Billy and I can run this farm by ourselves."

"Yes, we can, Floyd," I chimed in. "I wish I were old enough to join up and I could kill me some Germans. But I'm not and I can't. So Joe and Jim you go right ahead and I'll do your share of work and you can kill some Germans for me. Floyd, I'll quit school and work on the farm full time. We can manage the farm that way."

"No! Billy. No!" Ma said. "You're such a good student. I want you to finish school and maybe go to college. I want you to make something of yourself."

"Don't worry, Ma. I'll finish high school and perhaps go to college. It'll just happen a little later than I figured on. It'll happen after the war's over."

Instead of riding the bus, we took the car to school the next morning. We cleaned the books out of our lockers and went straight to principal's office. We could see through the window of his door that Mr. Davis was in his office and he was filling out paper work. We knocked on his door and he looked up, saw us and waved us in.

"What can I do for you boys?" Mr. Davis asked.

"We're quitting school and joining the army," Joe said.

"You just enrolled yesterday. What made you change your plans?"

"There was a telegram when we got home yesterday," Jim said. "We found out that our older brother, Kevin, was killed."

"Oh, yes. I remember Kevin. I'm sorry to hear that boys." Mr. Davis swiveled his chair until he could look out over the schoolyard. "War is such a terrible thing. So many of my former students have lost their lives." He turned his chair back and looked at Jim and Joe. "I'm supposed to try and talk you out of quitting school. I'm supposed to remind you that you're seniors and have only nine months of school left. But I'm not going to do any of those things because if I were in your place I'd do the same thing myself." He opened his desk and took out a couple of forms and handed one to Jim and one to Joe. "Fill these out and take them to the superintendent's office and check in your books." Jim and Joe took the forms and turned to leave. "Just a minute," Mr. Davis said. He scribbled a note on a piece of paper and handed it to them. "Give this to the office also. I think under the circumstances you should get full refund for your books."

When the twins were gone Mr. Davis turned to me and said, "What can I do for you, Billy?"

"I'm quitting school too," I said.

"But why, Billy? You're too young to go into the army."

"I know. But I'm not too young to do a man's work on the farm. With Jim and Joe gone, Floyd needs me fulltime."

Mr. Davis sat and looked at me for a good while. Finally he said, "You're such a good student, I hate to see you quit school. Maybe there is a different way. Maybe you can stay in school and work on the farm also. What classes are you in?"

I named them and he wrote them down. "Can you stay here just a little while, Billy. Let me see what I can do."

"Yes Sir."

He left me then and I sat there. I watched thirty minutes tick off on the clock. Jim and Joe came by, saw that I was still in the office and Mr. Davis wasn't, so they came in.

"We've been looking for you, Billy," Joe said.

"Here I am," I answered.

"What's happening?" Jim asked.

"Mr. Davis is trying to find a way for me to stay in school and still work on the farm."

Mr. Davis came back in and Jim and Joe left saying, "We'll meet you at the car."

"Billy, I think I have found a solution. Do you think you could attend school two days a week?"

"Probably."

"I've checked with all your teachers and cleared it with the superintendent. Because you're such a good student and because there is a war on, if you can come to school two days a week we can keep you enrolled. Would Tuesdays and Fridays be good days for you?"

"Yes sir."

"It's going to be hard for you, but you're a smart boy and I think you can do it."

If Mr. Davis thought I could do it, then I knew I could.

I left the office with the books I had intended to sell back still in my hand. I went to my locker and put them back in. I went to the car and found Jim and Joe waiting for me. I drove them to the house and they ran inside. Each of them had a paper sack with a change of clothes in them. They picked them up and carried the sacks outside where Ma was waiting for them. They hugged Ma goodbye and got back into the car. As I drove off, I looked back and saw Ma was crying.

I drove them to Red Moon but we got there just as the train was pulling out, heading down the tracks to Cheyenne. I put the car in gear and we went racing to Cheyenne and we reached the depot just as the train was pulling into the station.

I watched as Jim and Joe used their book refund money to buy their tickets and I waited until they went aboard and the train pulled out heading to Clinton. When the train was out of sight, I started the car and drove home with an empty, lonely feeling.

Chapter Nineteen

Somehow Floyd and I managed. We just had to work harder and longer and some things we did a little bit different. I went to school every Tuesday and Friday and those days I turned in my assignments and got new ones and took tests. I got A's on all my work but it was a lot harder to do than when I went to school every day. I seldom listened to the radio any more but spent my time working on my schoolwork.

When I was at school, I couldn't avoid Betty Ann since she was in all of my classes, but I could, and I did, avoid seeing Betty Ann and Bobby Woods together. It still hurt too much.

With the twins gone, Ma fed us breakfast while it was still dark, and there was only a faint trace of pink in the eastern sky when I saddled up Blue. By first light, I was in the pasture looking for the milk cows. They never wandered far at night and I usually had them in the milking pen before sunup. It took twice as long to milk without the twins. It was the second day after the twins left, Floyd and I had finished the milking and I was separating the cream when Ma came down to the milk house. She just stood and watched for a while and then said, "Let me try to do the separator, Billy."

I stepped aside and let her take the handle.

"How fast do you turn it, Billy?"

Of course I already had it up to speed so I said, "Hear that little bell going ding, ding , ding? You're supposed to keep that little bell going at just that regular rate."

Ma listened for a while as she turned the crank and then she asked, "Does that still sound about right?"

"Yes, ma'am," I answered. "You're turning it just right. Keep turning it just at that speed."

She looked into the separator bowl and asked, "Do you think you can empty that last bucket of milk into the bowl?"

"I think I can." It almost run it over but I poured the last bucket of milk in.

"What do you do with the milk when you have separated it?" Ma asked.

"Floyd takes the first half and feeds it to the hogs. That's where he is now. I take this last half and divide it among the calves."

"Then go do it, Billy. I'll separate the last of the milk."

I left Ma separating the last of the milk and carried the two buckets of separated milk down to the calf pen. I was about half way through feeding the calves and was about out of milk when I glanced back and saw Ma lugging the last two buckets full of milk down the hill to the calf pen.

"Ma, you shouldn't be doing that," I said. "That's men's work."

"Billy," Ma said, "my boys shouldn't be in the army and learning to kill people and Kevin shouldn't have been killed. There are lots of things going on in this world that shouldn't be. There's women building tanks and guns and that should be men's work. There's women building airplanes instead of being home doing housework as they should be. There is no reason in the world why I can't learn to separate the cream, slop the hogs and feed the calves and help you and Floyd out a bit. That will give you and Floyd more time to do the farming.

"Okay, Ma, I'll show you how to feed the calves and I'm sure Floyd will show you how to feed the hogs. But," I said grinning, "you can only do it of a morning."

"And why is that, Billy Harshburger?"

"Because neither Floyd nor I can cook worth a durn, and somebody has to cook supper."

After we showed her how, Ma separated the cream, slopped the hogs and fed the calves and Floyd and I went to work right after we finished milking. This gave us an hour to an hour and a half of extra time to work.

Five days later when I brought the cows in, Ma was down at the corral with Floyd.

"Ma," I said, "when Floyd and I finish milking we'll bring the milk up. Why aren't you in the kitchen washing dishes?"

"Those dishes can wait. I came down here to help you boys milk."

"You know how to milk?"

"Sure I know how to milk. I milked all the time until I started having children to look after. I reckon it's something you never forget. I might be a little slow to begin with but I'll get it back."

113

She was and she did. She was a little slow when she first started that morning but at that nights milking, she matched Floyd and I cow for cow.

Would Ma ever cease to surprise me? As I watched Ma on a milk stool milking cows, I could almost see her as a young woman, milking cows and doing other chores while Pa and his brothers were out plowing the fields.

Since Floyd didn't drive, it was me who took Ma and her eggs and cream to town Saturday evening. I couldn't help but notice as I drove to town and back, that Ma was watching me closely. We were coming home two Saturdays later and as soon as we got off of the pavement onto the dirt roads, Ma said, "Stop the car, Billy."

I thought that something was wrong, that there was an emergency of some kind so I slammed on the brakes and went skidding sideways down the road.

"You didn't have to stop that fast, Billy."

"What's wrong, Ma?"

"Nothing, Billy. I just want to learn to drive."

"What?"

"I think it's time I learned to drive and you're going to teach me," Ma said in her 'that's an order,' voice.

"Well, okay, Ma," I said, reluctantly.

"Well, turn the motor off."

"Why?"

"If I'm going to be driving I guess I need to know how to start the car."

I got out and walked around the car and got in the passengers seat while Ma scooted over behind the wheel. Before I could give her instructions on how to start the car, I saw Ma turn on the switch, reach down with her left foot and push down on the starter button. When the engine came to life, Ma pushed in on the clutch, took hold of the gear shift, put it in gear and we were off. Her start was a little jumpy, but she did right well for the first time.

She drove about half a mile in first and then she pushed in on the clutch and with only a little grinding of the gears, she had it in second. "It's a little harder to shift gears then it looks," Ma said, staring down the road and gripping the steering wheel tightly.

"It just takes a little practice, Ma," I said, gripping the edge of the seat with both hands. We were just a little ways from home before Ma put the car in high, and we drove on home. Floyd was out in the fields and didn't see that it was Ma who drove the car into our yard.

It was the following Tuesday and I had just gotten off of the bus and started walking home when I heard a car coming over the hill from behind me. I stepped to the edge of the road and looked back. It sure looked like our car, but of course it couldn't be. But the closer it came the more it looked like our car. Then it glided up beside me, stopped and I saw it was Ma.

"You want a ride home, Son?"

"Sure, Ma," and I climbed in. I looked at the gas gage and said, "You're about out of gas, Ma."

"I know, Billy. I don't know if we have enough ration stamps to fill it up again," Ma said.

"It don't make any difference," I said. "We don't have enough gas to make it to Cheyenne anyway."

"What'll we do, Billy?" Ma asked, putting the car in gear and starting off as pretty as you please. As she shifted gears and drove on down the road as if she had been driving all her life, I knew where the gas had gone.

"Let's go on down to the Burns' place and put in some tractor gas."

"We're not supposed to do that, are we?" Ma asked as she drove on past our driveway and headed on down to the Burns place.

"No, we're not," I said. "But this is an emergency."

"Who cares? Just as long as we don't get caught," Ma said. I looked at Ma and grinned. And all this time I had thought that us boys had inherited our streak of outlaw from Pa.

Friday when I came home from school and walked through the kitchen door, Ma said, "Let me show you something, Billy."

She reached into the pocket of her dress and brought out a shinny new drivers license.

"All right, Ma!" I said, and hugged her.

I continued going to school on Tuesdays and Fridays. I would turn my completed assignments in, take tests, and get my new assignments. I still got straight A's, but it was a lot harder to do.

I didn't listen to the radio with Ma and Floyd anymore. I'd listen to the fifteen minutes of news and when that was over, I would go to the kitchen, light a lamp, spread my books and papers out on the kitchen table and go to work.

The days I went to school, I tried my best to stay away from Betty Ann and Bobby when they were together but one Friday during lunch hour, I went around a corner and saw them kissing. They didn't see me so I turned around and went back the other way, the old familiar aching hurt still down deep inside. Times like these made me wonder if school was worth it.

I finished plowing the wheat field for the last time mid afternoon on Saturday. The next morning it was cloudy and by noon it was raining. It wasn't a thunderstorm like we usually get in Oklahoma, but just a good, hard, steady rain. It had stopped by the time we went to bed and I knew that in a couple of days I'd be drilling wheat. When I went to school, I told them I wouldn't be able to come back for a week or maybe more.

I started drilling wheat on Wednesday and kept right on going. Ma and Floyd let me out of doing chores so I could spend that time in the field and so I rode the tractor from first light until dark. Ma protested when I headed to the field on Sunday, but I reminded her that the ox was in the ditch, and she didn't say anymore.

I finished drilling wheat in the middle of the afternoon on Tuesday, so Wednesday I rode the bus to school and that afternoon I rode the bus home with an arm load of catch up work to do. That night I didn't even listen to the news. Right after supper I spread out my books and papers and went to work. When the grandfather clock in the living room chimed twelve times, I gave up and went to bed. The next night was the same but when I turned in my work on Friday and got it back on Tuesday, I had all A's.

I didn't argue much anymore and pretty much let Floyd make all the decisions when it came to running the farm but when Floyd mentioned it was getting close to time to head the maize I put my foot down. "We're not going to head the maize this year, Floyd."

"What do you mean, Billy?"

"I mean we're going to hook the John Deere to the binder and we're going to bundle the maize with the heads on it."

"But we've never done it that way before. We've always headed the maize and then bundled it."

"Why?"

"I don't know, Billy. We've just always done it that way."

"But Floyd, we've never been short of help around here like we are now. Let's try it and see if it doesn't work."

We tried it and it worked. We had it bundled and shocked in less time than it would have taken us to head half of the maize.

We had no more than hauled in the bundles and stacked them when we got a frost and the cotton started opening. So soon we started picking. I had been picking cotton for two weeks, except on Tuesday and Friday, when school turned for cotton picking. It was slow going with just Floyd, Ma and me but we finally got a bale picked and it was me who hooked the wagon onto the tractor and took the cotton to the gin. Cotton was still at a good price and Floyd had me sell it. Floyd also asked me to see if I could find cotton pickers, but there were none to be found at that time.

Shortly after school was out for cotton picking we were able to hire the King family, minus Ted who was fighting in the Pacific. The Kings hadn't picked for us last year but had gone straight from picking their own cotton to picking for the Woods.

Like year before last, Mary Lou chose a row right by mine and we headed up the rows picking cotton. We were soon in front of everyone else. When we were out of earshot, Mary Lou said, "It's like old times, isn't it, Billy?"

"Not hardly," I answered.

"What's wrong, Billy? Don't you still love me?"

"No, Mary Lou, I don't."

"Are you mad at me, Billy? Do you hate me?"

"No, I don't hate you either. I don't love you, I don't hate you, I don't have any feelings for you whatsoever." With those words, I bent over and started picking on down the row leaving Mary Lou pouting behind me.

When I got to the end of the row, I weighed my cotton, wrote down the weight, dumped my sack into the wagon and picked a row that nobody was on and started picking towards the other end of the field. I was a man now and I was big enough and strong enough to pull two rows of cotton in my sack.

The wagon was full by mid afternoon. "Should I sell it, Floyd?" I asked, as I hooked the tractor to the wagon.

"If the price is still up," Floyd answered.

The price of cotton was actually a little higher, so I sold it. After they gave me the check, I walked uptown to the bank and cashed it. That was the law of the Harshbuger household. After the bank failures of the thirties, Harshburgers never put money in the bank again.

I didn't get home in time to help Ma and Floyd milk, but I did get home in time to help Floyd separate the cream. I gave the money to Floyd and took over the separator while he went to slop the hogs and start feeding the calves.

"Billy," Floyd said over supper that night, "the wheat is ready to start grazing. You're as good a judge of cattle as I am and besides you can drive. There is a cattle sale in Cheyenne tomorrow and I would like for you to go and see if you can pick up some steers to put on the wheat pasture."

"Be glad to, Floyd," I said. "Anything to get me out of the cotton patch.

"There's something else," Floyd said.

"What's that?"

"Ma and I have been talking it over and we've decided not to pay you anymore for picking cotton."

"And why the hell not!" I exploded.

"Billy, don't cuss in my kitchen," Ma said. "Floyd, you didn't have to break to him that way."

"I know, Ma," Floyd said. "I just wanted to see Billy explode. Billy, instead of paying you to pick cotton, we've decided to give you a fourth of the cotton crop. With buying steers and getting them on the wheat pasture, you're not going to have time to pick much cotton." Then he reached into his pocket and took out the money I had given him. He counted out a fourth of it and handed it to me. It was much more than I would have ever made picking cotton. "Now that's only if it's okay with you."

"It's better than okay," I grinned. I took the money up to our room and put it into the Prince Albert can.

The next few weeks I became a real cattle buyer. I went to the sales at Cheyenne, Elk City and Sayre. When the trucks brought the steers in I was down at the Burns place to show them what pens to put them in. I liked to keep the cattle up for a few days when they first came in so that I got to know them and they got to know me before I herded them out to the wheat pasture.

When I had spent all the money Floyd had allowed me for steers, I took almost all of my money from the tobacco can and kept going to the sales. When I was through, I owned seven bred, black angus cows with calves at their sides, and I was just about broke. Darned if I wasn't becoming a farmer after all.

Chapter Twenty

By the time school took back up after cotton snapping, we had the farm work pretty well laid by for the winter. Leastwise laid by enough so that Floyd could handle it and I could go to school on a regular basis. I figured it would sure make it easier to keep up on my schoolwork.

The second Monday morning after school took up that Betty Ann got on the bus and came back and sat with me. This surprised me somewhat, but nothing like her riding all the way to school without saying a word. She just sat there holding her books and stared straight ahead. She never even said "Hi, Billy," when she got on.

I knew something was very wrong when Betty Ann didn't go racing across the school to meet Bobby, but instead went into the school house, down the hall way to her locker, put all her books except her math book in her locker, closed the door and marched up the hall to the math room which was our first period class, and went in.

I put my books except for my math book in my locker and followed her into the math room, and the teacher wasn't even there yet. She was just sitting there looking at the clean blackboard and didn't even seem to notice me when I came in. I knew that something was very wrong but I had no idea of what it was. I sat in a desk beside her and took out my homework. I figured Betty Ann needed to get her mind off of whatever was bothering her and she needed a friend.

I fiddled with my homework and then asked, "Betty Ann, how did you work problem number five? I think I worked it right but I'm not for sure."

That was a lie. I knew for darned sure I had worked it right but it was one of the harder problems and it had taken me a while to figure it out.

She got out her homework and we compared how we had worked the problem and we had both worked it the same way. We compared other problems and as we discussed them I saw her began to brighten. She was almost her same old self by time the bell rang and the other students came in.

I made a point to be by Betty Ann's side in all of our morning classes and at noon I found out what her problem was when I saw Bobby Woods talking and flirting with Mary Lou.

I made double sure I sat by Betty Ann in the afternoon classes. I saw some of the other girls look at Betty Ann out of the corner of their eyes and some of them even snickered. This made me even more determined to let Betty Ann see that she had a friend.

When I got on the bus to go home Betty Ann sat in the seat with me. She didn't say anything for a ways then she turned to me, took my hand and said, "Billy, don't think that I don't know what you have been trying to do for me all day, because I do. Thank you. It's so nice to have a friend who doesn't make demands on you."

Then before I could say anything she let go of my hand and faced the front of the bus but not before I saw the glimmer of tears in her eyes. I rode the rest of the way home with her in silence.

At home I found a cold biscuit, buttered it and ate it on the way to the corral to saddle up Blue. I rode down to the wheat field to check on the cattle. I counted the steers and came up one short, so I counted them again and was still one steer short. I started riding the fence line and sure enough I soon found the place where he had gotten out. Now why would a fool steer leave a luscious green wheat field to go wandering around, I thought to myself as I started tracking him down. His tracks went up a canyon and I followed them. I soon found him wandering around as if he was lost. It was an easy task to head him back to the wheat field because I think he was lonesome for others of his kind, and I think he missed the green wheat. I had just finished cobbling up the fence so it would hold them until I got back to do it right when I heard a horse come splashing across the river. I looked up to see Betty Ann riding Old Stocking come out of the trees that grew along the river. I waved at her and she waved back and came on up to me.

"Thanks for being my friend, Billy," she said as she dismounted and looped Stocking's reins over a fence post. "I really need a friend right now."

"I'm your friend, Betty Ann. I always have been and I always will be. Anytime you need a friend, well, here I am." I spread my arms and she came running into them and I held her as she cried over Bobby Woods.

When her crying let up I asked, "Do you want to tell me about it?"

"Bobby dumped me," she said.

"And you were madly in love with the guy?"

She turned me loose and stepped back, a funny expression on her face. "That's the funny part about it. No, I wasn't. Mr. Woods and my Dad are very close friends. They kind of pushed us together. I do have to admit, however, that Bobby is good looking, charming, fun and exciting to be around. But he's not like you, Billy. He's not willing to work for what he wants and he doesn't have to. Anything he wants, his daddy gets for him. He's a spoiled bastard who thinks just because his daddy gives him anything he wants everyone else should do the same. No, I didn't and I don't love him."

"Then why are you crying over him?" I asked.

"I'm not crying over him dumping me but the reason and the way he did. It makes me so damn mad," and she stamped her foot in anger.

"So you're not so heartbroken as you are mad?"

She smiled at me and said, "You know me so well that sometimes it's scary."

"Do you want to talk about it, Betty Ann? Do you want to tell me what happened?"

"Yes, I do and I know I can trust you not to spread it all over school." She stood there a while, thinking, remembering, sorting her words out. I stood there patiently until she said. "Bobby and I went to the movies Saturday night and then after the first show, we went to the drugstore and had a coke. By the time we were finished with our cokes, it was time for the preview to start so we went to it.

"After the preview we started home and I noticed that Bobby didn't have much to say. When we got to a hill about a mile from my house, Bobby started to pull to the side of the road. I told him it was late and that I should be getting on home, but he parked anyway. I tolerated him for a while but then he started to get bold. So very, very bold. I pushed him away and told him to stop but he wouldn't take no for an answer and came back at me again. I had to fight him off kicking and screaming and as soon as the chance came, I got out of his clutches, opened the door and got out, my torn clothes and all.

Bobby was angry and he shouted, 'If you won't put out, Betty Ann, I'm going to find me a girl that will'. 'Well, I'm not going to put out to you so go ahead.' If Bobby Woods thinks I'm going to lose my virginity to him and fall shit-faced in love, he's got another think coming. He reached over, slammed the car door and drove off.

"How did you get home, Betty Ann?"

"I walked, how else?"

"Now I understand why you're mad at Bobby Woods."

"You do?"

"Yeah, Betty Ann. You don't like to walk."

"Billy Harshburger," she squealed and as she bent over to pick up a clod of dirt, I turned and started running. I felt the clod shatter between my shoulder blades and as I turned back to face her I saw her running towards me. She ran up to me and put her arms around me and I felt her lips brush against my cheek.

"Thanks, Billy. You're the best friend a person could ever have. I feel so much better." With those words, Betty Ann ran to ole Stocking, gathered the reins, stepped in the saddle, kicked Stocking in the ribs and in a flurry of hoof beats, they were gone.

As they disappeared in the trees, I wondered to myself if that girl knew a horse could walk or trot, and I heard them splash across the river and go thundering into the distance.

But I felt good all evening and the next morning Betty Ann got on the bus and sat beside me with a "Hi, Billy," and continued chattering all the way to school. Yes, God was in the heavens and all was right with the world. Or at least my part of it.

Things got better at noon. After lunch I went into the rest room and found Bobby, Travis and Troy standing by the open window sharing a cigarette. They were holding the cigarette out the window and when they would take a puff they would blow the smoke out the window. Bobby was bragging about having sex with Betty Ann and about his sexual exploits with her.

I walked over to Bobby and said, "You shouldn't be telling lies like that about Betty Ann. You know they're not true but some stupid son of a bitch might believe them."

"What's wrong, Billy?" Bobby said. "I've seen you sniffing around Betty Ann. Are you trying to get just a little of what ole Bobby got a bunch of?"

I hit him then. My left fist went to his right eye and his head bounced against the cement wall. And it felt so good I hit him in his left eye and then hit him in his nose and mouth as hard as I could. I got a good right uppercut to the point of his chin as he went sliding to the floor. I don't have many scruples in a fight but I do have one. I'd never hit or kick a man when he was down but I have no scruples about reaching down, standing him on his feet and hitting him again. And that's what I was fixing to do when Travis and Troy grabbed me, one on each side and pulled me back.

"He's had enough, Billy," Troy said.

"I can't give that lying son of a bitch enough," I said.

"You just about kilt him," Travis said. "Why do you keep saying he's lying?"

"Betty Ann told me yesterday afternoon that he tried to rape her Saturday night. She was able to fight him off and get out of the car and then he drove off and left her by the side of the road. She had to walk home."

Travis looked at Bobby moaning on the floor with disgust. Then he turned to me and said, "Get out of here, Billy, we'll take care of it."

"I came in here to piss and I'll leave as soon as I'm through," I said.

As I unbuttoned my pants at the trough I heard Travis say to Bobby, "We were in here horsing around and you tripped and fell into the heat radiator. That's our story and we're sticking to it."

"Well I'm not," Bobby said. "I'm going to tell my Daddy and he'll get that German bastard thrown out of school and maybe put in jail."

"I wish you hadn't mentioned jail, Bobby," Travis said. "The mention of jail makes me wonder. You see, Billy told us what really happened Saturday night and now you bring up jail. It makes me wonder how long a sentence attempted rape carries."

"And you believed him. I thought you were my friends," Bobby said.

"Now us being friends is a subject in question," Travis said. "As far as believing him, we could always talk to Betty Ann. But then everything would be all over school and if Betty Ann backs Billy up, well, I don't want to be friends with an attempted rapist, do you, Troy?"

"No sir," Troy answered. "I don't want to be friends with a guy that has to rape a girl to get a little."

"Do you want the whole school know you tried to rape Betty Ann, Bobby?" Travis asked.

I saw Bobby shake his head no as I buttoned up my pants.

"And honestly all I saw was you trip and fall into the radiator. What did you see, Troy?" Travis asked.

"I saw exactly the same thing. I don't know exactly how it happened, but I saw Bobby trip and fall into the radiator. See, it's even loose." and I saw Troy give the radiator a couple of hard kicks and sure enough it was loose.

"Bobby, I sure wouldn't want to be friends with a guy who tried to get Billy in trouble just because the guy was clumsy."

I headed out the door then but I heard Travis ask, "Now Bobby, what really happened to your face?"

I heard Bobby say, "I stumbled and fell into the radiator," as I headed up the hall.

I had two classes with Bobby. One right after lunch and one the last period of the day. Bobby was a little late for the first class after lunch but Travis and Troy had gotten him cleaned up and he made it. During the first class after lunch and during the last class of the day, I got a warm, fuzzy feeling inside me every time I looked at Bobby's face and saw the two black eyes and his swollen up nose.

"Bobby sure messed up his face when he fell onto the heat radiator in the boys restroom," Betty Ann said as she sat down beside me on the school bus.

"He sure did," I answered.

"Was he telling lies about me, Billy?"

"How would I know?" I said, but continued, "but knowing Bobby Woods, he probably was."

Betty Ann reached over and took my hand in hers. She turned my hand over and ran her finger across my bruised knuckles. "You should know," she said.

"Let it go, Betty Ann Payne," I said angrily, jerking my hand away. "You're not going to do anything but cause a lot of people a lot of trouble," and I stared angrily out the bus window. That Betty Ann, why did she have to keep prying? Why couldn't she leave well enough alone?

But I could never stay mad at Betty Ann for long. I turned to her and said, grinning, "You have to admit, Bobby Woods does look good wearing those two black eyes and busted nose."

Betty Ann laughed. "Yes, he does, doesn't he? Don't worry, Billy. I'm not going to breath a word to anybody or anything." We rode in silence until the bus stopped to let me off. "Thank you, Billy," Betty Ann said, as I stood up to get off. "Thank you so very much."

Chapter Twenty-One

Travis and Troy claimed they never said a word about what happened in the restroom, other than they saw Bobby fall into the heat radiator. Betty Ann may have had her suspicions, but she didn't know anything for sure. You can darn well bet I didn't say anything, since it would be me that got in trouble.

Things began to change in the life of Bobby Woods. For some reason the other students began to shun him. Maybe it was instinct or maybe it was suspicion, I don't know. But the life of Bobby was never the same again. Where girls had stood in line for a date with Bobby, now the only one who would have anything to do with him was Mary Lou.

He tried to act as if nothing happened, as if everything was the same as before, but it didn't work. Even though he still tried to pretend like he was a big man on campus, the other kids were laughing at him behind his back.

I thought that if I were to be friendly with him he would go back to being the same old Bobby, but it didn't work. Every time I got around him, he got all nervous and jumpy. It was then that I realized that even though the marks on his face I had put there were all healed up, the marks I had put deep inside him were still there. I tried to feel bad about it but somehow I just couldn't.

One cold afternoon in February, Betty Ann got on the bus all excited. "Did you hear the rumor that's all over school, Billy?"

"No. I don't pay much attention to rumors."

"The girls are saying that Mary Lou is pregnant."

"Are they also saying that Bobby's the father?"

"They say that Mary Lou claims that he is," Betty Ann said. "He probably is but I wouldn't bet everything on it."

"I guess Bobby found what he was looking for."

"What's that?" Betty Ann asked.

"A girl that would put out," I answered. "I hope he's happy with it."

But the word around school was that he wasn't happy with it. The word around school was that it was Bobby's dad who made him marry her, not Mary Lou's. The story was that Bobby and his dad had even gone so far as to have a fistfight over it. I don't know whether that was true or not but I do know that Bobby supported a black eye and it was for once one that I hadn't give him. He still looked good in it, though.

Whatever the case might be, Bobby and Mary Lou were married the last of February. They took out of school and when they returned, they were both wearing wedding bands.

That afternoon as I was on Blue counting the cattle in the wheat field, out of the corner of my eye I caught a flicker in the trees by the river. On closer look, I saw it was Betty Ann on Stocking. After I had finished counting cattle and saw they were all there, I rode over to her.

"Are they all there, Billy?"

"Every one of them," I answered. "What did you think of the Woods family this afternoon in school?"

Betty Ann shuddered. "Just think. That could have been me if I hadn't fought him off. What a horrible thought."

"What is?" I asked. "Having a baby or being married to Bobby?"

"Having a baby would be okay, just as long as it wasn't Bobby's baby. I'd sure hate to spend my life with that guy. Now that the cattle are counted, what do you do next, Billy?"

"I have some fence to fix, Betty Ann. It seems as if I can hardly keep up with it. When the war is over one of the first things I want to do is to buy some new wire. This old rusty wire seems to break faster than I can fix it."

"If you don't mind company, I'd like to ride along."

"I'd be happy to have your company, Betty Ann."

We rode the fence line stirrup to stirrup with Betty Ann chattering all the way. She pointed out a cardinal in a cedar tree and blue jays flickering through the brush. And so I rode with Betty Ann and Betty Ann pointed out this and that to me, I saw a new world through Betty Ann's eyes. A wonderful beautiful world.

And as we rode along I faced the fact that I loved Betty Ann. Not the infatuation I had had over her in the seventh grade but a strong, deep down, warming love. I finally worked up the nerve to ask, "Betty Ann, would you like to go to the movies with me Saturday night?"

"Billy, there is nothing I would want to do more, but I can't."

"Why not?"

"My dad would kill me if I told him I was going out with you. He would practically skin me alive."

"Then don't tell him, Betty Ann. Just walk down to the road and I'll come by and pick you up."

Betty Ann thought for a long moment and then shook her head, no. "If I were to go to the movies at Cheyenne or Reydon, the word that I was out with you would beat us home and my dad would be down at the end of the driveway waiting for us. I'm sorry, Billy. I really and truly am. I don't know why my dad hates the Harshburgers so."

"I do," I said and I wished I could have pulled the words back in just as soon as I said them.

"Tell me, Billy."

"No, Betty Ann."

"Come on, Billy. You can tell me. I'm a big girl now."

"No."

"Why not?"

"Betty Ann, you don't have a mother and your father is the only family you have, besides your aunt Vie. The Harshburger version of the story is not complementary to your father. I am not going to tell you anything that you would either disbelieve or would cause you to lose respect for you father. He's all you have, Betty Ann, so just leave it alone."

"Leave it alone like I was suppose to leave it alone when you fought Bobby Woods when he was telling lies about having sex with me?" Betty Ann, asked, a crooked smile on her face.

"Whoa, now girl. I never, ever admitted to fighting Bobby," I said, grinning at her.

"Billy, did you actually believe that Travis would be as quiet about the fight as you were? Especially when I promised to let him copy my homework and copy off of me during test time so he could pass math and graduate."

"That son of a bitch. And he promised me."

"Can you tell me when the problem between your folks and mine started, Billy?"

"It was during World War One," I answered. "Before we were even born."

"That was such a long time ago," she said.

"Some people have a hard time forgetting."

"Do you hate my dad, Billy?"

I looked at her and grinned. "I have to admit that right now he's not my favorite person in this world but the reason is, because

128

of him, you and I can't date. But no, I don't hate him. I don't even know him."

"I'm glad to hear that, Billy. You know I never knew my mother. Aunt Vie comes out a lot from Oklahoma City, but she's only an aunt. My Dad is the second most important person to me in this whole wide world."

"Second? Who's first?"

"You are, Billy. Bye, Bye." And with those words she wheeled Stocking around and was off in a flurry of hooves.

I watched her leave, ole Stocking in a full gallop. Nope, that girl couldn't walk or trot a horse if her life depended on it. I sat on Blue and watched her enter the trees on the riverbank, and then the last words she had said hit me and I was astonished. Did she really mean it? Did Betty Ann have feelings for me?

Betty Ann started showing up quite often when I was out checking the cattle and I very much enjoyed the time with her. "Does your dad know where you are, Betty Ann?"

"Yes and no. He knows I'm out riding, but he doesn't know where."

It was the second week of March and I was down at the wheat field cutting out ten steers to take to Red Moon the next day when Betty Ann showed up. I had the steers I wanted cut out but was having trouble herding them down to the corrals at the Burns barn. Without a word she put Stocking to work helping me. I was surprised at how well Betty Ann and Stocking worked the cattle. With their help it was a fairly easy task to herd the ten steers into the corral.

"Thanks a lot, Betty Ann," I said as I closed the gate on the steers. "You and Stocking make a good team when it comes to herding cows."

"Billy Harshburger, do you think all I do is sit around the ranch house and paint my fingernails. Dad won't let me plow or work in the hay fields but he doesn't hesitate to call on me and Stocking when it comes time to move cows. What are you going to do with those steers anyway?"

"I'm going to herd them to Red Moon tomorrow and put them on the train to Oklahoma City," I answered.

"Can I help?"

"Tomorrow is a school day. What will your dad say about you missing school?"

"He won't know. He's always gone when I leave to go to school. I'll just take Stocking out as if I'm going for an early morning ride, which I often do before going to school, only this time I won't come back. I'll come here and help you instead."

True to her word, Betty Ann was waiting for me when I got to the Burns place. With Betty Ann and Stocking helping me, we got the steers to the railroad at Red Moon and put them in the cattle pens.

We had just started back when Betty Ann, true to her nature, kicked ole Stocking into a gallop. I kicked Blue in the ribs and he took off after her. Blue, being much younger than Stocking, soon caught her and we pulled on ahead. Blue and I rounded a bend in the road and I saw a large cottonwood tree shading the road. I pulled back on Blue and when she stopped, I dismounted to give her a breather. Betty Ann and Stocking came thundering around the bend and saw us and she pulled Stocking to a halt.

She dismounted and stood beside me, her hat on the back of her shoulders, held by a thong around her neck, and she was laughing, her black eyes sparkling. Her lips were slightly parted and she looked so lovely I couldn't help it, I kissed her. I put my arms around her and pulled her yielding body against mine and kissed her and she kissed me back.

"We shouldn't be doing this, Billy," she said.

"I know." And I kissed her again.

"This is something that 'just friends' don't do."

"I know," I answered and kissed her again. And in those kisses I tried to tell her how much I loved her, how much I worshiped her.

After a while we broke apart. She and I mounted up and started home. For once, as we rode, we rode in silence. Betty Ann didn't say a word.

"Betty Ann, I probably won't see you in school tomorrow. I have to go home and start listing. Until the listing and planting are done, I'll probably be going to school only on Tuesdays and Fridays."

"I wish there was some other way, Billy. I know it's hard for you. I wish you could go to school every day."

"I do too, Betty Ann. But I can't."

When we reached the corner, I reined Blue one way and Betty Ann reined Stocking the other. There were no tender good-byes.

She just kicked Stocking in the ribs and I saw them go over the hill in a cloud of dust.

I began listing that afternoon and when the listing was done, I started planting. I went to school on Tuesdays and Fridays and it was hard, but I still made A's.

Early June, Floyd and I started wheat harvest. I drove the tractor and Floyd run the combine. Ma was down at the Burns place when the first load of wheat was ready to go to town.

"When you take the wheat to the elevator, I want to go with you, Billy," Ma said.

"Okay, Ma," I answered. She watched me closely as I drove the truck loaded with wheat to Cheyenne. After I had sold the wheat and cashed the check, Ma said, "I want to drive the truck back."

By the time we got back to the Burns place, Ma was handling the truck as if she had driven it all her life. That mid afternoon when we had the truck loaded again it was Ma who drove the load to Cheyenne and Floyd and I kept cutting.

When wheat harvest was done, all three of us went to the cotton patch and started chopping cotton. We all three chopped cotton until the night it rained, then I knew it was time to hook up the Farmall to the one-way and soon as it was dry enough, start plowing.

Chapter Twenty-Two

Around and around the wheat stubble I went, slowly but surely getting the wheat ground plowed. In the afternoon when I started to get sleepy, it became my habit to hike up to the deep hole in the river and go swimming. I always felt a little guilty to swim instead of plowing, especially when I could see Ma and Floyd up in the cotton patch chopping cotton, and so I worked especially hard and long to make up for it. Instead of listening to the radio after supper, I would saddle up Blue and go ride the fence line, fixing the fence that always needed worked on, until dark.

I had just dove into the water one afternoon and when I came up and shook the water out of my eyes, I saw Betty Ann bending over to pick up my pants. I didn't holler at her or say nothing, I just splashed to a shallow part and quickly waded ashore. She already had my britches in her hand when she saw me coming towards her. She turned and started running up the riverbank but I was too fast or she was too slow or something, and I quickly caught her.

She squealed when I grabbed her around the waist from behind and pulled her up close to me. "Turn me loose, Billy."

"Drop my britches," I said.

"Not until you turn me loose."

"Well, I'm not turning you loose until you drop my pants." And so we had what you would call a stalemate. I didn't mind though. It felt so good holding Betty Ann.

But soon, as I held her, I felt myself becoming aroused and I knew that Betty Ann could feel it. It was embarrassing but I couldn't help it. She was so warm and soft against me. But I knew this wouldn't do so I turned loose of her waist with my right hand and reached down and picked her up. I started carrying her towards the water.

"What are you doing?" she asked.

"You're going swimming," I answered.

"No, I'm not," she said, and started wiggling and squirming as I carried her. But it wasn't any use, I just gripped her tighter.

"No, Billy, no," she cried as we neared the water. "I'll get my clothes all wet and how will I explain that to my dad?"

"You could tell him you fell in the river, or there is another option and I like it best," I said as I set her feet down in the sand, still holding her and we faced each other.

She dropped my pants and struggled only a little when I put my arms around her and unfastened her halter top and threw it back upon the bank. "Now it will stay dry," I said. She struggled not at all when I unbuttoned her shorts and she actually wiggled her hips to help me as I pulled them down. She stepped out of them and I picked them up and tossed them to join her halter top up on the bank.

Then I looked at her. I had never seen a naked woman before. Never in my life. But if all girls looked like Betty Ann naked, then there should be a law against women wearing clothes. For a long while I just stood there looking at her. I examined every detail of her young body. It was breathtaking.

"Do you like the way I look, Billy?" Betty Ann asked, arching her back so that her breast stood out proudly.

"You're beautiful, Betty Ann. No, that's not strong enough. You're stunning, you're gorgeous. No, none of those words are strong enough to describe you. I wonder if you'll look as good wet," I said as I stepped forward and picked her up.

This time she put her arms around my neck as I carried her into the deep hole of the river. I looked deep into her eyes and she look into mine and she smiled as only Betty Ann can smile.

"You had better stop looking at me that way, Betty Ann, unless you want to get kissed."

I didn't get a chance to kiss her before she tilted her head up and kissed me. I carried her on into the water, our lips still together. Her body became lighter as we went into deeper and deeper water and still we held the kiss. I stepped into the deep hole and we went under, still holding the kiss. I turned her loose when I ran out of breath and we came bobbing to the surface.

"That's a first," Betty Ann said, laughing, as we treaded water, facing each other, catching our breath. "I've never been kissed underwater before."

"The first time was so much fun let's make it a second," and I reached for her and she came into my arms. Again we sank and held the kiss until we ran out of air and again we came bobbing to the top.

"That's no good," I said.

133

"Didn't you like it? Don't you like to kiss me under water?" Betty Ann asked, a look of puzzlement on her face.

"I liked it just fine. It's just that I ran out of air too soon and we had to stop. Let's go to a more shallow spot." And we swam toward the shore until our feet touched the bottom.

We just stood there then. Stood with the river water flowing below our chins and I pulled her to me and we kissed and as we kissed my hands began to know Betty Ann's body and her hands got to know mine and when we broke the kiss we were both gasping for air. "I love you, Betty Ann Payne," I said.

"Those are strong words to be speaking, Billy," and we kissed again.

"I know they're powerful words," I said when we broke the kiss. "But it is a mighty powerful feeling I have for you."

"I love you, Billy Harshburger. I always have and I always will," she said, as she pressed her body even closer to mine. Our lips met and I felt her tongue dart into my mouth and her finger pads kneading my back. I kissed her back the same way, my hands reshaping her breast. We broke the kiss and I picked her up and carried her to the shore and knelt in the soft river sand. I laid her down so softly and gently in the warm sand of the river shore and I laid down beside her, and again I took her in my arms and she pressed her body closely against mine and in the kiss I told her how much I loved her and how much I wanted her. Wanted her not in lust but in love. I looked into her eyes and saw they were a misty black, shinning in passion.

"Be gentle, Billy," she said. "Be gentle. This is the first time for me."

"I will, Betty Ann, I could never be anything but gentle with you. This is the first time for me, too. You'll have to show me how."

All afternoon while I was plowing, I remembered how it was. It had been so wonderful I felt myself becoming aroused again just thinking about it. I had just thought I was in love with Betty Ann before, but now I knew that what I had felt before had been a mere shadow of the real thing. Now I was so in love with her it hurt, hurt to be away from her. I wanted to be with her, to hold her, to kiss her every hour of every day.

And yet I felt guilty. She had given herself to me and it had truly been her first time. I remembered the small yelp when I had entered her and I remembered the small spot of blood on the warm sand of the riverbank. She had chosen me for her first time and I felt guilty and hoped I would be worthy.

I thought of her as I rode Blue home from the Burns' place late that evening, herding up the milk cows on the way. I thought of her as I rode the fence line after supper, fixing the weak spots in the fence and wishing I could hear the drum beats of Stocking's hooves as she carried Betty Ann to my side. I missed her so much already and we had only separated for a few hours. When it become too dark to see, I rode Blue home, climbed exhausted into bed and my last wakeful thoughts was of Betty Ann.

The next morning I thought of Betty Ann as I check the white faced cattle and my herd of black cows and calves on the way to the wheat field. When I reached the Burns corrals, I unsaddled Blue and turned her loose to graze. I had taught Blue to come to me when I whistled so I knew she would come to me when I needed her that evening. I cranked the tractor to a start and started around the field. I thought of Betty Ann all morning and even made up songs to her and sang them as I guided the tractor around the field, keeping the right rear wheel in the furrow of the previous round.

When the sun was straight overhead, I stopped the tractor as close to the shade tree where I had stashed my lunch as I could, and killed the motor. At first I thought I was dreaming when I saw Betty Ann leaning against the tree with a sack in her hand, but then I knew I wasn't after I had taken several quick steps towards her and took her warm, vibrant body in my arms.

"I thought I'd ride down here and eat lunch with you if you don't mind," she said.

"The trouble is I'm not hungry for lunch," I said. "I'm only hungry for you." Her lunch sack fell to the ground and she threw her arms around me when I kissed her. She didn't protest when I reached behind her and unfastened her halter-top. She shuddered and moaned when I began kissing her nipples and sucking on them.

But when I reached to unbutton her shorts, she grabbed my hands saying, "No, Billy, no. We can't."

"Why, Betty Ann? Why not? We did it before."

"I know, Billy, and that was very foolish of us. If we keep on doing it, I know I'll get pregnant and then what would we do?" Betty Ann asked as she slipped her halter top back on.

"We'd do the same as Bobby and Mary Lou. We'd get married."

"Billy, can you imagine facing my Dad and telling him that a Harshburger wants to marry his daughter because he got her pregnant?"

"Betty Ann, for you I'd face any man or beast."

"That's sweet, Billy. Almost as sweet as the songs you were singing about me though I could barely hear you over the tractor motor."

My mouth must have fallen open as I asked, "How long have you been here?"

"Long enough," she said, winking at me. "Let's sit down and have lunch."

Betty Ann's chatter was melodious music to my ears as we sat and ate lunch in the shade of a giant cottonwood. After lunch we kissed and petted until Betty Ann said, "Billy, you'd better get back to plowing."

"You're right of course, Betty Ann. But what we're doing now sure is a lot more fun."

She kissed me goodbye and I started back towards the tractor. Soon I heard the hoof beats of Stocking thundering out through the hills. I wondered if Stocking ever got to walk or trot when Betty Ann was on his back. I cranked the tractor to a start, climbed aboard and started around and around the field with the taste of Betty Ann still on my lips. That afternoon I didn't get sleepy at all but just kept on plowing. Nothing like a little loving to keep you awake all afternoon I discovered.

Thus we began a routine while I was working on the Burns place. At noon I would stop for lunch and Betty Ann would be there waiting for me in the shade of the cottonwood. After I would finish my lunch she would often reach into her sack and hand me a cookie or a cupcake she had made. We always kissed, necked, and petted some but she would only let me go so far before saying, "Stop, Billy. I want to as bad as you do but we have to be strong."

When the wheat field was plowed, I went to the cotton patch and chopped cotton with Ma and Floyd. However in the evenings after supper, I'd ride out to the Burns pasture to check the white faces and my small herd of black cattle. Some where along my route, Betty Ann would always show up and we would ride along together.

"How do you always know where I am?" I asked her one evening when she came riding up beside me.

"Us women have mysteries we can't reveal," she answered, smiling at me. Then she turned and pointed to a tall red hill with a flat top across the river. "See that hill? From there I have a view of the whole Burns' place. You'll think I'm forward if I tell you that I sit there and watch for you won't you?"

"No, Betty Ann. I'll just think you love me and want to be with me almost as much as I love you and want to be with you."

After we had checked the cattle, we would ride to the top of a hill and dismount. As the horses munched the green grass in the pasture, Betty Ann and I would hold each other and tell one another how much we loved each other. We would stay there long after dark and watch the stars and the moon and listen to the coyotes yelp in the distance. When it was time for us to part, Betty Ann would jump up and run to Stocking, quickly mount and go galloping away.

"Betty Ann, I wish you wouldn't run Stocking after dark the way you do when you leave me," I said, after the first time it happened. "It's too dangerous."

"I know I shouldn't, Billy. But I'm afraid that should I linger, I might not ever go."

"That would be okay with me," I said, smiling at her.

"It would be okay with me too, but you know I can't. That's why I have to leave in a hurry and not look back."

And again when we parted that night I heard the thunder of Stocking hooves long into the distance and could see her racing shadow in the moonlight.

We got a good rain and after the weeds had sprouted it was time to plow the wheat field again. And again Betty Ann showed up at noon to eat lunch with me. Now not only were we spending lunch together, but we were together in the evening when I went out to check the cattle and ride the fence line. It was wonderful. Especially at night, we kissed and petted and I went as far as she would let me. I always respected her wishes even though it was hard to do, especially when we were both breathing heavily.

August came and I started to school. It was hard to do but we acted as if we were just friends. Sure, we sat together on the bus and sometimes at lunch, but we didn't hold hands and we didn't walk around the school yard with our arms around each other, but we did take the same classes again as we had last year.

I couldn't go to school on a regular basis. I had to work but when I did go to school on Tuesdays and Fridays, I picked up armloads of home work. Then I would sit until late hours of the night and do the homework. It was tough, but that's the way it was. The way it had to be.

It was September and we had just had a good rain. I was out by the buses telling Mr. Davis that I wouldn't be coming back to school until after the wheat was planted when Bobby Woods drove up. I don't know why he came to school, he had graduated the spring before, along with Troy and Travis, but he did.

He walked right up to me in front of Mr. Davis and Betty Ann and asked, "Have you been able to get in Betty Ann's pants yet like I did, Billy?" I guess Bobby felt safe saying that to me with Mr. Davis standing there but he was powerfully wrong.

Mr. Davis reached to grab hold of me but he was much, much too slow. I give Bobby the same treatment as I had given him before. A right to the left eye, a left to the right eye, a hard right to the nose and this time I was able to work in a left hook that snapped his head to the left before he started down and I caught with a hard right uppercut that snapped his head back before he hit the gravel, moaning. I reach down to pick him up so I could hit him some more and I actually had a hold of his shirt collar when I felt two hands firmly but gently on my shoulders pulling me back and heard Mr. Davis say, "Let him go, Billy, he's had enough."

I sighed, "Bobby Woods never seems to get enough. He's either the dumbest person in the world or he enjoys me beating on him."

"See, Mr. Davis," Bobby said. "Now you have to expel him for fighting. He picked a fight and he did it right in front of you."

"Bobby, let me explain to you what I saw," Mr. Davis said.

"I saw Billy, a student of this school, strike Bobby Woods several times for insulting Betty Ann Payne who is also a student of this school. Let me also emphatically explain that Bobby Woods is no longer a member of this school, but is actually trespassing on school grounds. Expel Billy? Expel him for what? He was not fighting another student, he was fighting a man who dishonored a friend of his. Bobby Woods, I am now going to order you to never set foot on these school grounds again while school is in session."

"I'm going to go home and tell my Dad and he'll have Billy Harshburger's ass thrown in jail," Bobby said.

"Wait until I get Billy on the bus and on his way home and I'll go with you," Mr. Davis said.

"You don't need to," Bobby said.

"But Bobby, I insist," Mr. Davis said. "Billy get on the bus."

I did as he told me and walked down the aisle to sit by Betty Ann, who was staring out the window. The driver started the bus, put it in gear and start down the road. I saw the driver looking at me in the mirror and when he saw me looking at his reflection, he smiled, nodded his head up and down and gave me a thumbs up. I felt Betty Ann take my hand, turn it so she could run her finger up and down my bruised knuckles. I turned to look at her.

There was pain in her eyes when she asked, "Was that the way it happened in the boy's restroom?"

"Pretty much," I answered.

"Why did you stop, Billy?"

"Mr. Davis got hold of me and told me to. At that time I figured I was already in more trouble than I needed and I didn't need any more by disobeying him, though it was mighty tempting."

"I mean before Mr. Davis got a hold of you. Why did you reach down to pick him up?"

"I was going to pick him up so I could hit him again, Betty Ann. It felt so good hitting him that I wanted to do it some more and I never hit a man when he's down."

"I kind of wish you didn't have such scruples, Billy. I wish you had of stomped him in the balls, kicked him in the head and stomped him in the gut."

Then she came into my arms crying. I held her and patted her on the back as she cried into my chest. "It's okay, Betty Ann. We both have reason to know that he was lying."

"Yes, we do, don't we," and she wiped the tears from her cheeks with her bare hands as she smiled wickedly at me. "But what about other people. They don't know what only you and I can know and they might believe him. Especially now."

"What do you mean, especially now, Betty Ann?"

"Never mind, Billy," she said, as she came back into my arms with the whole bus watching.

"Aren't you afraid some one will tell your dad that Billy Harshburger held his daughter on the school bus all the way home?"

"Somebody is," she said. "That somebody is going to be me. I'm going to tell him exactly what Bobby said and what you did to him and how you comforted me all the way on the bus until you got off."

It felt so good holding Betty Ann, that I hated for my bus stop to come up, but it did anyway.

That evening after supper when I rode out to check the cattle, Betty Ann showed up and we rode together.

"What did you're dad say when you told him?" I asked.

Betty Ann laughed as she said, "First thing I had to do after I had told him was to calm him down some. He was going to go to the Woods' and see if there was something more that needs to be done on young Bobby. I assured him that you had done an adequate job. Then he said he would like to shake your hand if you weren't a Harshburger and then he made me promise to tell him if you had any trouble over this. He said that he had enough on Mr. Woods that he could guarantee that any trouble you had with Mr. Woods would stop immediately."

That night I went to sleep dreaming of Betty Ann and I wished that I was holding her in my arms.

Chapter twenty-three

In October school turned out for cotton picking but I wasn't doing much snapping. The wheat was up and ready to be grazed and I was going from sale to sale buying steers. I had one pen full I was just waiting for them to calm down so I could put them on the wheat pasture and another truck load was due in that afternoon.

When the truck showed up, I helped unload them, paid the driver and the truck left. The cattle were milling around anxious and I stood by the corral talking to them, trying to calm them down. Blue neighed his greeting and I turned around to see Betty Ann on Stocking riding up from the river.

"I see you got another load of steers in," she said.

"Yeah. They're a little anxious right now, but they'll calm down in two or three days and I can put them on the wheat. I think if I buy one more truckload, it will be all we need."

"Did you buy all these, Billy?"

"Floyd give me the money so I guess you could say the Harshburger family bought them."

"But it was you who went to the sale barn and bought them?" Betty Ann asked.

"Yeah. That's what I've been doing all week. It keeps me out of the cotton patch though."

Betty Ann reined Stocking around the corral looking at the steers in the pen. She rode back to me and said as she dismounted, "You've got a good eye for cattle. They all look like good steers. A little skinny though."

"That's the way I like them. Tall and lanky. A few months on wheat pasture and they'll fill right out."

I looked at Betty Ann and saw her shiver. "Are you cold?"

"A little," she answered.

"Put Stocking in that empty corral and we'll go into the house and I'll build up a fire."

She did as I suggested and we walked to the house together holding hands. I stopped on the porch and gathered an arm load of wood and took it in. One thing Ma and Floyd insisted on was that I keep a supply of wood chopped and ready on the porch just in case I should get caught in a blizzard while I was on the Burns place and couldn't get home. Betty Ann wandered around looking at the house and furnishings as I built up a fire.

"I've never been in the Burns' house before but I imagine it's the same way it was when he lived here," Betty Ann said as the fire began to roar and heat the place up.

"Mr. Burns left everything here but his suitcase full of clothes when he left for California," I said.

"It's nice," Betty Ann said. "It has everything a person could need. I wouldn't mind living here."

Now that was a strange thing to say for a girl who lived in a big fancy ranch house on a hill. It was warming up real nice and I helped Betty Ann out of her light jacket and took off mine. I took her in my arms and began kissing her. I kissed her on the mouth and began unbuttoning her shirt and trailing kisses down her throat. She shuddered and moaned when I bared her breast and kissed her nipples, extended in passion. I was surprised when she didn't stop me from unbuttoning her jeans but I didn't say anything but with a pounding heart, stripped them from her and she stepped out of them and came nude into my arms. I kissed her and as our tongues battled I felt her hands unbuttoning my shirt. I started to help her but she took hold of my hands saying, "Let me do it, Billy."

When we were both nude and holding each other tightly I realized that I had put too much wood in the stove and the house was becoming too hot, but it was much too late to be thinking about that.

"I suppose Mr. Burns left a bed in one of those bedrooms," Betty Ann murmured in my ear.

I picked her up then. I picked her up and carried her to a bedroom. I bumped her head on the door facing as we started in.

"Ouch," Betty Ann said. Then Betty Ann started laughing. "Thanks for the romantic thoughts, Billy, but put me down. I think I can find the bed."

I put her down and watched as she walked to the bed and stripped the top covers back, still laughing. She lay down in the bed and beckoned me to her and I quickly obeyed.

We made love. Not like the first time, soft and gentle, but strong and powerful and yet playful and experimental. Try this and see what happens and try that and see what happens and all too soon it was over and we lay there holding each other and panting.

"I guess this is what it is like to be married folks," I said.

"Better get used to it, Billy. That is if you aim to keep your promise."

"What promise?" I asked.

"The promise you made to marry me if I become pregnant."

"What! You mean you're pregnant? You mean I'm going to be a father?"

"Hell, yes, you're going to be the father," she shouted and started pounding on me with her small fists. "I never done it with anyone but you."

"I never questioned whether or not I was the father. Calm down. I was just surprised, that's all. We only did it once that is before now."

"Apparently once is all it takes, Billy."

"And we've been strong and restrained ourselves all these months. What a waste."

Betty Ann started laughing as she came back into my arms. "Billy, I bet you're the only guy in the world whose only regret when he finds out his girlfriend is pregnant would be that they could have been doing it more since she was already pregnant. You're one of a kind and I love you so for it."

One thing led to another and when we were through for the second time, I said, "I'll come up and talk to your dad after supper tonight. We can go to Cheyenne tomorrow and get our blood test and in three days we should be able to get married."

"Do you want me to tell my dad before you come up, Billy?"

"No. No, just wait and we'll tell him together."

That evening after the chores were done and we had eaten supper, I asked Ma to stay in the kitchen with me when Floyd went into the living room to listen to the radio.

We sat at the kitchen table across from each other and I didn't know how to tell her so I just blurted it out, "Ma, I would like for you to write a letter giving me permission to marry Betty Ann Payne."

Ma looked at me in surprise and silence for a long while before she said, "Are you sure you want to get married now?"

"Yes, Ma, I'm sure."

"Billy, do you love her?"

"Ma, I love Betty Ann more than anything in this world. I love her more than life itself."

"I supposed you and Betty Ann have discussed this at length, Billy."

"Yes, Ma. She came down to the Burns place this afternoon while I was trying to get the steers that had just came in calmed down. Yes, we discussed it."

"Have you discussed it with her father?"

"No. But I plan to go up there this evening and discuss it with him."

"You're both awfully young, Billy."

"We're not to young to have a baby."

"You mean you have gotten her pregnant?"

"Yes, Ma'am."

Ma's face broke into a smile as she got up to search for a pen and paper. "I feel like it's time I become a grandmother, Billy."

It was with my heart pounding in my throat that I turned the car up the Payne's driveway. It was with sheer determination that I kept my knees from knocking together as I stepped upon the porch. Betty Ann was waiting for me at the door and let me in.

"Who was that who just drove in, Betty Ann?" I heard Mr. Payne's voice boom from another room.

"It's Billy Harshburger, Dad," Betty Ann called back.

"Billy who?" he asked as he came into the room and saw me. "What the hell are you doing here? You know I don't allow no Harshburgers on my land or in my house."

"I know, Sir. But we have some serious talking to do."

"Well say your piece and be gone. The sooner the better."

"I'm afraid it's not that simple, Sir."

"Well say it. Out with it."

"I want your permission to marry your daughter."

"Is that supposed to be a joke, because if it is, it's not funny."

"No, Sir. It's not a joke. I'm dead serious. I want that Betty Ann and I get married."

"Over my dead body. Now go on, get out of here," Mr. Payne said.

"Dad, I'm pregnant," Betty Ann said.

"You're what?" Mr. Payne said, startled.

"You heard me," Betty Ann said. "I'm pregnant and Billy's the father."

Mr. Payne's face turned beet red as he took a step towards her. "You little whore! Bobby Woods was probably right. You've been spreading your legs for every boy in Roger Mills county. You're nothing but a whore!"

144

"No, Billy, no!" Betty Ann shouted as I took a step towards Mr. Payne. "Please don't, Billy." And she rushed between Mr. Payne and me.

Mr. Payne turned to face me. "Oh, you were going to hit me," Mr. Payne said, and I swear I saw a look of admiration on his face.

"No, Sir. I'd not have just hit you but I'd have whipped your ass but good. I might still do it if you don't apologize to Betty Ann for what you said. We only did it one time last summer and it was the first time for her and for me for that matter."

"But I'm a man and you're just a boy," said Mr. Payne.

"You're going to find out how much of a man I am in a fight if you don't apologize to Betty Ann, and right quick."

"Please, Dad," Betty Ann implored her father. "Do as Billy asks. I love you and I love Billy and I don't want to see either of you get hurt."

Mr. Payne looked down at Betty Ann and said, "Do you think Billy can whip me?"

"I don't know, Dad. I know I have seen him fight and I know he's fast and vicious. I do know that he'll hurt you and I don't want that to happen. You'd probably hurt him also and I love him and I'm carrying his child. We only did it once and Billy is right. It was the first time for me. I've never done it with anyone else."

Mr. Payne looked at me standing there with my fists clenched and ready to explode with fury. Then he looked at Betty Ann. "I apologize for calling you all those ugly names. You're my daughter, my only child and you mean more than life to me."

"Oh, Daddy," she said as she went crying into his arms.

"Does this mean you'll write us out a note giving Betty Ann and me permission to get married?" I asked.

"I guess I have no choice," he sighed. "Come with me."

Betty Ann and I followed Mr. Payne into his office where he wrote and signed a note giving us permission to get married and handed it to Betty Ann.

"I want some rules clearly understood though, young Billy."

"What are they," I asked.

"Rule number one; Betty Ann can come over and visit me anytime she wishes."

"I wouldn't have it any other way, Sir," I said.

"Rule number two; when the baby is born, Betty Ann can bring it over anytime she wishes."

"Of course, Sir."

"And rule number three; you never ever set foot on this place again."

"That'll be the easiest rule of all to follow, Sir," I said.

Mr. Payne studied me for a while before he asked, "Billy, does it ever get heavy?"

"Does what get heavy, Sir"

"That chip you're carrying on your shoulder."

Four days later Betty Ann Payne became Betty Ann Harshburger. We moved into the Burns' house and with very little effort set up housekeeping. Ma and Floyd insisted that I bring a milk cow down to keep Betty Ann and me in milk. Ma also gave us a dozen laying hens so we could have fresh eggs and insisted to Betty Ann that the cellar door was never locked and that she should help herself at any time. She also strongly hinted to Betty Ann, that she would welcome all the help she could get next summer during canning season.

At last on those days that I could go to school, I had a girl I could walk around the school yard with during lunch hour, even if the girl was also my wife.

Chapter twenty-four

"Betty Ann, I don't know why those fool steers want to get out of the wheat pasture and go wandering around," I said as we followed the tracks of a half dozen steers through the two inches of snow that cold December day.

"They do it for me, Billy."

"The steers get out for you? How do you figure?"

"It gives me an excuse to get out and ride Stocking. Otherwise I wouldn't get to," Betty Ann said.

There were two things Betty Ann insisted on taking with her when we moved onto the Burns place other than her clothes. One was her car and the other was Stocking. I wasn't there, of course, but Betty Ann said her dad didn't argue with her even a little bit. I think Mr. Payne was beginning to wish that he wasn't quite so stubborn.

Truthfully I wish he had argued about Stocking. I really didn't like for Betty Ann to be riding since she was six months pregnant.

"I'll sure be glad when this war is over and I can buy some new barbed wire," I said. "I know for sure now that the old rusty wire is breaking faster than I can fix it. You know the place where the steers got out?"

"Yes."

"Well I fixed that exact same spot of fence yesterday. It's getting mighty discouraging."

"Keep plugging along, Billy. From the sounds of it the war will be over soon."

"It can't be over soon enough for me. There they are," I said, pointing to the six steers wandering along the floor of the canyon as if they were lost.

Betty Ann took one side of the canyon and I took the other and we eased our way to the front of them. It was easy with two people to turn the steers and start them back the way they had come.

We were out of the canyon and onto the flats when two of the steers decided to go their separate ways and cut off to the right, the side Betty Ann and Stocking was on. Stocking being the cow horse she was, wheeled to take off after them but when she wheeled, she did so on ice and she fell, Betty Ann with her. Stocking jumped to her feet but Betty Ann lie there in the snow. The steers forgotten, I kicked Blue in the ribs and we went to her at full gallop. I hit the ground running when we got there, and ran to her. "Betty Ann, Betty Ann, are you hurt?" I cried.

"The baby," she cried. "I'm afraid I'm losing our baby. I'm bleeding."

I looked and sure enough she was. I picked her up and carried her to Blue where I set her sideways in the saddle. "Steady, Blue, Steady. Betty Ann, can you hang on to the saddle horn and stay there until I get mounted?"

She nodded her head yes and I ran around to the other side, put my foot in the stirrup and swung up behind Betty Ann. I worked my other foot in the stirrup, picked up Betty Ann and held her in my lap as I slid into the saddle. I kicked Blue into a lope and we headed to the house with me guiding Blue mostly with my knees and Stocking following. I rode Blue up beside Betty Ann's car.

"Can you hold on to the saddle horn until I get down?" I asked.

She nodded her head yes and I eased myself behind the saddle and set her in it. I quickly dismounted and went to the other side where I lifted her down and carried her to the passenger side of the car. Somehow I opened the door and gently set her in the seat. "Hang on, Betty Ann," I said as I shut the door. I unsaddled Stocking and Blue and let the saddles drop into the snow. I pulled the bridles off and tossed them on the saddles. I ran to the car, opened the door and got in, praying all the while that the car would start on this cold December day.

God must have heard my prayer because the engine roared to life on the first try. We started for the doctor in Cheyenne. I wanted to give Betty Ann as smooth a ride as possible but at the same time I was in a hurry. On those rough country roads it was kind of hard to do. I looked over at Betty Ann and I could see that the crotch of Betty Ann's jeans were soaked in blood. When I saw that, a smooth ride didn't matter any more.

I braked the car to a stop in front of the doctor's office, got out and rushed to the passenger side, opened the door and picked Betty Ann up. I kicked the door shut as I started rushing Betty Ann into the doctor's office. The nurse at the desk took one look at us and jumped to her feet, saying, "Follow me, young man."

I carried Betty Ann down the hallway and followed her into an examination room. "Put her right there," the nurse said, indicating an examining table. I lay her on the table and the nurse pulled out a leaf at the foot of the table for Betty Ann to rest her feet on. She rushed out and down the hallway and I took Betty Ann's hand in mine and held it. Her hand was cold and her face was pale. A very short time later I heard the click of heels and the Doctor came into the room with a different nurse and they closed the door behind them.

"What happened?" the Doctor asked.

"She's six months pregnant and her horse fell with her," I answered.

"And what is her name?" the Doctor asked as he began to unbutton her shirt.

"Betty Ann Harshburger," I answered.

He listened to her heart before he asked "And what is your name?"

"Billy Harshburger," I answered.

"You her brother?"

"No. I'm her husband."

"I see," was all he said as he began to unbutton her jeans. He peeked in and said, "Billy, you should go up to the office and sign some paper work. It's just routine but it has to be done. If you'll wait out there, I'll come and get you when I know more."

I went up to the office and signed papers admitting her to the doctor's care and I signed papers promising to pay. I didn't know where I'd get the money but I'd get it from somewhere. When the paper work was filled out I turned it in at the office and the receptionist took it and looked it over.

"It all seems in order, Billy, but who's going to pay?"

"I will," I said. "I don't know how right at this minute, but you'll get your money and that's a promise. Just make Betty Ann well."

The receptionist frowned before she said, "We'll do all we can, Billy. Betty Ann, the name sounds familiar. What was a maiden name before she married you?"

"It was Betty Ann Payne," I answered.

The receptionist smiled as she said, "Oh, don't worry about paying. I'm sure Mr. Payne will take care of it."

"No, he won't," I said. "Billy Harshburger takes care of his own family and pays his own debts." I stormed out of the office and almost ran over the Doctor.

"There you are Billy," the Doctor said. "Come with me."

I followed the Doctor down the hallway and instead of taking me to Betty Ann, he took me to his office. "Have a seat," he gestured to an empty chair as he closed the door.

He then went behind his desk and sat down. "Is Betty Ann going to be all right?" I asked.

"She's going to be just fine. We want to keep her here a few days just to make sure, but she will be just fine."

"Thank God," I muttered.

"However, she did lose the baby, Billy, and she's taking it pretty hard."

"Can I see her?" I asked.

"I think you should. She needs cheering up and if anyone can do it, I think you could."

"Show me where she is"

I followed him down the hallway until we came to a door, which he opened and said, "Betty Ann, Billy's here to see you."

I walked in and looked at her. She looked so small and frail lying there in her hospital gown. I saw she was crying. The Doctor left and I pulled a chair up to her bed and sat down. I reached out and took her hand in mine.

"I lost our baby, Billy."

"I know. The Doctor told me."

"I'm not pregnant anymore, Billy. You've done your duty. You don't have to stay married to me."

"Whoa there girl. What are you talking about? You think I married you because it was my duty. Do you think I married you just because you were pregnant? If you think that, you're wrong. You being pregnant just gave me an excuse to marry you, which I desperately wanted to do anyway. If we were not married and you were not pregnant, I'd ask you to marry me all over again if I thought there was a chance of you saying yes. I'm married to you for ever and ever, that is if you still want me."

"Want you? Billy, I love you with all my heart and soul. This past two months have been the happiest days of my life."

"Mine, too, Betty Ann. Mine, too. Don't worry about loosing the baby. We'll just make another one. It's so easy and so much fun to do."

She started laughing then. "Don't do that to me Billy. It hurts too much when I laugh. Now get out of here and go home. I need to rest."

"Anything you say, Betty Ann," and I stood up and put the chair back where I got it.

"Billy," she said, as I started towards the door. "I know it's an awful lot to ask, but would you go by and tell Dad?"

"Betty Ann, I promised never to set foot on his land again."

"Oh, Billy, don't be such a stubborn fool. Dad will want to know. He'd probably shoot you if you didn't go by and tell him."

"And he'll probably shoot me when he sees me anyway. Poor Billy Harshburger, damned if he does and damned if he don't."

"Stop it, Billy, you're making me laugh again."

I dreaded it but all too soon my headlights were pointed up the Payne driveway. I stopped at the house and walked up on the porch and knocked on the door. The door opened and I saw Mr. Payne standing there.

"I'm sorry to be intruding, Sir, but I have some bad news concerning Betty Ann and I thought you would want to know."

"Betty Ann?" and I saw his face pale. "Come in. Tell me about it."

I stepped in and said, "Betty Ann was riding Stocking today and Stocking slipped on the ice and fell with her."

"Betty Ann? Is she okay?"

"She is about as well as can be expected. They're keeping her at the clinic in Cheyenne for a few days. But she lost the baby."

"Why did you do such a damn fool thing like letting her ride a horse in her condition in this kind of weather?"

"Mr. Payne, did you ever stop Betty Ann from doing something she truly wanted to do?"

His lips twitched, but he didn't smile. "Betty Ann is strong willed often enough. It must be inherited, she must have gotten it from her mother," and then he really did chuckle. I couldn't help it, I smiled.

"Thanks for coming by and telling me, Billy. Maybe we should alter rule number three about you never setting a foot on my land."

"No, sir," I said. "I like it just fine the way it is."

"Billy, did you ever make a mistake?"

"Yes, Sir. Quite often. But I'm not making one this time."

151

"That chip on your shoulder must get mighty heavy sometimes. Maybe someday somebody will do you a favor and knock it off."

"Perhaps," I said. "I haven't met the person who could yet, but perhaps someday I will."

I went by and apologized to Ma and Floyd about missing out helping them do the chores and told them about Betty Ann. I then went home, milked our cow, washed up and went to bed. I knew I should have eaten something, but I wasn't hungry.

Early the next morning I got up and cooked myself a half dozen eggs and after I had eaten, I milked our cow, saddled Blue, herded Stocking into her stall and fed her. I then rode Blue up and herded the cows in to milk. After the chores were done, I rode Blue to the wheat pasture and cut out four of my black steers and drove them to the corral by the barn at the Burns place. I shut them up, took care of Blue and then went to Cheyenne to see Betty Ann. We visited for a while and then I went home. Again I saddled Blue and herded the four steers to the pens at Red Moon to catch the train to Oklahoma City and the sale. I wish I could have kept them until spring, they would have put on a lot more weight and brought a lot more money, but I had Betty Ann's doctor bill to pay. I hoped the steers would bring enough.

I got the check back in the mail for the steers the day I was to bring Betty Ann home. I took the check to the bank and cashed it. When I went to get Betty Ann, I stopped at the office to pay her bill.

"Her bill has already been paid," the receptionist said when I ask her how much I owed.

"Who paid it?" I asked

"Mr. Payne paid it," she said.

"How much was it?" I asked.

She looked at the sheet and said, "One hundred and sixty-five dollars."

"Thank you," I said and went on back, got Betty Ann and helped her to the car.

"You're awfully quiet, Billy," Betty Ann said on the ride home. "Is there something wrong?"

"Nothing I can't handle, Betty Ann."

When we got home, I built up a fire and the house soon warmed up. "I'm a little tired," Betty Ann said. "I think I'll lay down for a while. Maybe I'll take a little nap."

"You do that, Betty Ann. I'll be gone for a short time. I have a little something to do. I'll be back soon."

I started up Betty Ann's car and drove to the Payne's ranch. I'm sure playing hell with rule number three, I thought as I turned into the Payne driveway. I drove into the yard, stopped the car and got out.

Mr. Payne must have heard me drive up because he was at the door when I reached it. "Come in, Billy," he said. "How is Betty Ann?"

"She's just fine, Sir. She's at home resting."

"What can I do for you, Billy?"

I didn't say anything, I just walked to the table and started counting out money. When there was a hundred and sixty-five dollars on the table, I put the rest back in my pocket and turned to go.

"Wait, Billy. What's that for?"

"It's to pay you back for Betty Ann's doctor bill. It was my bill to pay and the Harshburgers always pays their debts, whatever they may be."

"I see. But where did you get the money, Billy?"

"I had to sell four of my Black Angus steers."

"You mean your family's steers, don't you? What's the difference between your family paying and Betty Ann's family, namely me, paying?"

"No, Sir, they weren't the Harshburger's steers. They were mine. I bought seven Black Angus cows with calves at their side, fall before last. I bought them with my own cotton money. No, Sir, they were mine alone."

"But Billy, this was the worst time in the world to sell them. Couldn't you have kept them until spring? They would have put on a lot more weight and brought a much better price."

"I know, Sir. I didn't really want to sell them but I had a debt to pay."

"Billy, you know Betty Ann is my daughter and I am responsible for her."

"Not any more, Sir. She's my wife and I'm responsible for taking care of her."

I walked to the door and just as I started out, Mr. Payne said, "Billy, we're going have to do something about rule number three."

"No, Sir," I said. "We don't need to do anything. Let's leave it just as it is."

Chapter twenty-five

It was early March and it was time to start thinning the cattle on the wheat pasture. Betty Ann and I both had skipped school and we were cutting out fifteen steers to drive to Red Moon. The war was winding down in Europe but the cattle prices were still high and it was time to start selling the steers off of the wheat.

The evening before, Betty Ann had gone to the ranch house to see her dad. She was gone longer than I expected and I was beginning to worry. That fool girl, I thought, you don't suppose she was running Stocking in the dark and had had another accident. It grew later and later. I had just walked out to the corral to saddle up Blue when I heard the drum of Stocking's hoof beats coming home.

"You fool girl," I shouted, as Betty Ann came loping up, "You know better than run a horse after dark."

"I know and I'm sorry, but I stayed at the ranch so long I knew you'd be worried so I wanted to hurry home."

"Don't ever run Stocking after dark again, Betty Ann. And yes I was beginning to worry," I said, as I took the bridle off of Blue.

"I won't, Billy. I promise. The reason I was so late starting home was because Aunt Vie is out visiting."

"Your Aunt Vie from Oklahoma City?"

"Yes. You know, Billy, she's the closest thing to a mother I ever had."

"I know, Betty Ann. I wish I could meet her."

"You can. She's going to be here three weeks. Let's both of us go up to the ranch some evening and you can meet her."

"Betty Ann, you heard your dad. You know I can't."

"Oh, Billy. I really and truly believe he's changed his mind about you. I think if you and I were to go up there, he'd welcome you."

"No, he wouldn't. He's hated us Harshburgers much too long for that."

"You're as stubborn as my dad. I wish you two could get along. Anyway you might meet Aunt Vie anyway. She's halfway promised to come down and visit us some evening."

Today I was using Blue to cut out the steers I wanted to sell first and Betty Ann was holding the small herd together with Stocking.

I cut out the fifteenth steer and worked it up to the small herd. "That's it, Betty Ann, let's take them to the corral. It'll be lunch time by the time we get these critters home so we'll just put them in the corral and eat lunch before we take them to Red Moon."

"That's my Billy, always looking forward to the next meal," Betty Ann said, smiling.

"Betty Ann, it takes a lot of food to keep up the energy I use working." I looked at her and said, "I work hard both day and night."

"You're not complaining about your night work are you," Betty Ann said, smiling that wicked smile of hers.

"No, not at all. Actually I was thinking that after lunch."

"So that's how I rate. Your stomach comes first."

By that time we had the steers in the corral and I shut the gate to hold them in. Betty Ann had dismounted and was looping Stocking's reins over a fence post. I walked up to her and took her in my arms and kissed her. "Maybe we should unsaddle the horses and put them in the corral. We may take a long lunch."

So we did, and we didn't go into the kitchen upon entering the house either, but we headed straight for our bedroom, shedding clothes as we went. Afterwards we ate lunch and had just stepped outside to go to the corral when I heard the drumming of hoof beats coming from across the river and heard the splash as the horse crossed the water.

"It's Aunt Vie," Betty Ann said, when the rider came into view. "I wonder what's wrong?"

We were soon to find out.

"It's your Father, Betty Ann," Aunt Vie said, as she skidded her horse to a stop and quickly dismounted.

"What's happened?"

"I don't know. He and Jerry were arguing out in the yard just a little while ago when he suddenly got beet red in the face and he collapsed. Jerry loaded him in the pickup and took him to the doctor in Cheyenne."

"Betty Ann, you and Aunt Vie get in the car. Aunt Vie, I'll take care of your horse before we drive to Cheyenne."

I led her horse into the corral with Stocking and Blue and stripped the saddle and bridle off. I then ran to the car, started it up and we went tearing out. I didn't know what was wrong with Mr. Payne, but it sounded bad. I wanted to get there as fast as I could for Betty Ann's sake, so there wasn't any dust that fell on the car as we went flying to Cheyenne.

"He isn't here," the receptionist said, when Betty Ann asked about her father. "The doctor did all he could do and then they put him in an ambulance and took him to Elk City."

"So we go to Elk City," I said, as I head out the door and to the car at a run. I had the car started and ready to go by the time Betty Ann and Aunt Vie got in and closed the door.

Betty Ann was silent on the ride over there and I looked at her once and saw she was crying. I turned loose of the wheel with my right hand and put my arm around her and hugged her. "Everything's going to be all right, Betty Ann."

"Do you really think so Billy? Tell me the truth, do you think Dad is going to be okay."

I was coming upon a car mighty fast so I had to turn loose of her and put both hands on the wheel. I look ahead and I saw a car coming in the distance but I knew I could pass before the oncoming car got there.

I waited until I had passed the car before I looked at Betty Ann and said, "Truthfully, I don't know, Betty Ann. But we can always hope, can't we?"

At the intersection I turned east and headed for Elk City rather than go straight ahead to Sayre. At the hospital I found a parking spot close to the front entrance and we got out and went hurrying in.

"The doctor is working with him now," the receptionist said. "We'll let you know as soon as we know something. You can sit over there," and she indicated a row of chairs.

I looked over where she was pointing and saw Jerry, Mr. Payne's foreman sitting there. I went over and sat beside him and Betty Ann followed me over and sat down. I took her hand in mine and turned to Jerry. "What happened, Jerry?"

"You know Mr. Payne don't like you much, Billy Harshburger, and I don't like you much either, after what you done to Betty Ann."

"Okay Jerry, you don't like me, what happened?"

"Mr. Payne and I were arguing, but that wasn't unusual, we argued a lot. He wanted me to fire a newly hired hand because the fool kid had run his horse through a prairie dog town and

157

the horse stepped into a prairie dog hole and broke its leg and we had to shoot the horse. Anyway he wanted to fire him and I didn't want to. Hired hands are hard to find and we need every one we've got and could even use another one or two if we could find them. Besides I think the kid will learn and eventually make a good hand. As we argued, he got madder and his face got redder. All at once he just fell to the ground. I hope no one thinks it's my fault."

"It wasn't your fault, Jerry," I said, patting him on the shoulder. "With Mr. Payne's temper, it was just a matter of time until something like this happened."

"Thanks, Billy. But I still don't like you."

"That's okay, too. Fortunately you don't have to be around me so it should work out just fine."

A nurse came walking into the waiting room, looked around spotted us and walked over. "Is this the Payne Family?" she asked.

"Yes, it is," Aunt Vie said.

"The doctor wants to talk to you now. Follow me."

We all got up except Jerry, he just sat there. "Come on, Jerry," I said.

"I ain't family," he said.

"Jerry, as long as you've worked for him, I doubt if Mr. Payne himself knows the difference," I said.

We followed the nurse to the doctor's office with Jerry coming along behind. I saw when we went in that there were only three chairs so I found an empty corner, leaned back against the walls and stood. The doctor came in shortly and sat in his chair behind his desk.

He looked at Betty Ann and said, "You must be the daughter?"

Betty Ann nodded her head yes.

"You must be the sister," the doctor said, looking at Aunt Vie.

"Yes. I'm his only sister. There were just two of us children, William and me."

That caught me by surprise. I had never known what Mr. Payne's first name was until now. I can't say that I really cared for the fact that he and I had the same first names.

"And you're the son-in-law," the doctor said, looking at me.

"Yes, Sir," I answered.

"And who are you?" the doctor said, looking at Jerry.

"I told them I shouldn't be here," Jerry said. "I told them that I wasn't family, but they wouldn't listen. I'm just his foreman."

"Then you're the one who took him to Cheyenne?"

"Yes, Sir."

"Then you should be here. What is your name?"

"Jerry."

"What happened to Dad? How is he?"

"Your Father has had a bad stroke. We have him stabilized at this time and I think he has passed the low point and will start improving from now on."

"Can we see him?" Betty Ann asked.

"In a moment. I want to talk to you about his condition first. He is paralyzed on the right side and his speech is slurred. He has the tendency to stutter quite often when he tries to talk."

"Will he get well again?" Aunt Vie asked.

"He will improve, I hope, but he will never be completely well again and improvement will take time. How much will he recover? Only time will tell."

"How much time are we talking about?" Aunt Vie asked.

"He'll be in the hospital at least three weeks. Then when he gets home, he'll have to have someone with him day and night for I'd guess six months. Don't be discouraged if at the end of the first year he is still severely handicapped, but at the end of two years he will probably be as recovered as much as he's going to.

"We're talking about a good bit of time," Aunt Vie said.

"Yes, we're talking about a good piece of time. Sorry, but that's the best we can do. If you're ready we can go see him now."

We filed out of the doctor's office and they turned to go down the hall and I turned to go back to the waiting room.

"Billy, aren't you coming?" Aunt Vie asked.

"Not unless you want to see your brother have another stroke," I said and continued on my way to the waiting room.

It was two and a half hours that I waited, but I didn't mind. I knew how important it was to Betty Ann. At last they all come back to the waiting room.

"Need a ride home, Jerry?" I asked.

"Nope. I brought the pickup down here."

We started on our way back home at a much slower rate than we had come down here. When we approached the driveway to the Burns place I asked Aunt Vie, "Don't you want me to take you on home?"

"No, but thank you, Billy. I'll ride the horse back that I rode over.

It was getting late when I pulled into our yard. "Betty Ann," I said, as I got out of the car, "I need to saddle Blue and take the milk cows home and I'll come back with our cow and milk her. Will you be all right?"

"Sure," she said. "Aunt Vie, will you stay for supper?"

"No, Betty Ann. Some other time. I will ride along with Billy, if he doesn't mind."

"I don't mind. In fact I'll saddle your horse for you."

When I led the two horses out of the corral I saw Aunt Vie hug Betty Ann, put her left foot in the stirrup and swing gracefully astride. I watched her as we rode to the wheat field and saw that she sat gracefully in the saddle. She caught me looking at her.

"What's wrong, Billy?"

"Nothing. I was just noticing how well you can ride. I didn't expect it for a city girl but I can tell you've been on a horse before."

Aunt Vie laughed and said, "That's a good point to live by, Billy. When you agree to ride with some one make sure you know how well they can ride. Yes, I grew up on horses. William and my parents started the ranch before Oklahoma was a state. Actually half of the ranch is mine but I thought it best to let William manage the whole thing. Since our parents died, I have put almost as much money into the ranch as he has. I let him go around like he owns the whole thing but he doesn't. I let him because it makes him feel important and it doesn't hurt a thing."

By that time we had reached the gate to the wheat field and I got off and opened it and let her ride through. I closed the gate and mounted back up and we rode through the cattle.

"Betty Ann tells me you're the cattle buyer for the Harshburger family."

"Yeah," I said laughing. "When my brother Floyd told me I had a choice, either buy cattle or snap cotton, you know which one I picked."

Aunt Vie laughed, "I can't say I blame you." We rode a ways with Aunt Vie looking at the cattle critically. Finally she said "Billy, you've got a good eye for cattle."

"Thank you, Aunt Vie," I said. By that time we had reached the end of the wheat field.

"This is where we part ways, Billy. Thanks for riding with me. Billy, we have some serious talking to do and to do soon."

"What about?" I asked.

"We'll talk some more tomorrow and I'll tell you then. I have to think it over some more and talk to William. Bye, Bye, Billy," and she wheeled her horse and took off at a full gallop.

I just sat there on Blue watching her. Doggone if I wasn't seeing Betty Ann twenty-five or thirty years from now.

Chapter twenty-six

The next morning after I had helped Ma and Floyd do the chores, I opened the gate and started herding the steers to Red Moon. It was a lot harder work and took a lot longer without Betty Ann and it wasn't near as much fun.

Betty Ann had left right after breakfast to pick up Aunt Vie and she had gone to Elk City to see her dad. I could tell there was something up in the air but I couldn't tell what it was.

I got the steers to Red Moon in time to put them in a cattle car and watched as the afternoon train pulled out with them heading for Oklahoma city. Then I rode back home and got there just as Betty Ann and Aunt Vie came in.

"Guess what?" Betty Ann said. "Aunt Vie is going to eat supper with us."

"Good," I said. "Let me go help Ma and Floyd with the chores and let me bring our cow in and milk her before you have supper ready."

"I'd like to ride with you, Billy," Aunt Vie said, "but I don't have a horse."

"Take Ole Stocking," Betty Ann said.

"You're sure you don't mind, Betty Ann, or you, Billy?"

"No. We don't mind," Betty Ann said.

Since Blue was already saddled, I just had to saddle Stocking. We rode along with Aunt Vie talking and me listening until we got to the gate to the wheat pasture and I dismounted and opened the gate.

"I see there's several Black Angus in the herd," Aunt Vie said.

"Yes, Ma'am. Those are mine."

"What do you mean those are yours? Aren't they all yours?"

"No. All but the Black Angus belongs to the Harshburger family. Those Black Angus I bought for myself using my cotton money."

"I see," she said. "Let me get this straight. You manage the Harshburger cattle herd but those Black Angus are yours?"

"That's right," I answered.

"What else are you responsible for, Billy?"

"Floyd pretty well manages the Harshburger place where we grow corn, maize and cotton. Of course we also have milk cows and we separate the milk for the cream. I mostly take care of the Burns' place. On the Burns place we grow wheat and raise white-faced cattle."

"Does Floyd also tell you when to harvest the wheat, when to plow the wheat ground and when to sow the wheat?"

"No, Ma'am. I pretty well decide that myself."

"I see," Aunt Vie said. "I know you took some steers to market today, but what are you going to do with the rest of the steers?"

"I'll sell them, ten, fifteen at a time. I've been keeping the younger, smaller steers over the summer and putting them on wheat another winter, but I don't know if I'll do that this year. I might just sell them all."

"And you make the decision whether to sell them or keep them. Your Brother Floyd doesn't tell you what to do?"

"No, Ma'am. That responsibility is mine and mine alone. Of course I know he would get irritated with me if I made a mistake, but so far he's been satisfied."

"Why wouldn't you keep the younger steers over for another year? Why not do as you have done in the past?"

"Because this war is going to be over soon and I figure when it is, the bottom is going fall out of the beef market."

"You've got a point, Billy. It's something to think about. Of course America is going to be feeding the whole world long after the war is over, so the market might stay up."

"It's a gamble either way and I've really not made up my mind."

By that time we had the milk cows herded up and had reached the barn where Ma and Floyd was waiting on us. I put the cows in the holding pen and dismounted and Aunt Vie did the same.

"Ma, Floyd, I'd like you to meet Betty Ann's Aunt Vie. Aunt Vie, I'd like you to meet my Mother and my oldest brother, Floyd."

"Pleased to meet you," they all said.

Aunt Vie watched as we milked the cows and she went with Floyd and me to watch us separate the cream. She went with Floyd when he went to feed the pigs and she then joined me while I finished feeding the calves.

"That's quite an operation your mother and Floyd have going, Billy," she said on the way home. "Are there any more children?"

"Yes, there were five of us, all boys."

"Where are the other three?"

"The twins, Jim and Joe are fighting in Europe and Kevin was killed in the air over Germany.

"I'm sorry to hear about Kevin, Billy. I hope the other two make it through the war."

We drove our milk cow to the barn on the Burn's place and while I unsaddled Stocking and Blue and started to milk, Aunt Vie went to the house to see if Betty Ann needed any help fixing supper.

After supper Betty Ann went into a back room while Aunt Vie cleared the table and started doing the dishes. I heard Betty Ann call, "I need you back here, Billy."

I went to her and asked, "What do you need, Betty Ann?"

"A kiss," she said as she threw her arms around me. When we broke the kiss, Betty Ann leaned back in my arms and asked, "Do you like Aunt Vie?"

"Like her?" I said. "I love her."

"Love her?" Betty Ann asked, startled.

"Yes, love her. When I watch her I can easily imagine that I'm seeing you twenty to twenty-five years from now. And I'll still love you then."

"I hope so, Billy. I really hope so. I hope you still love me and I hope I'm just like Aunt Vie. Now turn me loose, I'd better go help Aunt Vie with the dishes. You come too. She wants to talk to you."

By the time I got the firewood in for the night the women had just finished the dishes and had sat down at the kitchen table.

"Sit down, Billy. We need to have a serious talk," Aunt Vie said.

"Now Billy," Aunt Vie said, "you know the situation. You were there when the doctor told us that William would need around the clock care for the next six months."

"Yes, Ma'am, I was."

"Betty Ann and I didn't spend all day at the hospital. We looked around Cheyenne and we a found a day nurse for William. But a night nurse is not to be found. This means that Betty Ann must move up to the ranch house to take care of her father at night. Now she won't have to be in the room with him, but William mustn't be in the house at night alone. She must be close enough to hear him, should he call."

"But she can come and see me before school and after school?" I asked.

164

"We'll get around to that later, Billy. But you do see that Betty Ann does have an obligation to fill and she must fill it."

"Yes, Ma'am, I do," I said. "I would feel selfish if I were to ask her to do anything else and I would hate myself if I were selfish."

"Okay," Aunt Vie said. "We have William's night nurse settled. Now to the second problem. With William the way he is and the way he's going to be for the next year or two, we need a manager for the ranch. Someone who can write checks and make sure those things are done as they should be. Do you agree?"

"Yes, Ma'am."

"Billy, after I have seen what you have done here at the Burns place, as you call it, I have been impressed. I would like the ranch manager to be you."

"Whoa, Aunt Vie. You should know I can't do it."

"What's wrong, Billy. You think the jobs too big for you to handle?"

"You know that's not it. I could handle any job I don't care how big it is. But Jerry doesn't like me and Mr. Payne hates me, so you just tell me how I can manage a ranch under those conditions."

"William threw the same kind of fit as you did when I suggest it to him. But when I mentioned that I owned half the ranch and explained to him that you and Betty Ann would get the other half when he died, he calmed down some. When I told him how impressed I was with the way you managed the Burns place, he warmed right up to the idea."

"Why can't Jerry manage the ranch? He knows it and he knows the hired help?"

"Billy, there is not a better man in this world when it comes to knowing cattle and managing men. But when it comes to finances and managing a whole ranch, Jerry is completely lost. Will you do it, Billy?"

I got up and walked to the window and looked out at the darkness. It was a big task they were asking me to do. "You know I have an obligation to keep managing the Burns place," I said.

"I know," Aunt Vie said. "I'd lose respect for you if you didn't fulfill your obligations.

"I can't let Ma and Floyd do all the chores by themselves. I have to bring the milk cows in and help them milk."

165

"I know, Billy. As a ranch manager, you'd have to do very little actual work. Just see that the work that needs to be done is done."

I walked back to the table and sat down. I took a deep breath and said, "Okay, I'll do it."

"You can do it, Billy," Betty Ann said. "I just know you can."

"I just wonder how big a fool I am to even try. I already have two strikes against me and you don't get to first base on walks in this game."

"You'll just have to hit a home run on the next pitch, Billy," Aunt Vie said. "Don't worry. I'll stick around until William comes home and show you how he kept the books."

Aunt Vie spent the night with us and the next day she and Betty Ann went to Elk City to visit Mr. Payne while I cut out eight more steers and took them to Red Moon.

The next day we moved what little belongings we had to the Payne ranch house. We moved our stuff into Betty Ann's old room. It wasn't much of a job; we didn't have that much to move. The last thing we did was, I had Betty Ann take me back to the Burns place and I herded our milk cow over to the Payne ranch. I laughed to myself as I herded her over. I bet this ranch had never grazed a milk cow before.

Then I went back, put the saddle on Stocking and riding Blue, led her back home.

That night before going to bed, I took a hot bath and I didn't have to heat water for the tub. The Payne's had a gadget that heated water for you and when you turned a knob, you had hot water flowing right into the tub. They also had a wind charger, which produced electricity for their electric lights. As I looked at these luxuries, for the first time I realized how much luxury Betty Ann had given up to come and live with me and I was humbled. I just hoped that I would be worthy for her. As I went into her room to go to bed and wait for her to bathe and join me, I looked around the room. I saw the things of her childhood. I saw the stuffed animals setting on a shelf, I looked at her pink and frilly curtains. I looked at her walls where her childhood pictures, mementoes, and trophies hung, and I saw a blank spot on the wall where there was nothing.

When Betty Ann came into the room and dropped her housecoat from her nude body on the floor, I asked her, "Betty Ann, I see you have things hanging all over the wall. Well almost all over. Why do you have a blank spot on the wall?"

"Oh, that," she answered. "That's where Billy Harshburger's britches were supposed to go." She flipped off the light and jumped into bed giggling.

Chapter twenty-seven

Betty Ann had started back to school and since she and I were in all the same classes she was able to bring my assignments to me. Once she and I had caught up on our schoolwork, then it was easy for me to stay caught up. She would tell me when there was a test and what period it was scheduled, and I'd drive Betty Ann's car to school, take the test and then drive back home and to work.

All that driving played hob with the gas ration stamps and I have to admit more than just a little tractor gas was used in Betty Ann's car. But it run on tractor gas just fine.

I spent my days at first just riding around the ranch and getting acquainted. I had to grudgingly admit that Mr. Payne had things in pretty good shape and Jerry knew how to fix fence and herd cattle. But I also noticed that there was close to four hundred steers still on the wheat pasture and it was time to start taking them off. I rode through them and saw that three hundred head were plenty big enough to sell and about a hundred head could be kept over for another year.

It was customary for Betty Ann and I to sit down at the table right after she got off of the bus and do our school work. After that while Betty Ann helped Wilma, Jerry's wife, cook mountains of food for the hired hands, I would go into the office with Aunt Vie and we sorted through Mr. Payne's papers and book work. Little by little I was learning the operation of the ranch with the help of Aunt Vie.

That evening I looked at the tally book with Aunt Vie and saw I had estimated the number of steers on wheat pasture pretty close.

"It's time to start taking the steers off of the wheat and selling them, Aunt Vie," I said.

"Well, start the boys doing it, Billy. You're the manager," Aunt Vie said.

"I guess I am for a little while longer," I said. "At least I am until I give my first order."

The next morning I went to Red Moon and ordered enough cars for a hundred steers. The pens at Red Moon weren't big enough to hold any more steers than that and even then, the steers would be awfully crowded. I was told the cars would be there Wednesday evening. We could load them Thursday and the freight train would start them to Oklahoma City Thursday evening. That way they would be at the Oklahoma City stockyards in time for the Friday sale.

Thursday morning I got up early and had Blue saddled before it even started to show pink in the eastern sky. I was very nervous about today. Today I'd give my first order and see to it that it was carried out.

I hurriedly ate breakfast and was waiting outside when Jerry and the five hired hands came out.

"Jerry," I said. "I want you and the boys to saddle up and cut out a hundred of the biggest steers. I have cattle cars waiting down at Red Moon so I'd like for you and the boys to drive them down and load them up."

Jerry quickly whirled and said, "Who give you the right to tell us what to do on this ranch?"

"You know perfectly well who give me the right."

"Just because you married the boss's daughter don't mean you can boss us around."

I said as patiently as I could, "Mr. Payne and Aunt Vie asked me to manage the ranch until Mr. Payne gets back on his feet. I promised them I would and it's a promise I aim to keep."

"I ain't taking no orders from no German," Jerry said.

"I'm sorry to hear that Jerry. You're a good reliable man and could be a big help around here. But if that's the way you feel, come on into the office and I'll figure your wages."

"I ain't going," Jerry said. "Vie and Mr. Payne didn't need to put you in charge. I could have handled it. No, Wilma and I ain't going but you are Kid Kraut. Or at least you're going to be put in your place."

"I really don't want to fight you, Jerry. But if I have to I will. Besides it might be that you're biting off more than you can chew."

"What are you talking about? I'm a man and you're just a kid. Besides, I ain't ever been whipped before."

He started for me, his fists cocked and I punched a left straight from the shoulder and felt it connect. At the same time I felt him whack me along side of the head with his hard fist and I went spinning to the ground. I saw, just in time, his pointed

169

toed boot coming for my ribs. I reached out with both hands and grabbed the ankle. Instead of his boot kicking me in the ribs I let the momentum propel me to my feet. This surprised Jerry and while he was surprised I snapped his head to the right with a right hook. I followed it with a straight left from the shoulder and with all the power I could muster. Jerry went to the ground. I think he expected me to kick him because as soon as he hit the ground he started rolling away from me. He again seemed surprised that I hadn't even tried to kick him or hit him while he was down.

He got to his feet and we circled and measured each other. It was apparent to me that Jerry was stronger than I was and could hit harder. But I also saw that I was a tad faster than him and had a longer reach, so to win this fight I had to hit Jerry many more times than Jerry hit me. And win this fight I must. Betty Ann, Aunt Vie and even Mr. Payne were depending on it. To lose meant that I might as well find a hole and crawl in it and pull the dirt in on top of me. So I fought, not only for myself, but also for Betty Ann and our life together. Jerry fought only for his pride.

So I circled Jerry and jabbed, jabbed, jabbed with my left and whenever I could, sneak in a hard right, straight from the shoulder. I hit him and hit him and he hit me and whenever he did, I went down. But I had learned a trick from Jerry and whenever I went down, I quickly rolled away and got hurriedly to my feet.

The last few times I hit the ground, it felt so good to be there that I thought about just staying. Then I would think about what I was fighting for, and I would quickly get to my feet. This was the longest I had ever been in a fight and I was growing weak and tired. I looked at Jerry and I could tell the same thing was happening to him. I circled him some more, jab, jab, jab and then a right. I know it was only minutes, but it felt like hours, that I circled him, trying to stay out of his reach, and hit him.

We were both breathing hard and heavy and I honestly wondered how much longer I could last when Jerry hit me and I didn't go down. I staggered, but I didn't go down. It was then I knew that my punches were weakening him. Jerry wouldn't last much longer. I was a way past tired of this fight and I was ready to end it. I moved in and began to put blows to his midsection. Right, left, right, left, I rained the blows and I felt him swat me weakly along the side of the neck. I knew the fight was about over. I stepped back measured him and hit him with all my power with a straight right from my shoulder to his chin. He went down then.

He went down and didn't even try to roll away. He just sat there shaking his head.

"Had enough, Jerry?" I asked.

"Hell, no," he said, staggering to his feet, his knees wobbling.

I waited until he was standing and then I hit him again and again he went down.

"Had enough now, Jerry?"

"You ask me that once before and the answer is still the same. Hell, no."

He started to get up and got half way there when his knees buckled and he went face first into the dust. He pushed himself up and tried to stand but it wasn't any use. His legs just wouldn't hold him and he went down again.

"I damn well hate to admit it," Jerry said, gasping for breath, "But I've had enough."

That's when the other hands started towards me. All five at once. Oh God, I thought, I can't fight anymore. I'm just too tired.

That's when I heard a commanding voice say, "Stop it boys. Leave him alone."

"But Boss," I heard one of them say.

"Don't call me boss," I heard Jerry say as I stood there gasping for breath. "He's the Boss. He whipped me fair and square. You do as he says." I was thankful to see them back away from me and go instead to help Jerry up.

"I guess I had better go tell Wilma to pack up. I've been here a long time and I'm leaving a lot of memories behind," Jerry said.

"There's no need to, Jerry," I said.

"What are you talking about? You mean you ain't going to fire me?"

"Not only am I not going to fire you but I'm going to try to whip your sorry ass again if you try to leave. I'd hate for that to happen. I might not be so lucky next time."

"Luck had nothing to do with it, Billy boy. You're hell of a man," Jerry said and then he turned to the other hired hands and said, "You heard the Boss, let's get down there and cut out a hundred big, fat steers and take them to Red Moon."

I rode with them and did my share and even though every bone in my body including my head ached, I tried my best to not let it show.

We had sold all the steers except the ones I had decided to keep and those we had pushed back on grass by the time they brought Mr. Payne home. I wasn't there when they brought him in, I was in the back section of pasture farthest from the house. I was checking on cattle back there, making sure none of them were sick and making sure they had water. I found the windmill running but it wasn't pumping any water. I found the problem and fixed it temporarily, but knew I would have to come back over tomorrow in the pickup and bring the parts.

Riding in the pickup would be a pleasant change of pace because I had been riding Blue from sunup until dark everyday since I had agreed to manage the ranch. I guess I could have sat in the office like some managers, or could have been negligent in my job and gone to school, but I felt I had to still prove myself. Not prove I was the best man in fighting, I had already done that, but prove I was the best ranch manager Mr. Payne could have. I felt that to do that I had to know the conditions of all the cattle and the conditions of the range. To do that kept me in the saddle day after day after day.

Also I had Ma and Floyd to think of. I had to herd in the milk cows in to milk, help them do chores and look after the cattle on the Burns place.

So it was well after dark when Blue and I plodded into the corral the day they brought Mr. Payne home. I ate supper and had just finished my schoolwork when Betty Ann came out of her father's room and told me her dad wanted to see me.

"Are you sure?" I asked.

"I'm sure," she answered. "He wants to talk to you."

I got up and Betty Ann led me back to his room. I was shocked when I saw him. The last time I had seen him he was standing up and threatening to whip me and now he lay there all shrunken.

"Get out, Betty Ann," Mr. Payne slurred from the left side of his face. "Billy and I have some man talk to do."

"Now don't you and Billy go to arguing, Dad. You know he's doing the best he can."

"Just leave, Betty Ann. Close the door behind you."

She did as he had asked and after she had left, he just lay there for a while studying me. Finally he asked, "Do you smoke, Billy?"

"No, Sir," I answered. "I never cared to add another bad habit to the ones I already have."

"Good, good. Smart boy," he said. "It's a terrible habit to get into." He lay there a moment and then said, "Billy, will you look in the second drawer of that dresser over there. I think there's a sack of Bull Durham and papers. Would you get it out and see if you can roll me a smoke?"

I looked and sure enough there was. I got it out and on the second try, I had a halfway decent cigarette rolled. It had a few bumps and humps in it but I figured it would burn and he could smoke it. I handed it to him and he looked at it critically. "That's the worst damn cigarette I have ever seen in my life."

"I know, Sir," I said. "Maybe I'll get better with practice."

"If you are going to practice, the next time you're in Cheyenne, you had better pick up a half dozen sacks, as much as you wasted rolling this pitiful thing."

"How about I buy you a carton of tailor made?" I asked.

"Bah, those sissy cigarettes. I wouldn't put one of those in my mouth. Well, don't just stand there. Find a match and light this sorry thing for me. We'll see if it smokes better than it looks."

I lit his cigarette for him, found an empty coffee cup for an ashtray and he lay back, inhaling the smoke. "This cigarette looks bad but it sure tastes good. This is the first one I've had since Jerry hauled me off to the doctor."

He lay there a while smoking and then he said, "Speaking of Jerry, how are you and he getting along?"

"We've reached a working relationship," I said.

"I bet you have. I don't see too many bruises on you and when I talked to him this afternoon, he referred to you as Boss."

"You don't see many bruises on me, Sir, because I heal fast."

He chuckled then. "I guess I got even with you for stealing my daughter."

"Got even. How's that? How did you get even?"

"I let Vie talk me into letting you manage this ranch."

Chapter twenty-eight

The war was over in Europe in early May and the last we heard from the twins, they were expecting to be shipped out to the Pacific. In early June, we began wheat harvest. Jerry saw to the harvest on the Payne ranch, but it still left Floyd, Ma and me to harvest the Burns place. Betty Ann came down to help Ma drive the truck on the days that she could but there were a few days when Ma had to haul the wheat alone.

Right after we harvested the wheat on the Burns place but before we had finished harvest on the ranch, it came a good soaking thunderstorm. As soon as it was dry enough, I started plowing the ground on the Burns' place while Jerry and the boys finished harvesting the wheat on the Payne Ranch.

With managing the ranch and also helping Ma and Floyd, I was working from first light until dark. Even at dark, my work wasn't through. Fortunately, Aunt Vie had taught Betty Ann how to keep books right along with me and so I left Betty Ann to the books. Of course I would look over them at the end of each day for two reasons. One was to make sure Betty Ann hadn't made a mistake and secondly so I would know how the ranch was doing. I wanted to know every part of what was going on, from wheat harvesting, to hay bailing, to cattle buying and selling. I wanted to know where we were making our profits and what the profits were. If we were losing money, I wanted to know that, too.

After looking over the books, I would often sit there plotting and worrying what to do next. Invariably Betty Ann would come into the office and say, "If you're not too busy, Dad would like to talk to you." I always went into the room. After the first few times I went into his room I had learned to shut the door, open the windows if they were closed, and go to the dresser where his cigarette makings were. I would roll him a cigarette and light it for him and he would sit propped up in his bed, smoking and talking to me about the ranch.

I thought I was getting right handy at rolling cigarettes but invariably he would say, "That's one sorry looking cigarette. Well, let's light it up and see if it will smoke."

Every time I would broach a problem about the ranch he would say, "God damn it, kid, you're the manager. So manage."

I tried to help Ma and Floyd as much as I could but I knew it wasn't near enough. Ma was getting skinny from working too hard, but there was nothing more I could do.

We got a good rain the last of July and when it dried up enough I started plowing the field again on the Burns place every minute the ranch could spare me. One morning after I had herded the milk cows in and helped do the chores, I had to ride back to the ranch to see how the boys were doing. One tractor was just finishing up so after it was through I took it and made one round cutting the hay meadow in half and then turned back to Peter, one of the hired hands, and told him to finish plowing that part of the hay meadow. I knew that would fill his day and more.

"You sure you want me to plow that?" he asked.

"I'm sure."

"Holy cow, the old man's going to shit when he sees half of his hay meadow plowed up."

"Probably," I answered. Then I whistled for Blue and she came trotting to me. I mounted up and saw everything was going smoothly so I rode over to the Burns' place with the intention of plowing. I heard the motor of the Farmall running before I got there and I wondered if Floyd had decided to learn to drive a tractor after all. But when I broke through the brush and could see the wheat field, I saw it wasn't Floyd, but Ma, riding the tractor and singing at the top of her lungs.

She was on the other side of the field so I kicked Blue in the ribs and went to her in a hurry. She saw me coming and had stopped the tractor before I got there.

I loped Blue up beside the tractor and said, "What the hell do you think you're doing?"

"Don't cuss, Billy. As you can plainly see, I'm plowing the wheat field."

"But Ma, that's men work."

"Men's work, woman's, pshaw, there ain't no difference. You're working too hard, Son. I want to take as much off of you as I can."

"And you're not working too hard?" I said.

"This isn't work, this is fun. Although I have to admit it was work to crank the tractor."

I had to grin at the thought of Ma's little frame cranking the tractor. "Well, Ma, if you like it go ahead and do it."

"I intend to young man. If you insist on doing something, go help Floyd chop cotton."

I looked at Floyd in the cotton field hoeing one row at a time and there were a lot of rows to hoe. "No thanks. I just remembered something I have to do at the ranch."

By the first of August, Mr. Payne had improved enough that he could ride around in a wheel chair. It took Jerry and I both to get him in it, but that was mostly because he tried to help too much. Being able to move around from his room to other parts of the house and even out on the porch, improved his disposition considerably.

The first day he got the wheel chair, Jerry and I put him in it and wheeled him to the supper table. He smiled, criticized everything and everybody at the table. His same jolly old self. After supper he had me roll him out on the porch.

"Damn this feels good to be outside and out of the room," he said. "Roll me over to that corner out of sight of the kitchen."

Jerry was sitting on a bench smoking and watching as I rolled Mr. Payne where he asked.

"Jerry, you got plenty of makings?"

"Sure, Boss."

"Don't call me boss, call him boss," Mr. Payne said, pointing to me. "Roll me a smoke. Show this young man the proper way to roll a cigarette."

Jerry pulled out his Prince Albert can and papers and rolled Mr. Payne a cigarette and handed it to him. The cigarette Jerry had rolled didn't look much better than the ones I had been rolling. Mr. Payne took it in his left hand and looked it over critically. "Damn if this isn't a sorry looking cigarette. Young Billy can roll one almost as good. Can't anyone roll a decent cigarette around here? Well, let's light her up and see if she will smoke."

Jerry and Mr. Payne sat out on the porch smoking and visiting while I went back into the office, checked the books and started planning the next day's work. I had just finished when I heard Jerry rolling Mr. Payne to his room so I went in and helped Jerry get him out of the chair and into bed.

It was the evening of August the sixth and I was in the office going over the books while Jerry and Mr. Payne sat out on the porch smoking when Betty Ann, who had been listening to the radio, came running into the office laughing and a hollering. She threw her arms around me and kissed me hard. "I just heard it on the radio, Billy. The Americans dropped a new type of a very powerful bomb on the Japs and it blew them to smithereens. The war is all but over. They have to surrender now."

I jumped up and grabbed her around the waist and we started dancing around the office a hooping and a hollering.

"Hey, you guys in there. What are you hollering about? Come out and tell us," I heard Mr. Payne call.

We went out and I could tell by looking at them that they knew something was up, they just didn't know what it was. Mr. Payne was so anxious to hear what had happened that he forgot to put his cigarette out before Betty Ann and I got there.

"Dad, you know you're not supposed to be smoking!" Betty Ann said.

"To hell with that," he said, throwing his cigarette off of the porch and onto the bare ground. "Tell us what happened."

"A single B-29 dropped one bomb on a city in Japan named Hiroshima and that one new kind of bomb destroyed the whole city."

Mr. Payne grinned, "That ought to end the war. That'll teach those dirty Japs a lesson. Yep, the war is over."

He was almost right but it took another bomb to convince the Japanese that it wasn't any use to keep fighting. It wasn't any use and they might as well give up.

"This porch, this damn porch. I wish I could somehow get off of it," Mr. Payne complained. Jerry and the other hired hands heard him and they left. Soon they came back with a handsaw, hammer, nails and some two by eights.

I went into the office to check the books and plan the next day and when that was done since I hadn't heard Jerry bring Mr. Payne back in, I went back outside. Mr. Payne wasn't on the porch anymore but I could hear he and the boys out by the barn. Soon they were back and I watched as they pushed him up the ramp they had built.

It was in the evening the first week of September and when I herded the milk cows home, I didn't see anyone down at the barn. I started up to the house and damn if I didn't almost run over Jim and Joe, both with milk pails in their hands.

"Hi there, Billy," Joe said, as if we had just seen each other yesterday.

Before he had a chance to do anything or say anything more, I tackled him and took him to the ground. I felt Jim land on top of me and we rolled around on the ground until we heard Ma say, "Stop that, boys, get up. You're getting all dirty."

We all stood up grinning at each other. "It's about time you two got home and started helping out around here," I said.

We started milking the cows, and I said to Jim and Joe, "I hope you two are planning to stick around. It's awfully hard on Ma and Floyd to keep this place going with all the work there is to do."

"We plan on at least finishing high school," Jim said. "Then we may go to mechanic school and then set up a business in Cheyenne."

After we had milked, I let them finish the chores and I forked Blue and rode back to the ranch. It'll seem funny, I thought as I was riding back, to have four Harshburgers in the same class and graduating together.

"Where the hell have you been?" Mr. Payne asked as I rode up. It was still early in the day but Mr. Payne had conned someone into rolling him out on the porch, probably the day nurse.

"Helping the folks do their chores. Betty Ann already left for school?"

He nodded his head yes, and then asked, "What have you got planned for today?"

"A thousand little things, Mr. Payne. I have to check on the boys drilling the wheat and make sure everything is okay. I need to work on the windmill on the southeast section. I need to check the cattle today, the ones I didn't get around to yesterday. Just a bunch of little things. Oh, by the way, I'll be spending a lot less time over at home and much more time on the ranch. Jim and Joe came home last night."

"They're sending the boys home are they? Those that can make it."

"Yes, sir. Many never will come back."

"Boy, unsaddle Blue and put her in the corral. Take the pickup and do all those things you were planning to do today. You can do them from the pickup almost as easy as from the back of a horse."

"Take the pickup? That will use gas."

"To hell with the gas. I expect rationing to be over very shortly now that the war is over. Take the pickup and take me with you."

"I don't know about that, Mr. Payne. I don't know if you should be riding around in the pickup."

"Hell, yes, I should! I'm getting awfully tired of sitting here all day," and there was almost a plea in the old man's voice.

I unsaddled Blue and turned her loose in the corral. I pushed the wheel chair off of the ramp and down to the pickup. I opened the door and pushed the wheel chair right up next to the cab. He used his left hand to pull himself up using the doorframe. When he was standing on his left leg, I pulled the chair back out of his way. He hopped around until his back was to the pickup seat and then he sat down. I helped him swing around, lifting his right leg up and placing it on the floor of the pickup. I lay his right arm in his lap and closed the door.

"Better fold up that chair and put it in the back. Who knows but what this damn thing won't break down in the back pasture or something."

I got in and reached for the ignition when Mr. Payne said, "Just a minute, Boy." He reached in his pocket and pulled out a sack of Bull Durham and handed it to me. "Roll me a cigarette."

We drove down by the wheat fields and saw they were doing okay. As we came in sight of the hay meadow, Mr. Payne said, "What the Hell. It looks like you had them plow up half of my hay meadow. Why did you go and do a dumb thing like that."

"To plant wheat, Sir."

"Hell, don't we have enough ground in wheat already?"

"Yes, we do. But the way I figure with the war over, in a year or two the government is again going to put an allotment on the amount of wheat you can grow. I figure with planting half the hay meadow in wheat, when they cut us back we'll have just as much wheat ground as we've been having."

Mr. Payne looked at me shrewdly. "Did you figure that out by yourself?"

"Yes, Sir. There never seems to be anyone around to help me make decisions like that. I wish there were."

I noticed Mr. Payne looking at me occasionally. Finally he asked, "Have you quit school?"

"No, I go to school to take tests and Betty Ann brings my assignments home for me to do. Sometimes she helps me some."

"Do your homework for you, you mean."

"No, sir, I do all my own homework. That's the only way you can learn it."

"And you're passing everything and you are going to graduate?"

"Yes, Sir. The last B I got was in the seventh grade. My high school report cards are all A's"

"I see. How do you like farming, Billy?"

"Not worth a damn, Sir."

"And ranching. How do you like ranching?"

"It's a step above farming," I answered.

"Billy, what are you going to do when you graduate from high school?"

"As soon as you get well enough to take back over, or as soon as you fire me from managing the ranch, Betty Ann and I are going to move up north and I'm going to find myself a job."

"Billy, before you graduate there's going to be a million GI's discharged from the army. Had you thought of that?"

"No, Sir."

"And all of those GI's are going to be looking for a job."

"It doesn't sound good does it? I mean the chances of me finding a job when I graduate."

"Billy, you may have to spend the rest of your life here on this ranch. Would that be so bad?"

"No, Sir. I have to admit that it wouldn't be so bad as long as I could do things to your satisfaction."

He looked at me again with an odd expression. "Billy," he said, "I don't often say this but when I do, it is true. You're doing a damn fine job. I've seen enough, let's go back."

I was so astonished I didn't know what to say or do so I did as he asked. I turned the pickup around and followed the nearest pasture trail to the nearest county road. When we got to the gate I got out, opened it and drove through. I stopped the pickup, fastened the gate, got back into the pickup and started to turn to the left to go home.

"Turn right, Billy."

"But left is the way home," I said, thinking perhaps he had been turned around.

"I know how to get home, god damn it. I don't want to go home. I want to go to Cheyenne. I have some business to do with Justin E. Franklin, attorney at law."

When we got to Cheyenne, I helped him out of the pickup and into his wheel chair. I rolled him into the law office and he told me to leave. "Just a minute," he said, reaching into his pocket and giving me some money. "Go to the store and get me a half dozen sacks of tobacco. No, you'd better get a dozen sacks as much tobacco as you waste rolling those sorry cigarettes you roll. Come back in about an hour."

I bought his tobacco and killed the rest of the hour looking for barbed wire. I didn't think there would be any, but I was in luck and found a store that had one roll and I bought it and loaded it in the pickup. One roll of barbed wire wouldn't go far, but it would help some. Then I went back to the attorney's office. They must have finished their business because they were laughing and visiting when I went in.

"There you are, Billy," Mr. Franklin said as I came in. "I need you to sign a paper."

"What is it?" I asked.

"Never mind what it is, just sign the damn thing," Mr. Payne exploded. So I signed it.

"Now that was a damn stupid thing to do," Mr. Payne said. "Never sign anything until you have read it and know what it means. It's too late now so no use reading it. You've already signed it," he said but I kept right on reading anyway.

It seemed a little ridiculous to me. I had just signed an agreement to let Mr. Payne live in his ranch house as long as he wanted to and to provide for him as long as he lived.

"You're right," I said. "It was a damn fool useless piece of paper to sign. You know full well that Betty Ann and I will take care of you the best way we can as long as you live."

"I know, son. But Mr. Franklin felt that it was the proper thing to do under the circumstances. If you ever need legal work done, Mr. Franklin is the one you should get to do it."

"I'll remember that," I said, as I rolled him to the pickup and helped him in. I put his chair in the back and got in. "But I don't see any sense in signing a piece of paper promising to let you live in your ranch house on your ranch."

"Because it's not my ranch anymore, son. It belongs to you and Betty Ann. That's what took so long in there, signing the ranch over. Now you'll have to stay and I can watch my grandchildren grow up. Roll me a smoke and let's head for home."

Chapter twenty-nine

With the twins home my workload dropped tremendously and I was even able to go to school one or two days a week after the wheat was planted. The twins took care of the Harshburger place, except for the cattle buying, and it left me nothing to do but buy the cattle and manage the ranch.

We got a good three-day fall rain, soft and gentle, and after the sun came out the wheat really started growing. Mr. Payne had two trucks, or I guess I should say Betty Ann and I did, and after the twins had tinkered with them a bit, they ran like new ones.

The truck beds were equipped for grain sideboards so we could haul wheat, and also for stock racks.

Since the government wasn't buying tanks and guns anymore and there was steel available for other things, companies started making barbed wire again. I ordered two truckloads of barbed wire and as soon as it was in, Jerry and I took the two trucks and the hired hands and we loaded the wire on the trucks and brought it home. I rode all the fence lines and saw where we needed to start and put the hired hands busy building fence with the new wire. I knew it would be a job, which would keep them busy all winter.

The wheat was ready to graze by then so Jerry would line out the hands on fence building and then he would take one truck while I took the other and we would go to the cattle auctions. Even though the ranch had never done it before, I liked to keep the cattle we bought and brought back to the ranch in the cattle pens for a day or two and let them calm down a bit before we put them on wheat pasture. It was difficult to sleep with the cattle bawling and telling us how much they missed their old homes.

I had just checked over the books paying close attention on how much money we had left in the cattle account and since I didn't have to figure out what to do tomorrow, as Jerry and I were going to a cattle auction in Elk City and I had already lined the boys out on building fence, I wandered out on the porch. It was just at dusk and I saw Jerry wheeling Mr. Payne back onto the porch.

"Roll me a smoke, Jerry," Mr. Payne said. "I've been out looking at the cattle you've brought in, boy. They all look like good stuff."

"Not all of them, Sir," I said. "I had to take a few clunkers to get the whole herd."

"Are we broke, yet boy?"

"No, Sir," I said. "But at times it seems like I'm trying my darndest to break us."

When all of the ranch steers and heifer yearlings were bought for the ranch, I kept going to the cattle sales with Jerry, buying cattle for the Burns place and by the time all the money Floyd had given me was spent, school had been out for cotton picking for a week.

I usually saved Saturdays to do the long horseback riding and Betty Ann would go with me. Riding together on Saturday was really the only daytime hours we had alone. I had one more pen full of steers down on the Burns place to push out on the wheat and since Betty Ann wasn't in school, I asked, "Betty Ann, do you want to help me push the last of the steers out on the wheat down at the Burns place?"

She had just finished cutting up her Dad's breakfast steak and was just setting down the plate of steak and eggs in front of him when she answered. "I don't think so, Billy. I think I'll stay off of horses for a while. I remember what happened the last time when I was riding and I was pregnant."

I said, "Well, okay. I just thought- - - you're what? You're pregnant!"

"Yes," she answered, standing there by her dad with a huge smile on her face.

I jumped up from the table and rushed to her and hugged her as Mr. Payne pounded on both of us with his good hand. After the commotion was over, I sat down and finished my breakfast.

"I was beginning to worry," Mr. Payne said. "I was beginning to believe that one of you had gotten bashful."

It's such a beautiful day, I thought to myself, as I herded the steers to the wheat pasture. I herded the steers onto the green wheat and watched them immediately start eating. I led Blue through and shut the gate behind us. I mounted up and just sat there on Blue, watching the steers graze and thinking, there is no way today could get any better. Much too soon I glanced at the sun and saw that it was straight overhead which meant it was noon. I rode Blue on up through the wheat pasture, checking the steers I had previously bought on my way. When I got to the other end I went through the gate and up to the cotton patch where Ma, Floyd, the twins, and Mr. And Mrs. King were picking cotton. Since I ate lunch with them in the cotton field about every day, I knew Ma had packed a few extra cold biscuit and scrambled egg sandwiches. I saw they were just starting to eat lunch when I got there.

"Come to pick a little cotton, Son?" Ma joked as I dismounted.

"You don't see no cotton sack on me or my horse, do you Grandma," I answered.

"Grandma?"

"Yes, Grandma. And Uncle Floyd and Uncle Joe and Uncle Jim."

"Betty Ann's pregnant again?" Ma asked with a great smile on her face.

"Yes, and she's promised to stay off of horses this time."

"She'd better," Ma said. "If I catch her on a horse, I'll blister her behind until she won't be able to sit down for a week."

We sat there, ate lunch and visited and I knew the day couldn't be any better. I glanced down the trail that led to the cotton patch and saw someone coming at the distance. "Who's that?" I asked as he came closer.

"Who's what," Floyd asked.

"There's someone coming to the cotton field," I answered.

"I can't see him yet, but if he's got a cotton sack on his shoulder, he's hired."

As he came closer I saw that he did have a cotton sack over his shoulder and he walked with a slight limp. Then I felt myself pale.

"What's wrong, Billy? You're all pale," Ma said.

"It's nothing Ma," I said. "Other than the limp, that person coming up the road yonder walks and moves like Kevin."

As he came closer so did the twins. "What the hell!" Joe said.

"By god it is Kevin," I shouted, and started running down the cotton row to meet him with the twins following me. I met him and threw my arms around him and the twins got there about that time and we all went to the ground. Floyd was much more dignified, he walked hurriedly to us and then piled on.

"Get up, boys," I heard Ma say. We did and as soon as Kevin was on his feet, Ma threw her arms around him and I saw her shoulders shudder as she held him and cried. "Oh, Kevin, Kevin, Kevin," I heard her say.

Then she turned him loose and stepped back and looked at him. We went back to the cotton sacks and Mr. King shook Kevin's hand and Mrs. King hugged his neck and since they were through with lunch, they went back to snapping cotton. We sat down on the full cotton sacks.

"Kevin, you want some lunch?" Ma asked.

"No, Ma. Not today," Kevin answered. "I ate in Cheyenne on the way out here." Kevin looked around, "I only see four cotton sacks. Who's not picking cotton?"

"I'm not," I answered. "See that blue filly over there? It's on her back that I do my most of my work."

"What are you talking about?" Kevin asked puzzled.

"A lot has happened since you've been away, Kevin," I said.

"I married Betty Ann Payne and then old man Payne had a stroke and I'm now managing the Payne ranch and I just finished telling the others that Betty Ann's pregnant and you're going to be an uncle. But tell me Kevin, how come you aren't dead like the government told us."

"It's a long story. A piece of flack caught us right after we dropped our bomb load. Good thing we had dropped our bombs. Otherwise we would have been scattered all over the German Sky. I could tell by the way the plane was flying that there wasn't anybody at the controls, so I left my gun and went into the cockpit and sure enough, both pilot and copilot were splattered all over the cabin. I got what was left of them out of the way and took control, but the problem was, the plane was in a steep dive and some of the controls were shot away. I was able to get it leveled out just about five hundred feet above the ground. I suppose an experienced pilot could have done it sooner, but remember this was only the second time I had ever flown a bomber.

"We had lost one of the motors and the plane had lost too many parts and just flat didn't want to fly. I give it full throttle but we kept slowly but surely sinking closer and closer to the ground. Finally I gave up and picked the flattest place I could find and set her down.

"What did you do then?" Joe asked.

185

"Soon as that plane stopped scooting along the ground stirring up dust, I opened a door, jumped out and ran like hell. I found me a good place to hide and I hid."

"Kevin, were you the only that lived?" I asked.

"I don't know, Billy. From my hiding place, I saw German troops board the plane and they brought out some of the crew and they brought them out on litters and the others they brought out in bags, so I hope those they brought out on litters were alive and lived."

"Joe and I had the opportunity to walk over a good part of Germany and we saw that it was pretty heavily populated, or would have been if it hadn't been for the war," Jim said. "How did you manage to stay hid amongst all those people for that long."

"That's the point, Jim, I didn't," Kevin said. "For two weeks I stayed hid, living on wild berries and drinking from the streams. Then when I figured everything was quieted down some, I broke into a farmhouse and found some clothes that would fit me. I put the clothes on and found a shovel and buried my uniform and returned the shovel where I got it. Then I just walked out as bold as brass and joined in with the Germans. If someone asked me why I wasn't in the German Armed Forces, I simply tell them I had been, take off my shoe and show them the little bit of foot I have left. I am really thankful that Ma insisted that we learn to speak German right along with English.

"So you been in Germany all this time?" I asked.

"No Billy, I haven't. Doing odd jobs for this German farmer and doing odd jobs for that German farmer and never staying too long in one place, I gradually worked my way into France. Once into France, I was picked up by the French Resistance and worked with them."

"The French Resistance gave my battalion a lot of help once we were in France," Joe said. "What did you do in the French Resistance?"

"Joe, I did things I don't want to even think about, say nothing of talk about," and he sat there staring off into the distance with a bleak look on his face. Then he smiled, "I did learn to speak French though. Now I can talk to girls in English, German and French. French is the best language to talk to girls in."

I looked at the sun and saw it was mid afternoon. "I don't know about you guys," I said, "but some of us have to work." I mounted Blue and said, "I'll catch you later," and rode off.

I checked the cattle on the wheat pasture on the Payne place on my way home and then rode on to the ranch house. Betty Ann and her father were sitting out on the porch.

"Guess what?" I said, kind of laughing as I dismounted. "Kevin's not dead after all. At noon he came walking out to the cotton field as if he had always been there while we were eating lunch."

"Terrific," Betty Ann said as she came into my arms.

"How come he was listed as killed when he wasn't?" Mr. Payne asked.

So I told them the story that Kevin had told me. When I was through, Mr. Payne looked at me and said, "I don't like Harshburgers much but I do have to admit that they are tough sons of bitches."

"Oh, Dad," Betty Ann chided, "You like Billy and you like me and we're Harshburgers."

"I can tolerate Billy, mostly because I don't have no choice and of course I like you, you're my daughter. But daughter, you'd better get your butt in there and start helping Wilma fix supper."

"My God," I said, looking at the setting sun. "I've lost a whole half a days work."

Mr. Payne looked at me in amusement and said, "If losing a half day's work is the worst that ever happens to you, I want to be with you all the days of your life." He reached in his pants pocket then and pulled out his tobacco and papers. "Roll me a smoke."

I took the crumpled papers and the tobacco sack and rolled him a cigarette.

"That's one poor excuse for a cigarette," he said, as I handed the cigarette to him.

"I think that is a pretty good looking cigarette, considering how rumpled the papers are. Why don't you carry them in your shirt pocket so they won't get crumpled?"

"What? And let Betty Ann see them and think I smoked against the doctors orders?" he said, laughing and puffing on his cigarette as the sun sank in the western sky.

Chapter thirty

Betty Ann was right. Up on the tall flat topped hill, I could see all of the Burns' pasture. Because of this, I would head out towards that hill in the mornings when the sky had only a hint of pink and usually I was sitting there on Blue when the sun came up and it was light enough to see. From the top of that hill, I could see the cattle on the wheat pasture getting up to start their morning graze and I could see the Burns house where Kevin had moved. Jim, Joe and Floyd still lived at the house with Ma, but Kevin said he needed a place of his own and he had moved to the Burns house.

There was something different about Kevin. He was still the brother I loved, but he seemed to be more reckless and had developed an 'I don't give a damn' attitude. It seemed that he felt that since he had cheated death not only once but many more times, death could never claim him. Or perhaps he had looked death in the face and had seen it was real and would claim him one day so he wanted to cram as much living into each day as he could.

Often when I sat there on Blue on top of the hill waiting for it to get light enough to see, I would see another car parked beside Kevin's. When the sun had chased away the last of the night, I would see a woman come out the door way, turn and give Kevin a long kiss before getting in her car and driving away. I knew none of these women but it was obvious Kevin did.

Two weeks was the longest I ever saw the same car parked in the driveway and the same woman come out of the house. Then a week or so later there would be another different car and a different woman.

After the cars had left and the dust had settled, I would ride down to the wheat field, count and check the cattle and then ride on down to the house to have a morning cup of coffee with Kevin.

On those mornings after a woman had left, I would walk into the house after Kevin answered the door, and I would say, "My god, Kevin, this place smells like a French whorehouse after a busy Saturday night."

"Yes, it does, Billy. Yes, it does," and he would yawn as he poured me a cup of coffee and refilled his cup. "Doesn't it smell great."

It was a joke between us and I never let on that I couldn't smell a thing. While God had gifted me with eyesight that many men would envy and while I could see things at a distance that most men needed binoculars to see, God had slighted me when it came to a sense of smell. I could smell some things if they were strong, like smoke or a skunk, but most things I couldn't smell at all. The only reason I knew that Kevin had been busy the night before was that I had seen the woman leave the house.

Kevin and I would visit while we drank our coffee and then I would leave to check the ranch cattle and Kevin would leave to go help do the chores.

I knew Floyd didn't pay Kevin much to work around the farm but Kevin always seemed to have plenty of money to spend. One day I asked, "Kevin, how come you got all that money to spend?"

"Billy, do you realize that the Army Air Force give me back pay for all the time I was dead? And they paid me flight pay as well. Then I get a disability check because of this foot. That's where the money is coming from."

But I knew that only explained where part of the money was coming from. Kevin had spent and was spending more than that. He had a much better car than any of us and had a good pickup, which I couldn't see he needed, parked in the barn and he left the house right after the morning chores unless Floyd said he needed him awfully bad. Kevin left, saying he had chores of his own to do and he never explained them. Never explained them at all, these chores he had to do.

I hadn't seen a strange car in front of Kevin's driveway in over two weeks and thought perhaps he had worked it out of his system. Now, I thought, Kevin will find a nice girl, settle down and get married. I even suggested it to him over coffee one morning.

"Me settle down and get married? Never in your life, Billy. Life's too short for that. Of course life might seem a lot longer if you were tied down to just one woman."

"I don't know," I said. "I enjoy being tied down to Betty Ann."

"That's you and I'm me. We're alike in many ways, you and me, Billy. But in that way we're different. Tell me, did you ever lose a fight?"

189

"No, Kevin. But I came mighty close in my last fight. The fight I had with Jerry before he would follow my orders."

"I haven't either. But tell me, have you ever been in bed with a woman other than Betty Ann?"

"No, and I don't aim to."

"But you wonder. You wonder what another woman would be like to sleep with."

"Of course, I do, Kevin. But I know it couldn't be any better or any more fun than Betty Ann."

"She's that good in bed?"

"She's that good."

"Maybe I ought to try her and see if you're telling the truth," Kevin said, jokingly.

"Not unless you want to lose your first fight and lose it bad," I said and I wasn't joking.

"I'd never do that to my brother, Billy. Even if I could. The way Betty Ann is always looking at you I don't think I even could. You've got one of a kind there, Billy. You make damn sure you do whatever you have to do to hang on to Betty Ann."

"I aim to, Kevin."

It was three days later, as I was sitting on top of the tall flat topped hill, that I saw another car in Kevin's driveway. As it grew lighter, I could see that the car looked familiar. The woman came out and kissed Kevin good-bye before going to her car. There was something familiar about the woman and I knew I knew her. When she turned to look at the rising sun I saw her face clearly and knew then who it was. It was Mary Lou Woods.

When I knocked on Kevin's door and he let me in I didn't say a word, just walked to the table and let Kevin pour me a cup of coffee. I sat there in silence for while and then said, "Kevin, you ought not be fucking these married women."

This startled Kevin so much that he sloshed some of his coffee onto the table.

"Damn," he said and got up to get a rag. When he had cleaned up his mess, he sat down again. "How do you know who my night guests are?"

"I can see them Kevin. I can see them when they leave. I ride up on that big hill on the Payne's ranch and from there I can see where the cattle are on the whole Burns place. I can also see the house. This morning I saw Mary Lou King-Woods leave."

"So you've been spying on me," Kevin said coldly.

"No, not really. Mostly I've been watching and waiting for your girlfriends to leave so I wouldn't come riding up and catch you in what do they call it? A compromising position."

Kevin laughed then. "So you're not watching the house to spy on me but to make sure there isn't an embarrassing situation."

"Yeah," I grinned. "But Mary Lou is married and you could be breaking up a happy home. You shouldn't be doing that."

"Listen, Billy. Forget it. Mary Lou has been sleeping around for a good while and she'll continue to sleep around for a good while longer. It might as well be with me until I get tired of her. After all she is a good lay."

It was a cold January day and I had had to work on the ranch that morning. We had cows with calves at their side still out in the pasture and I had to drive the pickup around to the windmills and break the ice out of the stock tanks. It was a cold, wet job. I could have had one of the hired hands to do it but I had made it a practice to do the dirty jobs myself and never ask the hired help to do a job that I wouldn't do.

I was through by noon and drove the pickup home. I changed out of my wet clothes before I ate lunch. "Are you going back out again? Mr. Payne asked, "It's awful cold out there."

"I know," I answered. "But I have to check the cattle on the Burns wheat pasture."

"Why don't you have one of the boys do it?" Betty Ann asked.

"No, this is a job that only Blue and I can do. I will have Jerry roust one of the boys out of his bunk in the bunk house this afternoon and drive to all the windmills and break the ice though."

When I got to the Burns' place and counted the steers, I came up four short. I counted again and was still short. I started riding the fence line, looking for the place where they got out. I sure wish Floyd would let me buy more barbed wire and string it around the wheat field. But I knew Floyd wouldn't for a good while. Since the fence around the wheat field was used only when we were grazing the wheat and since we grazed the wheat at most only six months out of the year, putting new wire around the wheat pasture was on the bottom of Floyd's priorities.

At last I found where they had gotten out and I followed their tracks. This was slow going and hard to do since their tracks were made on frozen ground. And sure enough, their tracks headed up the canyon where it seemed that all the steers went when they got out. I wondered if in the future I could save myself some time and trouble if I would just cut across the pasture and go straight to the canyon. Heading up the canyon looking for them I was at least out of the wind, which had began to blow. As I started to come upon a bend, I swung Blue across the canyon so I could see better. As I crossed the canyon floor, I suddenly spotted pickup tracks and they were heading up the canyon. I pulled Blue to a halt and studied the tracks. Who would be driving around our pasture and who would be doing it on a day like this?

I went on around the bend and saw the steers and at the same time I smelled smoke. The smoke had to be powerfully strong for me to smell it so I knew the fire was somewhere near by.

I slipped around the steers and went on up the canyon and around a bend. At the head of the canyon I saw Kevin's pick up and a whisky still that I knew had to belong to Kevin, but I didn't see Kevin at all. So this is where Kevin is getting all that extra money, I thought to myself. Kevin's moon shining. A noise broke into my thoughts and I looked to my left and up the bend and saw Kevin coming down with a shotgun in one hand and a rifle in the other. There was also a pistol strapped to his waist.

"Spying on me again, Billy?" Kevin asked.

"No, I'm not, but what are you doing? Expecting an invasion of some kind?"

Kevin grinned, "I guess I am a little overloaded with hardware," and he walked to the pickup and put down the rifle and shot gun, but kept the pistol strapped to his waist. He came back to me and said, "Now tell me. Billy, what are you doing here?"

"Kevin, when you picked this canyon to hide out your still, you picked a piss-poor place. For some fool reason, every time a steer gets out of the wheat pasture, he heads for this canyon. That's the reason I'm here. Four steers got out and wandered up this canyon. When I found them, I smelled smoke and came on up to investigate."

"It's probably because of the fresh water spring which I use to make my corn. You're not going to tell anyone that I'm making shine up here are you?"

"Hell no. It's your ass if the law catches up with you and they throw you in jail and lose the key."

Kevin laughed, "I'm not worried about the law. It cuts a little bit into my profits but I've taken care of it. But the Biggs brothers is another matter."

"The Biggs brothers?"

"Yeah, they don't like competition. I've seen them sneakin around down at the river, trying to find my still, but I ran them off. They also threatened me but when that didn't work they tried to sneak up on me down at the house but I heard them. A couple of shotgun blasts in their general direction started them on their way and a few rifle shots kicking dirt up at their heels, and you never saw mangy critters run so fast."

"Be careful, Kevin. The Biggs brothers aren't to be trusted. Well, I've got to get those steers back in the pasture. Don't worry, I'm not going to tell anyone."

"Thanks, Billy. And Billy if you have to come up this canyon again, sing out loud and clear before you come around that bend. I'd hate to make a mistake that we'd both regret.

Chapter thirty-one

The old man raised one hell of a fuss, but when Betty Ann's water broke I rushed her to the car, loaded her up and headed to Cheyenne and none to slow either. It was just after supper and as I turned around in the yard, I saw Jerry pushing Mr. Payne towards the pickup and I knew they would be along shortly.

"What are we going to name it?" Betty Ann asked as we were driving towards Cheyenne.

We had discussed names for the baby before but now that the time was near, it was time to decide. "I like the name of Ann, but I would also settle for Andréa."

"I have thought of that and I like it," Betty Ann said. "But if it's a boy can we name it after my father?"

"I don't care much for the idea," I said.

"You still hate him, don't you?"

"No, I don't. Actually, I kind of like the old fart. The reason I question naming him after your father is that it will be confusing. We can't call him William without confusing him with your dad. If we call him Billy, well, you see the problem."

Betty Ann said, "My father's full name is William Dale Payne. We could name him after father and call him Dale."

"I'll go along with that," I said as we reached the Cheyenne doctor's office. I stopped the car, got out and ran around to the passenger's side. I opened her door and reached in to pick her up.

"I can walk this time, Billy. Let me. After all I'm just coming to the doctor's office to have a baby.

"Not to just have a baby," I said as I held her hand and we walked towards the office door. "You're going to have my baby."

"Wait out here, Billy," the nurse said. "We'll come and get you as soon as we get her settled."

I was standing looking out the window when the door opened and Jerry rolled Mr. Payne through the door in his wheel chair.

"I see you made it, Boy, and that surprises the hell out of me the way you tore out of the yard. I just knew you'd wreck before you got to Cheyenne. How is she anyway?"

"They're getting her settled in," I answered. "They said they'd come and get me when they were ready."

"God damn it, can't one of you guys see that I'm dying for a smoke?" Mr. Payne said, pulling out his tobacco and papers.

I took the makings and tried to build him a cigarette but my hands were shaking so bad I tore the paper and spilled the tobacco. I reached again for the tobacco and papers, which I had handed back to him, but he handed them to Jerry saying, "Here, Jerry, you do it. This kid ain't ever going to get it done."

After Jerry had rolled the cigarette and the old man was smoking it he said, "You two ain't going to have to roll my smokes much longer." He looked at Jerry, and then at me and said, "Watch this."

As we watched we saw Mr. Payne concentrate real hard and then we saw him raise his right arm from his lap and drop it by the wheel of his chair. As we continued to watch he concentrated hard again and raised his arm and hand back up and placed it in his lap. "It won't be long now," and he beamed through a cloud of smoke, "until I can build my own smokes."

A nurse stepped into the waiting room and said, "Billy, you can come back now."

"Keep us posted, Boy. We'll be right here," I heard the old man say as I followed the nurse back and when I entered Betty Ann's room I saw her face was in a grimace but it relaxed and I walked to the bed. "How you doing, Betty Ann?"

"Right now, okay. But sometimes it really hurts."

"Her contractions are a good ways apart," one nurse said. "It'll be a while yet." Two nurses were in her room and one of them picked up a damp washrag and wiped Betty Ann's sweaty brow.

I pulled up a chair beside her bed, sat down and reached for her hand. After a while her contractions started coming closer and closer together and my heart went out to her as I saw her face grimace in pain. I heard the nurse behind me say, "They're coming regular and every four minutes, I had better notify the doctor, and she left and there was only one nurse in the room with us wiping Betty Ann's sweating face.

Betty Ann went into another contraction and when it was over with she looked at me and said, "Billy, I know you want to be with me and I want you with me but you didn't change clothes before we left and you smell like cow shit and horse sweat. It's making me sick."

As I got up to leave, Betty Ann went into another contraction and the nurse looked at me, smiled and said, "That's not unusual, Billy. It seem that the sense of smell heightens in some women when they are having a baby and it makes them nauseous. It could be their husband's shaving lotion or cigarette smoke or fried foods. It could be anything so don't think anything of it. Go on out into the waiting room and we'll keep you posted."

Mr. Payne was smoking when I joined them. "How's it going, Kid?" he asked.

"Her contractions are between three and four minutes apart."

"The baby will be here before you know it," Mr. Payne said.

"I sure hope so."

"No need to be nervous," he said, stubbing out his cigarette in the ashtray. "Women have babies all the time. Jerry, what the hell does a man have to do to get a smoke rolled around here?"

"Coming right up, Boss," Jerry said, handing him a cigarette he already had half rolled before the old man even asked.

"You want to try one?" Mr. Payne asked as I paced up and down the waiting room. "It might help calm you down some. It helps with me."

"No, thanks," I said, looking at the ashtray which was already half full of Bull Durham home rolled cigarette butts. "I think you're smoking enough for both of us."

It was growing light outside and Jerry had emptied the ashtray twice and it was half full again when the nurse came into the waiting room and said, "Billy, she's having her baby now. Do you want to come in and watch?"

"Sure," I said and went swaggering down the hallway after her. She opened the door to the delivery room and I swaggered in. The screams of Betty Ann assaulted my ears, I saw her feet in stirrups and the doctor sitting on a stool with bloody rubber gloved hands, saying, "Push Betty Ann, push," and that's all I saw. The world started turning gray and then black and the next thing I knew I was laying on the hallway floor, my feet on a stool and the nurse was waving a foul smell tube below my nose and each breath made my nose sting. "Don't do that," I said.

"Don't be ashamed, Billy. You're not the first father to faint when they witnessed their wives in childbirth. Do you want to go back in there or do you want to go back to the waiting room until it's all over?'

"There's not a thing I can do to help in there, is there?"

"Not a thing. The nurses and the doctors have it under control and every thing is normal."

"Then I might as well go to the waiting room," I said, standing on wobbly legs. The nurse helped me back to the waiting room and I sat down.

"Couldn't take it, huh," Mr. Payne said. "I didn't expect you could. No guts."

Jerry roared with laughter.

"What are you laughing at?" I asked.

"Shut up, Jerry," the old man said. "Shut up or I'll fire your ass."

"You can't fire me. He's the boss," Jerry said, pointing to me.

"I still don't see what you're laughing at," I said.

"Now don't say a word, Jerry. If you're going to do anything, roll me a smoke."

"You should have seen the old man here when Betty Ann was born," Jerry said, rolling a cigarette. "They took him into the delivery room while Betty Ann was being born and he fainted dead away. He fell so hard his head bounced on the floor."

"That's nothing but a lie," the old man said. But I knew it wasn't. I knew it was the truth. And somehow it didn't diminish my respect for him but increased it.

It was eight thirty five in the morning when the doctor came into the waiting room and announced that William Dale Harshburger was now a member of the world. He also told us that Betty Ann was back in her room and we could go see her if we wished.

And we all wished. When I entered Betty Ann's room, she was nursing him with a peaceful and contented smile on her face. "Isn't he beautiful?" she asked.

I pulled the blanket back to see. "No he isn't," I said. "He looks too much like me."

"I know he does," she said. "Isn't he beautiful?"

I was sitting on her right side and she was holding the baby to her breast with her right hand. Mr. Payne had Jerry push him to her left side. I saw him concentrate and then he reached up with his right hand and took her hand. "Are you all right, sweetheart?"

"I'm just fine, Dad," she answered. Then she looked and exclaimed, "Dad, you moved your right hand!"

"I know," he said. "I want to be able to hold my grandson with both arms."

After a good while I said, "Betty Ann, I'm going to go now. I want to tell Ma and my brothers, but I'll be back soon."

"No need to hurry, Billy, I'm not sleepy right now but I think when I do get sleepy, I'll sleep for a week."

When I left her room Jerry went with me but we left the old man sitting beside her, holding her hand. Jerry sat back down in the waiting room and rolled a cigarette. "I'll catch you later, Jerry," I said as I went out the door and to the car.

The sun was shinning and the skies were blue as I left Cheyenne. I left Cheyenne driving at a leisurely pace, a lot slower than when I arrived. I think I'll go by and tell Kevin first, I said to myself. Ole Kevin will be one proud uncle.

I turned into the driveway at the Burns' place, thinking all the time of funny ways to tell Kevin that his little brother was a daddy. I drove into the yard and saw Kevin, all crumpled and bloody.

I slammed on the breaks, jumped out and went running to him. "What happened, Kevin?" I asked.

"It was the Biggs brothers," he whispered hoarsely. "They snuck up on me. They caught me by surprise and beat the hell out of me."

"It looks like they didn't use their fists much," I said, eyeing a bloody fence post and a bloody piece of iron pipe. He moaned when I picked him up and carried him to the car. For the second time in less than twenty four hours I went racing to Cheyenne, but this time a whole hell of a lot faster.

He was completely unconscious by the time I reached the doctor's office. Jerry must have been looking out the window because he came to help me as I carried him in. A nurse led us down the hallway and into an exam room and the doctor showed up immediately. He checked his heart and breathing and started an IV in his arm. All this time Kevin just lay there on the examination table on his back.

"He needs to go to Elk City," the doctor said. "He has a severe concussion along with broken ribs. But I'm afraid to move him anymore. I need to stabilize him first."

Kevin's breathing became ragged and the doctor prepared a shot and injected it into the IV tube. This seemed to help him some. Damn those Biggs brothers anyway, I thought to myself. When Kevin gets healed back up, we're going to pay them a little visit.

I stepped out into the waiting room and saw Mr. Payne with Jerry.

"I heard that Kevin's been hurt," Mr. Payne said. "Is there anything we can do?"

"Hurt, the Biggs brothers used fence posts and iron pipe and beat the hell out of him. Yes, there's something you can do if you don't mind. You can go by the Harshburger place and tell Ma and the boys that Kevin's been hurt. You could soften the blow a might by telling Ma she's a grandmother first."

I went back into the room where Kevin was. I saw he was breathing fast and he had his eyes open. I waved my hand in front of his face but his eyes didn't follow my hand.

"I'm sorry, Billy, there is nothing more I can do. If I try to send him to Elk City, he'll die before we get started. If he stays here, only a miracle from God can save him."

"Then let's start praying for a miracle, Doctor," I said.

"I have been, Billy. I have been," the doctor said, as he injected another shot into Kevin's IV tube.

But it didn't help none. Why don't Ma and my other brothers get here, I thought? Why do I have to face this alone? Kevin started breathing faster then before and he began to gulp like a fish out of water. I looked at his hands and saw there were purple splotches on them.

Then Kevin began breathing more shallow but just as fast. The doctor injected another shot into the tube but it didn't make any difference. His breath became shallower yet until he was hardly taking in any air at all. Then he breathed once and stopped, then breathed twice more and then he didn't breath at all. The doctor put the stethoscope over his heart and listened for a short while. "I'm sorry, Billy," he said and pulled the sheet up over Kevin's face.

I walked out of the room in a daze. Too much had happened and had happened all at once. I opened the door and looked into Betty Ann's room and saw she was sleeping with my newborn son in her arms. I closed the door quietly so as not to disturb her. I walked back down the hall and by the examination room where Kevin lay dead. I walked out into the waiting room where I had spent the night, the night I had spent in anticipation and joy. I walked out and sat down in the same chair and waited for Ma, Floyd, Jim and Joe.

Chapter thirty-two

We left the doctor's office, and I drove our car and Floyd rode with me and Joe drove the other car with Ma and Jim. We went by the funeral home and made arrangements and then we went to the sheriff's office.

"What can I do for you good folks?" the sheriff asked as all five of us filed into his office.

"I'll tell you what you can do for us," I said. "You can go out and arrest the Biggs brothers."

"Arrest the Biggs brothers? What for?"

"They beat Kevin with fence post and iron pipe. He just died," I answered. "You can arrest them for murder."

"Whoa, now. That's a pretty strong statement. Accusing them of murder. How do you know they did it?"

"Because Kevin told me they did before he died."

"I'll go out and investigate but you have to remember, it's just your word against theirs and your word is hearsay and not admissible in a court of law. But I'll sure investigate. Thank you for dropping in. I'm sure sorry about Kevin. Is there anything else I can do for you?"

"I guess that's all we can ask of you," Floyd said. "Come on, let's go."

"I think he was anxious to get back to dunking his doughnuts," I said to Floyd, as he got into the car beside me and I started it up.

"That was a complete waste of good time," Floyd said. "I doubt if he even gets his fat ass out of the office."

But the sheriff went out to the Burns' place and looked it over and then came to us and said there was absolutely no evidence that the Biggs brothers had done anything.

"I guess we know who pays off the sheriff," I said to Floyd after the sheriff had left.

"Pays him off? What do you mean?" Floyd asked.

"The Biggs brothers pays him to look the other way," I said.

"You don't mean that, do you, Billy?"

"Of course, I do. Kevin paid him too, Floyd."

"Kevin paid him? Why in the world would Kevin pay him?"

"Come off of it, Floyd. Surely you noticed that Kevin always had money to spend. Surely you must have wondered where he got it."

"Never gave it much thought," Floyd said. "I just supposed it was his back pay from the Air Force."

"Some of it was but he helped it along by making corn whiskey and selling it. That's why the Biggs brothers killed him. They didn't like the competition."

"You don't kill someone just because he competes with you in business. You just don't do it. It was murder, pure and simple."

It is bad enough to grieve for a brother dead once but no one should ever have to grieve for the death of the same brother twice. If it hadn't been for Betty Ann and my new son, Dale, I don't believe I could have stood it.

I went to see Betty Ann and Dale the next morning and she told me that she and Dale would get to go home the next day. I went to Kevin's funeral at two o'clock that afternoon. I didn't cry when they lowered Kevin's casket into his grave. No, sir, I didn't cry at all. But I wished I could have.

Jerry rolled Mr. Payne up to me after the funeral and Mr. Payne said, "I hear you think the Biggs brothers did it."

"I know they did, Sir. Kevin told me they did before he died."

Mr. Payne looked at me with those cold, steely eyes of his and said, "Don't be going off and do something stupid, Son."

I just walked away from him.

I helped the boys do the chores that night, sort of took Kevin's place, and then we all gathered in Ma's big kitchen and had supper. We ate in silence and when Floyd was through eating he got up from the table and walked out into the dark. One by one we boys finished eating and joined him.

"You all know what we should do?" Floyd said.

"Yep," I said, and stepped onto the porch and got a lantern. "I'll go get some rope," I said, lighting the lantern.

I found a couple pieces of big rope that was long enough, coiled them and put them over my shoulder. I found some smaller rope and took it also. By the time I got back, they had the team hitched to the wagon and had it pulled up into the yard.

Ma came out into the yard about then and she walked over and looked in the wagon and saw the rope. I expected her to raise the roof but she didn't. Instead she looked at each of us four boys and said, "Good. Hang those sons of bitches high."

I ducked my head and coughed in embarrassment. I had never heard Ma use that kind of language before.

"I wish I could come with you," Ma said. "I'd like to see them dangling from a stout limb. But I understand this is men's work and men have to do it."

"You could make us a pot of coffee, Ma," Floyd said. "We don't plan to leave here for a while. I want to arrive at the Biggs place about two or three o'clock. At that time they'll be sleeping the soundest."

We didn't say much, we just sat in the wagon and drank coffee while we waited. The horses dozed in their traces and Blue decided she was hungry and began to munch green grass near the place where she was hitched.

At last it was time to go and we handed the coffee cups to Ma, my other brothers got in the wagon and I mounted Blue and we started out. We didn't tell Ma goodbye or anything. We just left.

"This is about as close as we had better take the wagon," Floyd said, when we were about three quarters a mile away from the Biggs Brother's cabin. I hitched Blue to a limb of a hackberry tree and Floyd hitched the team to the fence. Floyd and I picked up a coil of small rope but we left the big rope in the wagon.

"Are we ready?" Joe asked, as he and Jim reached down, picked up hands full of dirt and began to rub it on their faces and hands.

Floyd sighed and said, "Let's go do it."

The twins disappeared. I mean one moment they were there and the next moment they weren't. I knew they had to be out there somewhere but I couldn't see them and I couldn't hear them. For all practical purposes, Floyd and I were alone.

Quietly, Floyd and I started walking down the road. Now I know I don't have much of a sense of smell but I could smell the Biggs place long before we got to it. It smelled like a dirty hog pen but ten times as strong. How can people live like that? I wondered, as we came into sight of the cabin. I still hadn't seen sight or sound of the twins.

I looked at the cabin and through the window I could see a dim light and it looked like a coal oil lamp turned down low.

Out of the corner of my eye, I saw Floyd sneaking up to the cabin. I suddenly tripped on something and stepped forward hard, making a crunching sound. I froze and looked over at Floyd and knew he had heard me because he was standing motionless. I looked down to see what I had tripped on and saw a hound dog laying on the ground, dead. His head was twisted at a grotesque angle and my admiration of the twins and what they had learned in the army went way up. I knew it had to be one of them who had sneaked up on the dog.

I looked at the dimly lighted window again and my heart went to my throat as I saw a shadow pass between the lamp and the window. It was then I heard hollering and cussing and crashing inside the cabin.

"You guys get on in here with those ropes," I heard one of the twins call out, but I couldn't tell which one it was. Floyd and I both rushed to the door and went in. "Turn up the lamp," Joe said. "We need to see what we're doing."

I turned up the lamp and saw that each twin had them a Biggs brother apiece, and they had the brothers on their stomachs sitting astride them with their arms pulled back behind their backs. The Biggs brothers were helpless, all they could do was wiggle a little bit and kick their feet against the floor.

"Get off of me, you son of a bitch," one of them hollered and the other one soon joined in.

While the twins held them down, Floyd and I tied their hands and feet. I tied mine good and tight and I could tell by the screaming and cussing that Floyd was doing the same with his.

"Let's drag them outside," I said, "It doesn't smell any to good outside but it's nothing like it stinks in here."

"I'll go get the wagon," Jim said, and took off at a run.

The brothers were still yelling and cussing and what they were saying didn't make much sense as I went back into the stinking cabin looking for a lantern. They had calmed down some by the time I had found a lantern, lit it and took it back outside.

"What is all this about?" one of them asked.

"In case you haven't heard, our brother Kevin, died," I said.

"What does that have to do with us?" the other asked.

"You should know," I answered. "You two are the ones that beat him with a fence post and an iron bar."

"It wasn't us," one of them said.

"Kevin talked to me before he died," I said. "He told me it was you and I believe him."

"So what? It's what the son of a bitch deserved. Who did he think he were, coming in here and start taking away our business. I'm glad he's dead."

No one said anything but the Biggs brothers and all they did was to cuss us and tell us how glad they were that Kevin had died. Not exactly the type of conversation one should be talking if one wished to be shown mercy. At last we heard the rattle of the wagon, and the horses and wagon pulled into the yard.

We loaded the brothers into the wagon and one of them said, "Go ahead. Take us to the sheriff in Cheyenne. We'll be out of jail in time to have an early breakfast in the morning."

Floyd climbed up onto the wagon seat and took the reins. He spotted the silhouette of a large tree and started the team towards it. The twins and I walked behind with me carrying the lantern.

"Hey, this ain't the way to Cheyenne," one of the brothers said.

"Where we going?" the other asked.

We stopped the wagon under a stout limb of the cottonwood and Floyd and I began to fashion nooses out of the big rope. It really didn't dawn on the Biggs brothers what was going to happen until Floyd and I put the nooses around their heads and snugged them up real close. Then they started yelling, cussing and tried to kick us with their bound feet.

The twins held one Biggs brother up and Floyd held the lantern so I could see while I threw the end of the rope over a stout limb.

"Leave some slack, Billy," Floyd said, as I started to tie it off. "We can at least be that merciful."

I backed the rope off some and gave some slack but not enough for the feet to hit the ground.

The twins stood the other brother up and I tied him off the same way.

"You can't get away with this," one of the brothers said.

"You killed our brother," I said. "You murdered him and the penalty for murder is to be hanged by the neck until dead."

Floyd and I jumped down from the wagon bed and the twins sat in the seat with Jim holding the reins.

"Okay," Floyd said, and Jim slapped the reins on the horses and hollered, "Hiyah."

The horses took off and the wagon was pulled out from under the Biggs brothers feet. I watched as they hit the end of the rope and started flopping around. I glanced over at Floyd and saw that he had turned his back on them and was staring out into the black night with his bad eyes.

The End

About the Author

Donovan Harrison grew up on a farm in Roger Mills County, Oklahoma. The family was so poor that even the poor people laughed at them. They scratched out a living by selling eggs, cream, and frying chickens in the small town of Cheyenne, Oklahoma.

Donovan married Mildred Clay when he was nineteen and she was eighteen. They said it wouldn't last, but forty-six years later, the marriage is still going strong. After marriage, Donovan attended college at Panhandle State University at Goodwell, Oklahoma.

After graduating from college, he taught mathematics in Texas, Colorado, Alaska, Oklahoma, and Kansas. After thirty-eight years of teaching, Donovan has retired and is now pursuing a second career in the field of writing.

Printed in the United States
24513LVS00004B/1-69